A MURDEROUS MISCONCEPTION

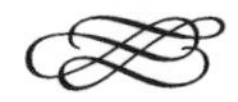

LORRAINE BARTLETT

GAYLE LEESON

Polaris Press

A MURDEROUS MISCONCEPTION

The recipe oven temperatures have been converted to Celsius and Gas Mark to make things a bit easier for non-US readers. However, ***please note all recipes were tested in Fahrenheit.***

❀ Created with Vellum

ACKNOWLEDGMENTS

Thanks to Pat O'Keefe for providing us with the perfect tarot spread for Rose.

Thanks to members of the Lorraine Train for their support: Mary Ann Borer, Amy Connolly. Linda Kuzminczuk, and Pamela Fry Priest,

Cover by Wicked Smart Designs

CAST OF CHARACTERS

Katie Bonner: owner-manager of Artisans Alley, the anchor on Victoria Square

Andy Rust: owner of Angelo's Pizzeria and Katie's boyfriend

Ray Davenport: former homicide detective and owner of Wood U on Victoria Square

Rose Nash: jewelry vendor at Artisans Alley and Katie's friend

Nick Ferrell: co-owner of Sassy Sally's B&B on Victoria Square

Seth Landers: attorney and Katie's friend

Don Parsons: co-owner of Sassy Sally's B&B on Victoria Square

Detective Schuler: homicide detective with the Sheriff's Office

Brad Andrews: Noted chef, hired to manage Tealicious tea shop

Roger Mitchell: works at Angelo's Pizzeria and also in construction for John Healy

John Healy: contractor renovating Katie's apartment over the Tealicious tea shop

Nona Fiske: owner of the Quiet Quilter on Victoria Square

Vance Ingram: vendor at Artisans Alley and Katie's second-in-command

Janey Ingram: wife of Vance, mother of VJ

VJ Ingram: teenage son of Vance and Janey Ingram

Izzy Jenkins: receptionist for Matt Brady Photography Studio

Matt Brady: owner of Matt Brady Photography

Moonbeam Carruthers: owner of The Flower Child flower and gift shop.

Ann Tanner: Co-owner of Tanner's Bakery and Cafe on Victoria Square, wife of Jordan

Jordan Tanner: : Co-owner of Tanner's Bakery and Cafe, husband of Ann

Erikka Wiley: Andy's assistant manager at Angelo's Pizzeria

Erryn Fletcher: Erikka's sister

Captain Spence: Officer in the Monroe County Sheriff's Office, Detective Schuler's superior

CHAPTER 1

Katie Bonner had no idea of the wretched turn her life was about to take. In fact, she started the day in a particularly cheerful mood. The renovations on her new apartment were coming along nicely, her boyfriend Andy Rust had been extra attentive for the past couple of days, and both of her businesses were doing exceptionally well.

Tealicious, the tearoom she'd bought earlier that year, was busy from the time it opened until closing time. This, even though construction was ongoing nearly twelve hours a day over the shop—it was where Katie's new apartment was being overhauled. Patrons didn't seem to mind the noise since the teas, sandwiches, and pastries were delicious. The piped-in music also helped.

Artisans Alley, the former applesauce warehouse bequeathed to Katie by her late husband and his business partner, had seen its share of rough times in the past. But now the consortium of vendors was consistently turning a profit and getting ready for the much-anticipated annual Harvest Festival.

Katie sat back in her chair in her Artisans Alley office and munched on a hard peppermint from the jar she kept on her desk. Delighted to have a few minutes of free time, she decided to check social media. In particular, she wanted to post about the upcoming Harvest Festival to get some buzz going among McKinlay Mill shoppers.

She opened her Facebook feed and the first thing she saw caused a cold fist of dread to encircle her heart, squeezing until she felt breathless. It was Erikka Wiley, Andy's assistant manager at Angelo's Pizzeria…lovely Erikka, with her luscious waves of dark brown hair, who Andy had driven home from work one evening not so long ago shortly after he and Katie had argued. Andy had sworn to Katie that nothing had happened between them. But here Erikka was holding a sonogram photo with the caption, "It's a boy! I hope he has big, brown eyes just like his handsome Daddy!"

Katie threw up in the trash can beside her desk.

After a few minutes, Katie recovered enough to go to the bathroom, wash her face, and down some water. She wasn't watching where she was going, and she nearly ran headlong into Rose Nash. Rose, a spunky seventy-something jewelry vendor, also happened to be one of Katie's closest friends. She was also far too observant to suit Katie that morning.

Rose grasped Katie by the shoulders. "Are you all right? Sweetheart, you're shaking like a leaf! What's wrong?"

"I'm feeling a little sick this morning," Katie said. "I…I guess I ate something that didn't agree with me."

Rose's mouth quirked into a knowing smile. "Oh, I was sick like that once." She lunged forward to hug Katie. "It took me about nine months to recover."

Katie backed out of her friend's embrace. "No! No, it's not that, I assure you." How utterly mortifying that Rose—rather gleefully—thought it was Katie who was pregnant. The poor woman couldn't be farther off the mark.

But Katie couldn't tell Rose that. She couldn't tell her—or anyone—what she'd seen that had upset her so badly...not until after she'd spoken with Andy.

"I'm going to step out for a few minutes," Katie told Rose.

Rose smiled. "A breath of fresh air will do you good. Maybe you should go to the drug store while you're out and pick up a test...you know, just to be sure."

Katie ignored her friend's suggestion. "Please tell Vance to call me if he needs me."

Vance Ingram was not only a vendor at Artisans Alley, but he was also Katie's invaluable second-in-command.

"Oh, don't forget about Mr. Brady," Rose said.

At Katie's blank expression, she elaborated.

"You told me to remind you to see Mr. Brady about his past-due rent today." Rose looked at her watch. "And you should probably try to catch him before he slips out. I don't know why he even keeps a studio. He certainly doesn't spend a lot of time there."

"He's *not* going to have one if he doesn't start paying his rent," Katie said.

She was fed up with Matt Brady, the thirty-eight-year-old photographer who was habitually late with his payments. Katie had to physically track the man down every single month. It was time for him to shape up or find a studio elsewhere. She'd had to turn away several businesses whose owners would love to have his space for Katie to have to jump through hoops every month to get paid the rent she was owed.

As soon as she got the bag from her wastebasket and put it into the dumpster out back, she'd find Brady and then she'd go talk to Andy.

They had a *lot* to talk about.

* * *

As Katie ascended the stairs for the building's second floor and the photography studio above the lobby, she considered the irony of Rose thinking that she was pregnant. Some would likely have thought Katie was jumping to conclusions about Erikka's pregnancy. But Katie wasn't. She knew just as sure as she knew her heart was beating that the baby Erikka bragged about belonged to Andy.

She'd known Erikka was in love with Andy almost from the moment the woman began working for him. And, lately, Erikka had become more brazen in her flirtatious behavior toward Andy, even in front of Katie. Who knew what she did when Katie *wasn't* around?

The memory of the sonogram photo and Erikka's triumphant smile swam before Katie's eyes.

Oh, yes. She was already certain of the truth. But she needed to hear—face to face—what Andy had to say for himself.

She strode into the photography studio. "Hello!"

A young woman stepped out from behind a backdrop. She wore ripped jeans, a tie-dye T-shirt, and black sneakers. Her pink-streaked hair was caught up in a messy bun.

"Hi," the girl said, before going back to snapping her gum.

"Do you work here?" Katie asked. If the man could afford an assistant, then he could absolutely pay his rent on time. If making the time to get around to delivering the check was the issue, he could have this little Girl Friday bring it down to Katie's office.

"Yeah...I mean, *yes*." It had apparently dawned on the young woman that she was supposed to be professional. "I'm Isabelle Jenkins, but you can call me Izzy. Most everybody does."

"It's nice to meet you, Izzy. I'm Katie Bonner. Is Mr. Brady here?"

"No."

"Do you know where I might be able to find him?" Katie persisted.

Izzy shook her head.

Katie tried one last time. "When will he be back?"

Izzy shrugged. "I don't know. I only started working here yesterday. The school sent me over."

"School?"

Izzy nodded. "The community college. I'm on a work-study program."

Now it made sense. Brady had found a way to get *free* help. Of course, if the job facilitated Izzy's education, Katie was all for it. She only wished Izzy had the authority to write a check to Artisans Alley for the rent Brady owed.

She smiled at the young woman. "Thank you for your help. I'll try to catch up with Mr. Brady later today."

"Um…you said your name was *Bonner*, right?"

"Yes." Was it too much to hope that Matt Brady had left the payment for her?

"Your husband was Chad?" Izzy asked.

Katie's smile faded. *Yes, of course, it had been too much to hope for*. She felt that the universe was truly conspiring against her today.

"Yes," she said. "I was married to Chad."

"When I was younger, my mom brought me here to pick out a birthday present." Izzy's expression softened at the memory. "I fell in love with one of Mr. Bonner's paintings, but we couldn't afford it. He heard Mom and me talking about it, and he gave me the painting."

A hard knot formed in Katie's throat, making it difficult for her to swallow or to speak. At last, she croaked, "That sounds like Chad."

"Anyway, one of the other vendors told me you keep some of his paintings here." She lifted and dropped one bony shoulder. "I looked around a little yesterday, but I couldn't find them."

The girl looked so hopeful that Katie asked, "Are you allowed to leave your post?"

Izzy smiled and nodded. "All I have to do is take my phone

with me. Mr. Brady forwards his calls to my phone when he's on a shoot."

Katie led Izzy inside Artisans Alley, up the stairs and to the room she called Chad's Pad where she displayed the remainder of her late husband's paintings. As they approached the small room, Izzy called out and Katie turned.

"Whoa! What's with the floor?"

Katie frowned and watched as Izzy pointed the toe of her right shoe and pressed several spots on the floor. "What's wrong?"

"This wood feels kind of spongy."

Izzy moved aside and Katie tested the floor for herself. It was indeed soft under her foot. She looked above and saw a water stain on the ceiling. It looked like the roof had leaked at some point. She'd walked the aisle hundreds of times and never noticed that spot on the old wooden floor. "I'll have to get this fixed."

"I'll say," Izzy agreed.

They continued along the aisle and, already irked, Katie felt an additional, and unreasonable, stab of resentment toward Chad as she and Izzy entered the room. She and Chad had been separated when a car accident had claimed her husband's life, but they'd been working on their issues. They'd almost reached the point of reconciliation. Had he not crashed that night, Katie wouldn't be going through this heartbreak with Andy now. She and Chad would be happy. Maybe. Probably. It wasn't like Katie to dwell on the past or on what might've been.

Besides, there was a chance that Andy would look her in the eye and tell her he'd never slept with Erikka, that the child she was carrying couldn't possibly be his.

Sure, there was a chance...a fat chance.

After giving Izzy a few minutes to browse Chad's work, Katie told the young woman that they'd both better get back to work. "I'll bring you back again sometime soon if you'd like."

"I'd like that a lot," Izzy said. "I'm studying graphic design in college, but it's my dream to be an artist."

"I wish you all the best, Izzy. I really do."

Katie closed and locked the door to the tiny room, then squared her shoulders and headed for the staircase. She'd put off the confrontation with Andy for as long as she could. As she walked, she took her phone from her pocket and called him.

"Hey, Sunshine," he answered. "I was just thinking about you."

I'll bet you were.

"Could you please meet me at the apartment?" Katie asked. She occupied the rooms above his pizzeria. "I'm on my way there now." She didn't want a scene to play out at Angelo's.

"Sure. Is…is everything all right?"

"I want to talk." She swallowed the lump in her throat. "Face to face."

"Yeah. All right. I'll have Roger watch the place for a few minutes."

She ended the call.

At the bottom of the stairs, she found Ray Davenport waiting for her. Ray was a former homicide detective who now owned and operated Wood U, a gift shop offering handmade products made with with materials from trees across the globe, and located on Victoria Square.

"Hi, Katie. Have you got a second?"

"Not really, Ray."

"This will only take a moment. I promise." He grinned. "It's about the new tenant on Victoria Square—Moonbeam Carruthers."

Moonbeam was what Katie's Aunt Lizzie would've called a hippie. She'd leased the shop owned by a group of the Victoria Square Merchants and had named the place *The Flower Child*. At The Flower Child, Moonbeam sold milled soaps, homeopathic remedies, crystals, candles, incense, and more.

"I'm sorry, Ray, I don't have time right now. We can talk about it later or, if you have a problem, you can take it up with one of the other building owners."

"Wait...what's wrong?" He took her arm. "Are you all right?"

"I'm fine." Katie avoided looking into Ray's eyes, sure that if she did, he'd be able to read just how very far from *fine* she truly was.

Katie and Ray hadn't been friends when she'd first taken over management of Artisans Alley. Their relationship had taken quite a while to grow. But once it had started, the two of them had become close...so close that Ray's three teenaged daughters began to see Katie as a rival for their late mother. They became bitter about their father's friendship with Katie, and Andy hadn't been thrilled about it either.

"I have to go," she whispered, hurrying past him and out of Artisans Alley.

Her phone rang as she climbed the stairs to her apartment. She thought the caller was most likely Andy and that he was wondering where she was. If it wasn't Andy, she'd return the call later. She needed to get this confrontation over with.

On legs heavy with dread, she pressed on. She needed to know the truth so she could decide what her next move would be.

She reached for the doorknob, but Andy flung open the door.

"I was getting worried about you," he said, stepping aside to let her into the kitchen.

"Ray Davenport stopped me in the hallway when I was on my way out of the Alley."

"Of course, he did," Andy said tartly.

"Don't start with that," Katie said quietly.

She looked up into those beautiful big brown eyes—the eyes Erikka hoped her baby would have—and pain wrenched through her gut. For a second, she thought she was going to be sick for the second time that morning. She tried to brush past Andy to go into the living room, but he caught her in his arms. She sank against him, wanting to let him hold her.

Katie hadn't realized she was crying until she pulled away and saw that Andy's shirt was wet. "Is it true? Is Erikka having your baby?"

Every muscle in Andy's body seemed to tense and he looked away. "Well…maybe."

White-hot anger, laced with a thread of utter betrayal, coursed through her. "Maybe?" Katie demanded.

Andy shrugged, looking sheepish. "I don't know if Erikka has slept with anyone else."

"Anyone else?"

"I swear, it was only one time," Andy said. "And I've made it clear to her that if this kid is mine, I will support him, but he will mean nothing to me."

"So, you've talked to her about this? You knew, and you didn't tell me? You let me find out on social media?" Was that why he'd been so attentive to her for the past couple of days?

"There's no reason to worry," Andy said defensively. "I won't let this come between us."

"If that child is your son, then he's already come between us."

"But I don't want to be with Erikka. I want to be with *you*."

Katie shook her head, taking a step back. "You made your choice the night—and I presume it was night…and probably after a bottle of wine—that you slept with Erikka."

"What do you mean?" Andy asked, sounding confused.

"I mean we're done."

"Katie!" Andy protested. "I made a mistake. I'm sorry. I'm *human*."

She went into the living room and sank onto the sofa. Her two cats, Mason and Della, realized something was wrong. Mason wound around her ankles, and Della hid under the chair and watched the couple furtively. Katie picked up Mason and buried her face in his soft fur.

Andy sat beside her, his hands in his lap. "Babe, I love you."

"Not enough." Her voice broke. "Not enough to avoid sleeping with Erikka. Not enough to even use protection."

"She said she was on the pill—I even saw them in her purse."

"And her explanation for the pregnancy?" Katie asked archly. "Was it a miracle?"

"She said she missed a couple of doses." He sighed. "Katie... Sunshine...what's it going to take to make this right?"

"I don't think you can." She placed Mason back onto the floor, stood, and strode into the bedroom.

Andy followed her as far as the door. "I'm not in love with her —you have to know that."

Katie took her suitcase from the closet and placed it onto the bed. She opened the case and began tossing clothes in it.

"What're you doing?" Andy asked.

"I can't stay here."

"Your apartment isn't ready yet. You can't stay in an unfinished apartment."

Katie grabbed a tissue off the dresser and wiped her eyes. "I can't stay here—under *your* roof...over *your* business—and watch your lover come and go every night."

"Don't call her that." Andy strode into the room and took Katie by the shoulders. "*You're* my lover...my world. I can't go on without you. Please, Katie, forgive me."

She looked up at him and saw the tears brimming in his eyes. "I want to."

He hugged her so tightly, she was almost afraid he was going to crush her. "We can get through anything. You know we can."

"I need some space...okay?" Katie gently pulled away from him. "I'm going..." Where? Where was she going? She knew she could stay with her pseudo big brother, lawyer Seth Landers, but that would take her away from Victoria Square, and she didn't want that. Instead, she'd see if Nick and Don had a room available at Sassy Sally's, their bed and breakfast across the Square. If not, Seth was her back-up, and if not...well, if not, she'd try to find a pet-friendly hotel. "I can't be here right now. It hurts too much."

CHAPTER 2

For someone so smart, Andy just didn't get that Katie could be so upset. Finally, she just asked him to leave so that she could finish packing what she'd need to be away for the next few days. The door had hardly closed on his back when she reached for her phone and called Nick.

"Hey, Katie, what's up?"

"I'm...um...wondering—"

Hearing the panic in her voice, he ordered, "Spit it out."

"Do you have any vacancies?" she asked timidly.

"What's wrong?"

Katie was quiet just a little too long.

"Where are you?"

"In my apartment over Angelo's."

"Stay there. I'll be right over."

When Nick arrived at the apartment five minutes later, he carried a thermos emblazoned with the Sassy Sally's logo. He sat the thermos on the counter and enveloped Katie in a hug. "Do you want to talk here or in the living room?"

"Living room," she said. "What did you bring?"

"Irish coffee, and given the way you sounded over the phone, it's not too early in the day to sip it." He took two mugs from her cabinet and carried them and the thermos into the living room. He shook up the mixture and then poured the creamy brown liquid into the mugs. "Drink up."

She tasted the coffee, surprised it was smoother than she'd anticipated. She took another drink as she closed her eyes and sank against the sofa cushions. "Andy cheated on me."

Nick's mouth dropped open, and then he grabbed the mug from Katie and refilled it.

"It wasn't empty yet," she pointed out.

"No, well, drink up. You deserve it."

"You haven't heard the whole thing." She gave a mirthless bark of laughter. "Want to know how I found out? I saw Erikka with her sonogram photo on social media."

Clutching at his chest, Nick drained the contents of his mug.

"What're you doing?" Katie asked.

"Girding my loins," he said. "I'm going downstairs to kill Andy."

"You can't. I need you here with me."

"Fine." Nick stood and paced. "Then, I'm calling Don and telling him we're having a spa day. We're not that busy at the B&B today. He can handle it."

Nick was a sweetheart, but he could be a diva about getting his own way. Katie sometimes thought Don must be the most patient husband ever.

"Don't tell him about Erikka," Katie said. "Not yet, anyway. I'm sure she's busy spreading the news all over town, but I don't want it to come from me."

"All right. But then you and I are having a spa day...on me. We'll even get you a manicure with long, red acrylic nails."

Katie looked down at her short, unvarnished fingertips. She *could* use a manicure. "Long, red nails?"

Nick positively grinned. "Yes, so you can scratch that cheater's eyes out."

* * *

KATIE LEFT her packed bags in her apartment, along with Mason and Della, until after her spa treatments with Nick. Before heading out, she made sure the cats had ample food and water until she returned.

As she and Nick reached the bottom of the stairs, Erikka got out of her car and strode toward Angelo's. She was wearing tight jeans, a pale-yellow maternity top, and a navy and yellow scarf. She smiled and waved at Katie and Nick.

"Oh, no, she didn't," Nick said.

"Just ignore her." Katie headed toward Artisans Alley and the salon within, but Erikka hurried over to intercept them and grabbed Katie by the arm.

"I take it Andy told you about *our* baby," she said and ran her hand over her belly.

"Sweetie, are you sure you're pregnant?" Nick asked. "That looks more like a few too many cinnamon buns than a baby bump to me."

Erikka huffed. "Goes to show what *you* know. Want to see the sonogram?"

"I already have," Katie said. "If you'll excuse us, we have somewhere else to be."

"Katie, wait. I want you to know I never meant to hurt you," Erikka said, her tone simpering.

Katie turned her blazing eyes on Erikka. "You didn't think sleeping with *my* boyfriend would hurt me?"

"I…well…" Erikka said and giggled. "We couldn't help ourselves."

"Yeah…Andy told me about the wine."

"Right. That's what pushed us over the edge the *first* time."

Erikka looked at Katie from beneath her lowered lashes. "But that merely kindled the flame to where we could barely keep our hands off each other...even at work."

Katie's jaw went slack for merely a moment before she regained control and walked away.

"Long, red nails with sharp tips," Nick muttered, as he caught up to her.

"Do you think it's true?" Katie hated hearing a tremor in her voice.

"Absolutely not. I might've bought her little performance had she not added the part about Andy *barely* being able to keep his hands off her at work." He scoffed. "Andy's hair being on fire couldn't distract him from his work."

"That's true." But Katie still wanted to know if Andy had drunk too much and had made a single mistake or if he'd been having a full-blown affair with Erikka.

* * *

TWO HOURS, one pedicure, and a manicure later, and Katie was still seething. "I should've had a better comeback," she grumbled, referring to her encounter with Erikka.

"It's all right. You'll get another chance." Nick held up Katie's right hand. "And now you have these lethal weapons."

Katie stretched out her fingers and looked at the tomato-red talons the manicurist had affixed to her nails. The tips hadn't been filed to a point, as Nick had suggested, but the appendages were still dangerous looking...and impractical. "How did I ever let you talk me into this?"

"It wasn't that difficult." He grinned. "You were vulnerable and open to suggestion. How about we get some lunch? I'm ravenous."

Katie shook her head. "My stomach is still queasy. I'm going to go back to Artisans Alley to take care of a few things. I'll be over to Sassy Sally's as soon as I finish up."

"If you need Don or me to help with moving anything, just give us a call." He kissed her cheek. "And don't go scratching Erikka's eyes out unless I'm there to watch."

Katie couldn't help but grin. "Deal. But with my luck, *I'm* the one who'll end up getting hurt by these claws."

"Nah, they'll grow on you."

"I certainly hope not!" Katie cried. "Their *growing* is the last thing I need!"

They parted and Katie decided to exit the building and walk to the back entrance to Artisans Alley to avoid prying eyes. Then she shut herself into her tiny office. She still needed to speak with Matt Brady, but she'd wait a while...*and* she'd call the studio before going in search of the photographer. No sense wasting a trip...and being the center of attention on a day when she wanted nothing more than to hide away from the pitying stares that were bound to be directed at her.

She took the Alley's checkbook out of her desk drawer, along with a folder filled with unpaid bills. Bill-paying was the only task Katie didn't feel comfortable putting off until tomorrow. However, she hadn't realized how one-inch long fingernails would impede her ability to grasp a pen. The task would take twice as long as it normally did.

Katie decided that when she was finished at Artisans Alley, she'd go get a pint of decadent ice cream, pack up the car, and hide out at Sassy Sally's for the rest of the day. She might even turn off her phone. She was tempted to go ahead and power down the device, but she was afraid one of her vendors, staff members, or contractor might need her.

She fumbled with the envelope of the last bill in her stack. "Geez Louise! It's like working with chopsticks attached to my hands!"

Without warning, Andy opened the door to her office, stepped inside, and slammed the door behind him.

Katie rose from behind the desk. "What do you think you're doing? You've got some nerve barging in here like this!"

"What have you been telling people?" he demanded.

"Nothing. You think I'm proud of the fact that my boyfriend got another woman pregnant?"

Andy stepped forward, immediately in her face. "Everybody on the Square has been giving me the stink eye today."

"Maybe you should've thought about that before you—"

"And then Ray Davenport came into my store and all but challenged me to pistols at dawn," Andy interrupted. "The old man seems to think it's *you* who is pregnant and that I've kicked you out of your home."

Katie wasn't sure she'd heard him correctly. "What?"

"I love you, Katie, and I'd be thrilled if *you* were carrying my baby." A look of comprehension spread over his face. "Wait...are you...?"

"No," Katie said quickly, sinking back onto her chair. "I probably have Rose to thank for this misunderstanding." She explained that Rose saw her this morning immediately after Katie was sick.

Andy came around the desk, knelt beside Katie's chair, and gently took her hand. "You had morning sickness?"

"No!" She blew out a breath and snatched her hand away. "When I saw Erikka's social media post, it made me throw up. In fact, I still feel nauseous."

"I'm sorry, Sunshine. I'd give anything if I could take it back."

Katie looked at him—the earnest expression in his deep brown eyes, the sadness and regret—but she wasn't ready to ask more questions or to hash the matter out. Her emotions were still too raw. "I'll make sure Rose knows I'm not pregnant. And I'll let her think I'm leaving the apartment for a few days because something's broken." *Because something sure* was *broken.* "You know, the water heater or…or something."

"Thank you," Andy said. He rose, then bent to kiss the top of her head.

Katie cringed, pulling away. Andy stood there for a long moment, but Katie refused to look at him. With a shaking hand, she managed to sign the check she'd been working on. She heard the door open and close as Andy left her office.

Ten minutes later, Katie had all the bills ready to go in the mail. She picked up the phone's receiver and hit the intercom button, asking Rose to come to her office for a moment. When Rose arrived, Katie could see by her sweet expression that the woman still seemed to be under the impression that Katie was trying in vain to keep a wonderful secret. Upon sitting at the chair at the side of Katie's desk, however, her brow furrowed.

"You look so pale, dear," Rose said. "Aren't you feeling any better?"

"No, I'm not. And to make matters worse, I'm going to have to clear out of my apartment for a few days."

"Really? Why?"

Katie shrugged, not wanting to lie to her friend but not ready to tell her the truth yet either. "It turns out, the apartment is part of what's making me sick."

"Oh." Rose's face fell. "So, you're not…?"

"No, I'm not. Anyway, Andy needs to…to make some repairs before he even thinks about renting the place to someone else. I'll be moving to my new place in a week or so anyway."

Rose smiled. "That's right! I'm looking forward to seeing it."

"And I'm looking forward to showing it to you," Katie said. "But, for now, I'm going to go get Mason and Della, head over to Sassy Sally's, and lie down for a while." She held the bills out toward Rose. "Would you please put these with the outgoing mail?"

"Of course. You concentrate on feeling better, dear."

"Thank you, Rose."

Depression weighed heavy on her soul, but Katie knew what she was doing was the right thing. It was just too bad she had to rely on the kindness of friends instead of being able to take care of herself. It left her with a bitter tang.

* * *

AFTER HITTING THE GROCERY STORE, Nick and Don helped Katie move her meager suitcases and Mason, and Della into their room at Sassy Sally's. The cats were cautiously inspecting their luxurious new, albeit smaller, surroundings while Katie lounged on the bed, plastic spoon in hand, plowing through a pint of salted caramel and chocolate chunk ice cream.

A tap sounded at the door. Guessing it was probably Nick, Katie called, "Come on in!"

Instead of Nick, Ray Davenport ambled into the room carrying a bouquet of yellow roses and white lilies.

Katie abruptly sat up and nearly dropped her spoon. "Um…hi, Ray. What're you doing here?"

The man's Adam's apple bobbed, and he cleared his throat. "I don't…." He shut the door, came closer, and carefully lowered himself onto the foot of the bed. "I realize I'm past my prime, Katie…and likely not your ideal choice as a partner to raise a child."

She started to speak, but Ray interrupted. "Hush. Let me get this out there."

Katie placed the ice cream carton on the nightstand and motioned for the man to continue.

"I care about you, I consider myself to be a pretty good father, and I'm prepared to do everything I can to help you and your child."

Irked at him for telling her to hush, she decided to have some fun at Ray's expense. "Both of them?"

His bushy eyebrows shot up. "B-both?"

She nodded.

"They're...you're having *twins?*"

"No. They're adopted." Katie looked at Mason, who'd jumped onto the bed to investigate Ray. "Aren't you, *baby?*"

Ray uttered a growl of frustration. "You know I'm talking about your unborn child."

"Mason and Della are my only children, at least, for the foreseeable future."

"You're not pregnant?" he asked, sounding confused.

"Nope."

He flung the bouquet onto the bed. "Damn it, woman! Why didn't you tell me that before I sat here and made a fool of myself?"

She held up her hands in mock surrender. "You told me to hush. I complied. But thank you for the flowers and the offer. I might take you up on it sometime. These two can be such a handful."

"Oh, sure. Ha-ha. Have a big laugh at the expense of the guy who was trying to do something honorable after your boyfriend kicked you to the curb." He stood and whirled toward the door.

Katie scrambled off the bed and grabbed Ray's arm. "Andy did *not* kick me to the curb! I left because I found out—"

Ray turned. "You found out what?"

Katie lowered her eyes. "I'm not the one who's pregnant."

Being a detective, Ray had no trouble putting two and two together. He muttered a string of expletives.

"And I wasn't making fun of you, Ray." She raised her eyes to his. "I—"

He didn't let her finish. He cupped her face in his hands and lowered his mouth to hers. Katie's lips parted in surprise, but then the kiss deepened. Ray's hands moved to her back as she slid her arms around his neck.

Finally, Katie took a step back. They stared at one another for long seconds and something in Katie's gut twisted once again. "I…I can't."

Ray leaned forward, gently kissed her forehead, then turned and left the room, closing the door behind him.

Katie let out a pent-up breath and sank onto the bed. With trembling hands, she retrieved her now-soupy ice cream.

What the hell just happened?

CHAPTER 3

After a night of fitful sleep, Katie awoke when Nick knocked on her room's door. "Katie, are you awake?"

"I am now," she answered, blinking.

"I've got my passkey and a lovely breakfast tray. May I come in?"

Katie frowned. "Sure." Heaving herself into a sitting position, Katie snuggled against the headboard and drew the bedclothes up and across her chest. The key rattled in the lock and the door opened. "I'm sure glad I'm not naked," Katie said wryly.

"You and me both. I'm also glad you're alone." Nick placed the tray between them and sat on the edge of the bed.

"And why wouldn't I be alone?" Katie asked with chagrin.

Nick shrugged. "Who's to say you and Lover Boy didn't kiss and make up? Maybe he called Erikka on her bluff."

Katie reached for the coffee cup. "You really don't think she's pregnant? Nick, I saw the sonogram."

"Sweetheart, we live in a world of digitally-altered photographs. Don't believe everything you see." He plucked a strawberry from the tray and popped it into his mouth. "But giving her the benefit of doubt and agreeing that the woman *is* pregnant, I find it hard to believe the baby belongs to Andy."

"Are you kidding? Andy admitted he slept with her," Katie blurted and then took a savage gulp of her coffee. Intrepid Mason strolled across the bed to check out the breakfast tray while Della remained poised to hop off the bed at the slightest disturbance.

"Oh, I'm sure the louse slept with her," Nick said. "But I seriously doubt he's the only one. Since Andy is the man Erikka is so obviously in love with, she *wants* the baby to be his. And she's convinced herself that it is."

"You think it's *obvious* that Erikka is in love with Andy?" Of course, Katie already believed it, but she didn't realize everyone else on Victoria Square acknowledged it as well.

Nick swiped another strawberry. "Duh. Why else would she have turned down an excellent job with benefits a few months ago in order to work as an assistant manager in a dumpy little pizzeria?"

He was right. Erikka had left her job with the local school system—a position with advancement opportunities, and an enviable benefits package with a retirement plan—to work with Andy.

"And why—if not for love—would a man bring a woman a bouquet on the day of her breakup with her boyfriend?" Nick asked, with a pointed look at the flowers on Katie's nightstand.

"It wasn't like that."

"Oh, it was absolutely like that." Nick smirked at her. "Are you blind to things right in front of your face?"

"It was a misunderstanding," Katie insisted. "And Andy and I aren't even officially broken up." She bit her lip. "I mean, we *probably* are, but..." She groaned. "Oh, I don't know."

"Your brain is as scrambled as those eggs, which are getting colder by the second," Nick said, nodding toward the tray. "So eat, get into your running clothes, and I'll be back to get you in fifteen minutes. Some fresh air and exercise will help clear your head."

"Good thinking. But let's make it twenty minutes," she said as Nick rose from the bed and left the room.

Katie reached for the fork on the tray. No more coffee for her until after their run. She didn't want to slosh.

* * *

KATIE HAD DAWDLED, so she didn't come downstairs to meet Nick for almost half an hour. She found him in the kitchen.

"Ready?" he asked, grinning

"As ready as I'll ever be," she groused as they headed out the back door. "I don't want to take my usual route around Victoria Square," Katie told Nick as they stretched in preparation for their run.

"Because you're avoiding *all* your boyfriends?"

Nick was clearly curious about what had happened between Katie and Ray yesterday. But Katie wasn't ready to discuss that encounter with anyone. She hadn't yet come to terms with it herself. Had she fallen into Ray's embrace and returned his kiss because she felt vulnerable and needed some sort of validation? Or was there more to it than that?

"I'm avoiding *everyone,*" she declared.

Nick grinned. "That's all right. I prefer to avoid everybody when I run. Otherwise, people think it's time for a street chat."

"I prefer to avoid running at all." Katie typically power-walked around the Square in the mornings. But today the sun was shining, the air was cool, and Katie thought a run would be invigorating. "I'm making an exception just for you."

Two minutes later, they finished stretching and started off across the Square at an easy pace.

Nick laughed when they jogged past The Flower Child.

"Moonbeam Carruthers. I have got to meet her. Anyone with a name like that has got to be a hoot!"

"Doesn't she though?"

"Haven't you met her?" Nick asked.

Katie nodded. "Just the one time. Gilda Ringwold-Stratten and I interviewed her. Seth," Katie's lawyer and pseudo big brother, "checked her references and handled the lease agreement. All other interactions between Ms. Carruthers and the partners have gone through him."

"We need to set up a proper meet-and-greet." It was then Nick nodded toward the vacant concrete warehouse that stood behind the south side of Victoria Square. "Should that door be open? It looks like someone is in there."

He and Katie jogged over to investigate. Katie's breath caught in her throat as she recognized the woman on the floor just inside the open door. It was Erikka Wiley, her body lying on the concrete. Katie knelt on the hard, chilly floor and placed her index finger against the cold flesh of Erikka's neck in the vicinity of her carotid artery, but there was no thrumming pulse. A navy and yellow scarf cut into her skin, leaving a visible bruise...the same scarf she'd been wearing the day before.

CHAPTER 4

Katie and Nick stood outside the warehouse and swatted the flies that were swarming while they waited for Detective Schuler and a newcomer, Captain Robert Spence, to emerge. Spence was a muscular man in his early forties who had clear blue eyes and a buzz cut. He was the physical opposite of tall, skinny Schuler, whose habit of staring down his hawkish nose with his beady brown eyes was annoying rather than the unnerving gesture Katie was sure he intended.

At last, Schuler approached them with his hands on his hips. "Interesting fingernails you've got there, Ms. Bonner. I didn't think you went in for long nails."

Katie looked down at her nails. She'd almost forgotten about them. "I had them done just yesterday."

"Well, I hope you're not too attached to them because they're about to be taken off by my forensic team."

Katie gaped at the man. Was he serious? "What?"

"You can't do that," Nick said. "I'm calling our attorney right now." He removed his phone from his armband and took a few steps away from them.

"He's right."

Katie saw Captain Spence approaching. Schuler's jaw tightened at the man's rebuke.

"That's a violation of Ms. Bonner's civil rights," Spence continued. "We can have the techs swab beneath her fingernails, but we can't cut them off. We have no evidence that she's involved in this crime."

"Her boyfriend was involved with the victim," Schuler spat out through gritted teeth.

Spence shook his head. "Circumstantial, sir. With all due respect, I believe your familiarity with the victim might be clouding your judgment...."

Schuler gave his superior a hard stare before addressing Katie. "Stay put until one of my technicians can swab your nails."

"Excuse me," Katie blurted, "but there are no scratches that I can see on the body. She was obviously strangled."

"That's for the medical examiner to decide," Schuler grated and stepped away.

Katie glowered after him.

Nick returned to Katie's side. "Seth is on his way. I know he's not a criminal lawyer, but he's all we've got right now."

Katie merely nodded.

A few minutes later, a female technician in a hazmat suit came and swabbed beneath each of Katie's fingernails. The woman was gentle but thorough, and she put the swabs in plastic bags.

Sweat trickled down Katie's spine, and it wasn't just from the heat and her previous exertion. A year or so before, she'd seen a documentary about a man falsely accused of murder because his DNA was found on a murder victim. The man had an airtight alibi—he was in the hospital at the time of the murder—and yet his DNA placed him at the crime scene. Investigators ultimately determined that the paramedics who took the man to the hospital earlier in the evening were the same ones who'd retrieved the corpse, and it was believed that the accused's DNA was inadvertently transferred to the victim by one of those paramedics.

Katie and Nick retreated to the shaded concrete steps on the west side of the building. Nick rested his arm around Katie's shoulder, and she was grateful for the gesture. They waited in silence until a black Mercedes pulled up and Seth Landers got out. He approached and without hesitation, gathered Katie into his arms for several long moments before pulling her away from the crime scene. "Everything's going to be all right."

"I'm scared," she whispered into his shoulder.

"Why is that?"

"I spoke with Erikka yesterday. She called to Nick and me when we were heading for Envy Day Spa." Her eyes probed his. "They swabbed beneath my fingernails. What if Erikka's DNA got under them somehow?"

"Did you touch Erikka when you saw her?" Seth asked.

"No."

"Did she touch you?"

Katie nodded. "Yesterday, she grabbed me by the arm."

"You should be fine." Seth gave her another one-armed hug.

"Innocent people go to jail, Seth," Katie asserted.

"You aren't going anywhere…except maybe back to work. I'll do some research and, if necessary, find you an excellent defense attorney." At Katie's quick intake of breath, Seth held up his hand. "I'm not saying you're going to need one, but it's always wise to be prepared."

It took an eternity—almost twenty minutes—before Seth was able to get Nick and Katie cleared to leave the area and despite the short distance, he gave them a ride back to Sassy Sally's. As soon as they arrived at the B&B, Katie left Nick to explain the situation to Don while she went upstairs and took a shower. For some reason, she felt incredibly dirty.

Katie closed her eyes and let the water from the rain shower head beat down on her head as she tried to comprehend the events of the past two days. Everything had gone from happy and fine to tragic and disastrous in a matter of hours.

Who could possibly want Erikka dead? And why was Detective Schuler so determined it was Katie? Only a few short months ago, Schuler had been convinced that Ray Davenport was responsible for the death of a local man, and he'd gone after Ray with an obsessive fervor only to be proven wrong. Was he planning to do the same thing to Katie?

It was ridiculous. Erikka's death had to have been a random mugging…or something. Almost everyone liked the woman. Some people liked her *too* much.

Like Andy.

Katie ran her hands down her face. *No. He wouldn't...he'd never.... Would he?*

She stepped out of the shower, toweled off, and dressed in jeans and a long-sleeved T-shirt. She padded out of the steamy bathroom barefoot and with her hair combed but still wet to find Andy sitting on the armchair in her room with Mason was on his lap.

A flash of anger coursed through her. How had he gotten in? Had she forgotten to lock the door? Surely, Nick or Don wouldn't have let him in. She took a deep, stabilizing breath before she settled on the edge of the bed facing Andy. Della came and pressed her head against Katie's hand, and she picked up the cat and snuggled her cheek against its fur. Neither Katie nor Andy spoke for a long moment.

"I'm sorry," Andy whispered at last.

Every muscle in Katie's body tensed. "Andy, please tell me you didn't—"

"No! You know me better than that. Don't you?"

"I thought I did," she said quietly.

"I'd never hurt anybody…especially not my—I mean *a* child."

"You almost said *your* child. So, you do believe the baby was yours."

He raked his hands through his hair. “He could’ve been. Now I’ll never know, will I?”

Mason hopped off Andy’s lap and stalked across the room.

“I imagine the coroner will run a DNA test on the baby.” Katie left out the fact that she guessed they’d do so to further narrow the suspect pool…that is if Schuler didn’t have *her* convicted by then.

“I’m sorry it was you who found her,” Andy said. “I’m sorry she was murdered. I’m sorry I slept with her.” He lowered his head and covered his face with his hands. His words were muffled when he said, “I wish none of this had ever happened.”

Katie sighed and resisted the urge to go over to him.

Andy looked up, tears brimming in his soft brown eyes. “I love you so much, Sunshine.”

Katie said nothing, merely looked at him. She felt numb. She, too, was sorry any of this had happened, but it had. And now what? What was going to happen next?

“Please tell me everything’s going to be okay,” Andy said.

Katie’s heart hardened. “I can’t do that. We’re both suspects in a murder investigation,” she told him. “We’re about as far from okay as we can get.”

* * *

KATIE’S first stop after sending Andy on his way was Tealicious. She wanted to see its manager, the celebrated chef she’d hired to manage the place, and she also needed to check the progress being made to her apartment on the building’s upper story.

When she stepped into the pale rose-colored room with the white wrought-iron tables and heard the soft classical music playing, Katie felt as though everything else happening in her life had to be a nightmare. How could her real life be such a mess in this beautiful, cheerful place? Tealicious’s soothing dining room looked like something out of a fairy tale.

And out of the kitchen came its handsome prince.

Chef Brad Andrews was tall, blond, and broad-shouldered. While his looks initially drew in the female customers, it was his food that kept them coming back. Okay, the food *and* his looks.

He rushed forward and took both Katie's hands in his. "How are you?"

"I'm—" It occurred to her that she didn't know. "I think I'm numb."

Brad nodded. "That makes sense. I've spoken with Nick. I'm going to make us all a special dinner this evening at Sassy Sally's. It'll just be the four of us."

"That sounds lovely. Thank you." She glanced at the floor, her heart heavy. "Every time I close my eyes, I see Erikka lying there on that dirty warehouse floor."

"I know. But tonight, we won't be talking about tragedies. We'll put this horrible business out of our minds for a couple of hours and enjoy some delicious food and lively conversation. All right?" His expression was so hopeful.

Katie sighed, unsure she could muster a positive reply.

Brad squeezed her hands before letting them go. "I understand as well as anyone how hard it can be to step back from one's emotions even for a second."

She nodded, remembering that he'd had to go to rehab for alcohol addiction. "I know."

"I just want you to remember that you have friends to lean on. We're here for you. Let us help."

Katie thanked him, giving him a heartfelt hug before pulling away. "Thanks."

A noise from above broke the quiet. "Your contractor is upstairs. He told me he needs your input," Brad said.

"Thanks. I'll go up there now."

Brad gave her an encouraging smile and Katie walked up the stairs to talk with John Healy, whom she'd hired to renovate the top floor of Tealicious into her new apartment.

"Just the person I hoped to see," Healy said when Katie walked into what was quickly becoming her living room.

Healy was in his early fifties with thinning salt-and-pepper hair, gray-green eyes, and a leathery complexion due to years working in the sun.

"Time to make a decision: Murphy bed or pull-out couch," Healy said. He took a tablet from his tool belt to show Katie the space ramifications.

Katie studied the space comparison. "I like the idea of the Murphy bed, so I can hide it during the day and then I can keep my love seat. Are you sure it won't fling me out of bed like a catapult and break an arm or something?"

He smiled. "I can put up a hammock to catch you."

"Sounds great." She smiled as she looked around, marveling at the work already finished. "It's really coming together."

"It really is," Healy agreed.

"Do you still think the place will be ready in a week?" she asked.

"Absolutely…barring any unforeseen problems."

"Thanks, John."

Despite the progress being made on her new home, Katie's feet felt heavy as she left Tealicious and walked across the vast expanse of asphalt toward Artisans Alley. At the moment, the new apartment was the one bright spot in her life …the one thing she had that she could happily anticipate. She simply had to get past this mess with Erikka…and Andy…and the cloud of suspicion that hung over her—them.

From a distance, she could see the CLOSED sign on the door of Angelo's Pizzeria. There was a note taped in the window as well. Katie could guess what it said—something to the effect that "Angelo's is closed as the staff grieves the loss of"…of what? Of one of their own? Of a beloved friend? Of the mother of Andy's unborn child?

Katie berated herself for the churlish thought. A woman and

her baby were dead...murdered. Erikka's circumstances and the role they played in devastating Katie's life were irrelevant at this point.

But they're not. They drove me to a point in my life where I doubt I'll ever be able to trust the man I love...loved?...again. And those circumstances also landed her in the center of a murder investigation.

Because of Andy's infidelity, Katie's life was now under a microscope—literally, thanks to those DNA swabs! She knew she should feel sorry for Andy, and she did...to some extent. But if he'd wanted Erikka so badly, why couldn't he have simply broken up with Katie? It would've hurt, but it would have been so much easier for her in the long run.

As she resolutely strode to the side entrance of Artisans Alley, she heard Ray call to her from somewhere behind her. She pretended not to hear him, and she tried to maintain her pace so it wouldn't seem obvious that she was ignoring him. She knew Ray either wanted to discuss what had happened between the two of them yesterday, Erikka's murder, or both.

She didn't have the energy to deal with any of it right now.

* * *

KATIE'S ATTEMPT TO update the Artisans Alley website with information about the Harvest Festival proved futile. She merely sat and looked at the monitor, not taking in anything on the screen before her.

Rose knocked on the open door, brandishing a box of the local confectionery's finest chocolates. "Sue Sweeney brought these over this morning."

She placed the box on Katie's desk, and Katie could see that the sweets were in the shape of baby booties piped with yellow frosting.

"I corrected Sue's misunderstanding," Rose said. "But she left the chocolates anyway. What should we do with them?"

"We should eat them. And all at once—every last one of them. Let's get some coffee."

Rose grinned.

The women went into the vendors' lounge, grabbed cups from the drying rack next to the sink, and poured coffee. Katie was relieved that they made it back to her office and closed the door before anyone else saw them. She was in no mood to chat with anyone other than Rose.

She and Rose spread out paper towels, and then Katie opened the box. She tried to pluck out a bonbon, but her long, unwieldy fingernails caused the chocolate to flip up into the air and plop into her coffee.

"Oh, well. I guess I'm having a mocha," Katie muttered.

Rose laughed. "What are you doing with those ridiculous nails anyway? They aren't your style."

"They were Nick's idea. He thought they'd make me feel better and, in a moment of weakness, I succumbed." Katie looked down at both her hands.

"And now you regret your decision?" Rose asked.

"More than you could possibly know." She speared a chocolate bootie with an index fingernail and then handed the box to Rose.

"Thanks." Rose popped one of the candies into her mouth, chewed, and swallowed. "These are delicious."

"They are," Katie agreed, as the hazelnut filling oozed into her mouth.

"I noticed that Angelo's is closed today," Rose said. "There's a note on the door, but I didn't get near enough to read it. Is the pizzeria having the same problems you were having at your apartment—the thing that made you sick?"

Katie shook her head. "No. It's because of Erikka, Andy's assistant manager. She...she was murdered."

CHAPTER 5

Katie didn't particularly care for website design. She could do it, but she didn't enjoy it...at least, not until she could preview her work and see that the site looked just as she'd hoped it would. The problem was that the final approved preview came after much tedious tweaking.

But, at last, there it was. Artisans Alley's homepage proudly announced the upcoming Harvest Festival with animation, vectors, and a full schedule of events. The page looked terrific, and Katie published the updated page. She then tried to massage the knots out of her neck. It was a futile effort—even her knots had knots.

There was a tap at her door. It was so light Katie wasn't sure it was an actual knock.

"Come in!" she called, just in case.

Katie's eyes widened when Sophie Davenport stepped into the office. Sophie was Ray's oldest daughter. Although Katie had once felt she and the Davenport girls were friends, one by one they'd begun to dislike her. She was almost certain the girls' animosity stemmed from Katie's friendship with Ray.

The memory of the kiss she and Ray had shared the night

before rose in her mind. Could that be why Sophie was here? Had Ray said something to his daughters? But what? There was nothing to tell.

While Katie's brain was going into overdrive, she realized Sophie was speaking.

"...I promise not to take up too much of your time."

"Of course," Katie said. "Have a seat. You'll have to excuse me. My brain is mush today."

"I can imagine." Sophie carefully closed the office door and sat on the chair by Katie's desk. "I heard about Ms. Wiley...and how you and Nick Ferrell found her."

"Yeah...that...um...that was rough." Katie studied the young woman carefully. "Your dad hasn't said anything, has he? About suspects...or motive?"

"No. You should know better than anyone that my dad is pretty much cut off from the Sheriff's Office these days, thanks to Detective Schuler."

Katie sighed. "Schuler made it clear to me this morning that he's no fan of mine, either." She took a peppermint from the jar and offered one to Sophie. "But this new guy—Spence—he isn't averse to standing up to Schuler."

Sophie declined the mint. "I'll ask Dad if he knows anyone on the force named Spence." She inclined her blonde head. "You seem worried."

"I am," Katie admitted. "I'm afraid Schuler will go after me the way he did your dad. To him, I'm a slam dunk—I found the body and, to his mind, I had a motive."

"But you're innocent. Dad won out in the end, and I'm sure you will, too."

Katie wished she could be as certain—or, at least, as cavalier—as Sophie was.

"That's not why I came by to see you," Sophie continued. "I wanted to tell you that I came back from college for a few days to ask a favor."

Katie's hackles immediately rose. "Oh?"

"I'd love to be able to tell my adviser that I'm going to have an unpaid internship at Tealicious with Chef Brad Andrews over winter break," she said sounding hopeful.

Katie silently mulled this over. Now Sophie's visit made sense. The young woman hadn't dropped in to check on Katie because she'd heard about Erikka's murder and Katie's finding the body. Sophie was no doubt thinking about how impressive an internship with Tealicious's celebrated chef would look on her resume.

Apparently uncomfortable with Katie's silence, Sophie quickly filled the void. "I know my sisters and I have been real brats to you sometimes, but...you know...that's how *close* friends behave with each other. You start to...accidentally...forgo the little niceties you extend to strangers." She forced a weak laugh.

Katie knew she could continue to let Sophie flounder a bit. Heck, she'd be perfectly justified in turning the girl down flat. But Ray was a good friend...good enough that he'd even offered to marry her and help her raise Andy's child.

"Yes," she said. "Of course, you can be an unpaid intern at Tealicious over winter break. The holiday season will be hectic, and Brad and I will be grateful for the extra help."

With a squeal of delight, Sophie hopped out of her chair to give Katie a quick hug. "Thank you so much. Well, I'd better run, but I'll be sure to ask Dad about that Spence guy."

"Thanks."

Katie hadn't been ready to talk with Ray yet this morning. Not about anything. But now she realized that she needed all the help she could get to keep Detective Schuler from arresting her for Erikka's murder.

* * *

AT LUNCHTIME, Katie decided that more than anything, she needed some fresh air. But, given everything that had transpired over the past two days, she chose to stay off the Square to avoid well-meaning people who'd want to talk about Erikka's death... and possibly her pregnancy, if they'd seen the sonogram posted on social media. So, she opted to eat a granola bar while strolling in the area where she and Nick had planned to run that morning.

Naturally, that course led Katie near The Flower Child, the shop operated by Moonbeam Carruthers. Any other time, Katie would've gone into The Flower Child to browse and to chat with the proprietress. Today, she sought solitude.

But it was not to be.

"Katie! Katie Bonner, is that you?" Moonbeam stood in the doorway of her shop, her mass of long chestnut curls framing her face.

Katie raised a hand. "Hi. Yes, it's me."

"Sweet henna! Get in here!"

Katie reluctantly closed the gap between where she'd been standing and The Flower Child.

Moonbeam put her arm around Katie, pulled her into the shop, shut the door, and put the CLOSED sign in the window.

"What are you doing?" Katie asked.

"You need an emergency Reiki session." Moonbeam propelled Katie into a room containing a massage table.

"Oh, no...I mean, thank you. I appreciate your concern, but I'm fine," Katie said as she tried to back out of the room.

"You are not even in the same ZIP Code as fine." Moonbeam's bracelets jangled as she flailed her arms. "Have you *seen* your aura?"

"No, I haven't," Katie said. "But I don't have time for a massage. Plus, I left my purse back at Artisans Alley."

"It won't take long, and this one is on the house." Moonbeam took Katie's arm and gently steered her toward the table. "If I let you leave here in the state you're in, I'd never forgive myself."

Katie expelled a defeated breath as she sat on the table. "All right. What do I do?"

"Slip off your shoes and lie face up."

Reluctantly Katie did as Moonbeam instructed and climbed onto the padded table.

"Now do your best to relax. I understand that's especially hard for you right now—"

"Because of the body?" Katie interrupted.

"What body?"

"Erikka Wiley. I...we...she was found in the warehouse this morning." Katie suppressed a shudder at the remembrance of Erikka's rigor-stiffened body lying on the warehouse floor. "Haven't the police been here to talk with you about it?"

"Nobody's been here to talk with me about anything. This is the first I've heard of it." She stretched her hands out over Katie's supine form. "I need you to relax and close your eyes."

"But if you didn't know about the body, how did you know I'm stressed?"

"Helen Keller could see that you're stressed, and not only was she blind, but she's been dead for more than fifty years." Moonbeam's tone sharpened slightly. "Now, shut your eyes and your mouth. I'm trying to help you," she said kindly.

Katie gave in and did as Moonbeam asked. As she lay on the table, she wondered why the police hadn't spoken with The Flower Child's proprietress. The backside of The Flower Child faced the warehouse. Moonbeam might've seen something important. Katie decided she'd question the woman herself, but as Moonbeam's soft voice droned on about chakras and energy, and her hands rested lightly but firmly on Katie's head, she thought it would be rude to interrupt. Her body felt as if it was melting into the massage table, and Katie wondered briefly if Moonbeam would be insulted if she dozed off.

Katie's thoughts drifted.... Should she have called Andy? Should he have called her or was it best to let things settle? Surely Schuler was looking at Andy as a potential suspect, too. Katie realized she should have called Seth to get advice, but as

Moonbeam continued her ministrations, Katie felt so drowsy that....

Opening her eyes, Katie realized she was still lying on Moonbeam's massage table. She looked around the room. The door was closed, and she was alone. Yet she heard Moonbeam's voice speaking with someone in another part of the building.

Katie sat up and slipped her shoes back on. Feeling awkward, she stepped out into the store. Moonbeam's customer was leaving.

Turning to Katie, Moonbeam smiled. "Ah, feeling better?"

"Yes. I'm sorry I fell asleep. I've—I've had a rough couple of days."

"I'm so glad you were able to relax." She smiled. "Your aura is much improved."

"I didn't do or say anything stupid, did I?" Katie asked, feeling awkward.

"Of course not," Moonbeam said and laughed. "I didn't hypnotize you. I only gave you a massage."

"Right. Yeah. I just—" Katie shook her head. "I don't know."

"You don't owe me an explanation. When you said you found a body, that told me all I needed to know." She straightened a tray of colorful crystals. "Would you like to talk about it?"

Actually, Katie didn't want to discuss her discovery of Erika's lifeless body, but she did want to know if Moonbeam had seen or heard anything that might lead to the killer's identity. "The victim was someone I knew. She worked with my boyfriend Andy over at Angelo's Pizzeria."

"The pretty brunette?" Moonbeam asked. At Katie's nod, she continued. "I remember seeing her around the Square. She had a muddy aura, which led me to believe she had some major negativity in her life...maybe even draining any positive energy from those around her."

"She apparently did have some major negativity in her life

because someone used her scarf to strangle her to death," Katie said.

Moonbeam clicked her tongue. "I'm ever so sorry to hear that. I'd hoped to help her. Every time I saw her, I encouraged her to come to see me at The Flower Child, but she never did."

"Did you happen to see her yesterday? Or perhaps last night?"

"I'm afraid not." Moonbeam handed Katie a red-orange crystal. "Put this in your pocket and keep it with you. It's a fire agate, and it'll protect you from all that negative energy."

"But Erikka's dead." Katie turned the crystal in her hand and thought it was pretty, but she didn't think it would protect her from anything. "Besides, you've done enough for me already."

Moonbeam refused to take back the agate. "Erikka is dead, but all the negative energy she carried had to go somewhere. Be on your guard, Katie." She said the words with such gravity that for a moment, Katie almost got sucked in.

"Have a good—better—day," Moonbeam wished her.

Katie forced a smile. "I'm sure I will."

She left the building and headed west across the tarmac toward Artisans Alley. She could feel the weight of the agate in her pocket and wished she believed Moonbeam's silly mumbo-jumbo. At that moment, Katie didn't know what she should believe—or, more importantly, whom she should trust.

CHAPTER 6

As Katie entered Artisans Alley's lobby, Ray was on his way out. "Hey, Ray," she said in a half-hearted greeting.

"I'm glad I caught you." He took her by the arm and led her through the length of the Alley, not speaking until they arrived at the vendors' lounge. "How are you doing?"

"I'm fine." Katie strode through the open doorway. "I've been at The Flower Child. What did you want to tell me about Moonbeam the other day?"

"It seems inconsequential now in light of Erikka's murder, but Moonbeam left Fairport because her business tanked after some people accused her of fraud."

Katie took a seat at her desk. "What sort of fraud? Her criminal background check was clean when Seth ran it before approving the lease."

"True. I didn't say *she* had a record." He sank onto the chair beside Katie's desk. "She was never convicted of anything. It didn't matter, though. The malicious rumors did her in."

"Why did you want to discuss it with me? Do you have reason to believe there's any validity to the claims against her?"

Ray shook his head. "No, and as I already pointed out, it

doesn't seem all that important anymore. But the other day, before everything turned upside down, I thought you should be aware."

"Thanks." She took a peppermint from the jar on her desk and offered one to Ray. He accepted.

"Sophie is thrilled about her internship with you and the pretty boy over winter break. Thanks for doing that for her."

I did it for you. "We'll be glad of the extra help. Sophie is an excellent cook and working with Brad will look great on her résumé."

"She mentioned your request for information on Captain Spence." Ray said. "I worked with him, of course, but I put a few feelers out anyway. Everyone I spoke with agrees he's a nice guy and a faithful cop. Totally by-the-book. I'm glad he's on this case."

"That's good to know. I appreciate your insight into him."

Ray's expression hardened. "Sophie said you're worried Schuler will come after you."

"Of course, he will." She pinched the bridge of her nose. "I believe he'd love to put me away for Erikka's murder. Don't you?"

"I won't let that happen." Ray gently clasped her wrists and pulled her hands away from her face, holding them in his. "I mean it. I'll discover the truth, and *you* will be exonerated."

Of course, it was then—with Ray holding her hands and looking earnestly into her eyes—that Andy burst into the office. And despite their actions being perfectly innocent and the fact that her boyfriend had so cruelly wronged her, Katie tugged her hands away from Ray as if he were on fire.

"What are you doing here?" Katie asked Andy.

He ignored her question and lit into Ray. "You'll take advantage of any opportunity, won't you, *old* man?"

Ray stood and faced Andy. "My, aren't you the pot calling the kettle black? Taking advantage of Katie, among other women, seems to be your forte."

Katie scrambled to her feet and put herself between the two

men, fearing they'd come to blows. "Don't do this. Don't make this about me or yourselves. We all have enough on our minds without adding petty insecurities to the mix."

"She's right," Ray said. "I came here to reassure Katie I'll do everything in my power to ensure Schuler doesn't pin Erikka's murder on her."

"So will I," Andy said.

"Then I'm glad we agree." Ray stepped toward the door. "Katie, thanks again for helping out Sophie."

"I'm happy to do it." She returned to her seat as Ray left the office and closed the door behind him.

Andy slumped on the chair vacated by Ray. "What did you do for Sophie Davenport? I thought those girls hated you."

"Hate seems a bit strong. I agreed to let Sophie intern at Tealicious while she's home on winter break."

"She's using you to pad her résumé ," he scoffed.

"And Brad and I are getting free help for three whole weeks," Katie said. "It's a win for everyone. So, what brings you by? I understand that Angelo's is closed today."

"Yeah. I thought that was for the best...you know, for everybody, to show respect and for—" His voice broke. "It'd be hard for them to work without seeing her or hearing the sound of her laughter."

Hard for them, *or hard for* you? Katie wondered. She knew it *had* to be hard on Andy—Erikka had been one of his best, most trusted employees. She'd also been his lover...at least once.

"I agree," she interrupted, tired of watching him flounder. "You made the right call."

"I wondered if maybe you'd go to dinner with me tonight," he said.

"I've already made plans to have dinner with Nick and Don at Sassy Sally's." She didn't bother to mention that it was Brad who would be preparing the meal.

"I simply hoped we could get out of McKinlay Mill for a few hours and start the healing process," Andy continued.

For some reason, Katie actually felt sorry for the man who'd betrayed her. *More fool you,* her Aunt Lizzie would have said.

"How about tomorrow night?" she asked, her voice low.

"Okay," he agreed, sounding ridiculously hopeful. "Of course, maybe I could join you guys tonight—"

But Katie cut him off. "No." She gave him no explanation.

Still, he was correct about the healing process. The rift between them was only going to get wider if they didn't address their problems. Katie got to her feet, which gave her a feeling of being more in command. "You're right. We need to begin to put Erikka's death behind us, and the best way to do that is to find out who killed her so Schuler will have to stop pointing the finger at us. We can discuss the murder and compare notes tomorrow."

He smiled with obvious relief. "Thank you, Sunshine."

As he moved in for a kiss, Katie dipped her head slightly. She still couldn't get the image of him embracing Erikka out of her mind. Would she ever be able to erase that imagined sight? *All* the imagined sights?

Andy kissed her cheek and said, "I'll see you later."

After Andy left, Katie sat back down at her desk and gave concentrating on her work a valiant effort. But she had so much conflicting information and stress assaulting her brain that she finally decided that maybe walking across the Alley to the photography studio and asking Matt Brady for his rent check would help soothe her nerves. If nothing else, it would provide her a change of scenery, and the errand might pay off, too.

As she scaled the stairs to the upper floor, Katie wondered if she should've called first to see if Brady was in. The flashing sign spelled OPEN so she walked right into the studio and found Izzy and Vance's son, VJ Ingram, standing near a decorative folding screen, lip-locked and clutching each other. Katie *definitely* should have called first.

Neither of the teens saw her, so Katie backed out and silently closed the door and went in search of Rose. Since Ida Mitchell was working the cash desk, Katie knew she'd find Rose in her booth.

"Hi, Rose. Have you seen Vance around?" she asked.

"He's around here somewhere." Rose looked up from the display case where she'd been rearranging her jewelry and glanced down the carpeted aisle. "Seriously, he was by here not five minutes ago." She slipped her hand into her slacks pocket and took out her phone. "I'll call him for you and—"

"No!" Katie clasped her friend's arm. "Don't call him. I don't want to see him yet. I wanted to talk with you first. I need your advice." She explained that she'd found Izzy, the college work-study student, and VJ, kissing in the photography studio. "Do you think I should mention it to Vance and/or Matt Brady?"

"How involved was this kissing?" Rose asked, her brow narrowing.

"Way more involved than appropriate for the workplace." Katie sighed. "But they're both good kids, and I don't want to get either of them in trouble." Well, she'd known VJ for two years. She'd just met Izzy, who had to be at least a year older than VJ, who was still in high school.

Rose's eyes widened, and she shook her head.

"What?" Katie asked. "Have you heard something? Is—?"

"Who are good kids?" Vance asked.

He'd come up from behind Katie. How long had he been standing there? Hopefully, he hadn't heard anything too incriminating.

"Not Vance Junior!" Rose exclaimed.

Katie closed her eyes. Of course, she realized Rose had been trying to cover their tracks by pretending they hadn't been talking about Vance's son; but that only made matters worse.

Vance, naturally, took umbrage with Rose's assertion. He drew himself up to his full height and glared down at the small, blonde woman. "Why don't you think VJ is a good kid?"

Poor Rose's face fell. "That's not what I meant. I think Vance Junior is a fine young man."

"We were discussing Izzy, the young woman working at the photography studio," Katie said. "She's a really sweet kid. She knew Chad."

"Then what did she do that you don't want her getting in trouble for?" Vance was nothing if not persistent. "I overheard you saying you didn't want *either* of the kids to get in trouble. Who was the other kid, and what have they done? As your second in command, I feel I have a right to know."

There were times when, although she knew she'd made the best possible choice, Katie regretted making Vance her assistant manager. This was one of those times.

"It's minor, and I'll handle it. You're needed for more important problems." She took out her phone and started walking away from the booth. "I'll talk with you later."

When she was certain she was far enough away from Rose and Vance, she called the photography studio. When Izzy answered, Katie said, "I need to speak with you and VJ so stay put. All right?"

"Y-yes, ma'am. How'd you know VJ was here?"

"We'll talk about that when I get there." Katie ended the call and headed back to the photography studio.

By the time she arrived, Vance was already waiting for her.

Katie pressed her lips together. "Let me guess—Rose told you."

"Yeah. She felt really bad about saying VJ wasn't a good kid."

"Will you let me handle it?" she asked. "Your son is going to be mortified to see you here. I don't want him to think I reported him for something this petty."

"All right," Vance said. "I just don't want him to get into any trouble…you know?"

"I know. And I'll stress that." She patted his shoulder. "If I get the impression you need to have a discussion with your son about Izzy, then I'll let you know."

"Thanks."

Once Vance had agreed to allow Katie to go in by herself, she went and took a seat in the studio's reception area. Both Izzy and VJ. were there waiting for her, and they were holding hands.

Katie stretched out her arms, Katie said, "I'm not here to embarrass you or make you feel uncomfortable. However, what I saw earlier was not workplace appropriate behavior. As the manager of Artisans Alley, it's my duty to ensure that vendors and their employees conduct themselves in a professional manner."

"It was all my fault," VJ said. "We're sorry."

Izzy quickly jumped to his defense. "No, it was my fault."

"I'm not blaming anyone. I'm simply asking you to keep your public display of affection to a minimum here."

At that moment, Matt Brady opened the door to his studio and demanded, "What's going on here?"

VJ got to his feet. "Nothing. Let me help you with your gear," he said and helped Matt carry in his photography equipment.

Matt looked at Katie. "What're you doing here?" he growled.

Finally, Katie thought, determined she would get her back rent if she had to turn the man upside-down and shake it from his pockets. But first….

CHAPTER 7

"What are you doing here?" Matt asked, looking from Katie to his employee, who still sat on the chair in the lobby with her hands folded in her lap. "Are you harassing my assistant?"

"Not at all. We were chatting while I waited for you. She's a terrific young lady," Katie said and smiled. "Izzy knew my late husband, Chad."

"Oh, well. Cool." Brady turned away and VJ schlepped the equipment into the studio.

Katie watched as they toted in the equipment. "May I please have a word alone with you?"

"Okay," VJ said.

"I meant with Mr. Brady," Katie groused.

"Right," VJ said quickly rejoining Izzy in the reception area.

Shutting the door behind them, Katie sat down in a chair in front of Brady's desk.

"Yeah, yeah, you want the rent check." Matt blew out a breath as he seated himself behind the desk and began rifling through the clutter.

A file folder fell off the edge of the desk, and photos spilled out. Bending to pick them up, Katie saw that the photographs were of Erikka and she was practically nude.

She turned one of the photos toward Matt. "What are you doing with pictures of Erikka Wiley?"

Having dug his checkbook out from under the papers, folders, and notes on his desk, Matt paused—pen in the air—to glance at the photo Katie held. He shrugged. "I don't usually take boudoir shots, but that client was anxious to impress some guy she liked. She paid me twice my going rate."

Katie turned the photo back around to get a better look. In it, Erikka wore a red silk bra and G-string panties. "When was this taken?"

"About two weeks ago."

"Two weeks ago?" Katie echoed. "Did Erikka ever come to pick up these photos?"

"Sure." Again Brady shrugged and handed her a signed check. "Those are my copies—to show clients who might want similar photos in the future."

"Whatever." She turned the photo face down on the desk, turning her gaze toward the deadbeat in front of her. "You need to be more efficient with your rent payments from now on. I'm tired of having to chase you down every month. If nothing else, maybe Izzy could take care of your bookkeeping. She seems to be a bright, capable young woman. Her talents shouldn't be limited to simply answering your phone."

"Yeah, well, she's only been here for a couple of days. I haven't had a chance to train her."

"From what I've observed, she needs more work to occupy her time."

Brady frowned. "I'll take your word for it." He turned his back on her.

Having been dismissed, Katie returned to her office, closed the door, sank onto her chair, and munched a peppermint. So Erikka had gotten sexy photographs made to *impress some guy.*

Katie felt certain that guy was Andy. Had he seen the photos? Did he have copies of them? Would he tell her the truth if she asked?

Then another suspicion crept in. Those photographs had, according to Matt Brady, been taken approximately two weeks ago. In them, very little of Erikka's physique had been left to the imagination, including her flat stomach. There was no way the woman in those photographs had been as far along in her pregnancy as the sonogram she'd posted earlier in the week had purported her to be.

Katie pulled up the social media page on which Erikka had posted the damning image. It clearly showed a well-developed baby, not a little kidney bean. Plus, Erikka already knew the baby's gender.

A little Internet research revealed to Katie that women typically have their first ultrasound between eighteen and twenty weeks of gestation. Could Erikka have faked her pregnancy? If so, why?

* * *

KATIE FED MASON and Della and apologized to the cats for the fact that they didn't have a lot of room to roam around at Sassy Sally's.

"I promise, our new home will be finished soon, and you'll have an entirely new place to explore." She neglected to mention that it wouldn't be a whole lot bigger than their current digs.

She showered and changed into a light, summery dress for Brad's promised dinner. As she applied her lipstick using the mirror over the dresser, she caught a glimpse of the flowers Ray had brought the night before. Dropping the lipstick into her makeup bag, Katie crossed to the nightstand, picked up the vase of flowers, carried them into the bathroom, and refreshed the water.

The flowers were lovely, and it had been sweet of Ray to bring them…not to mention offering to help her raise another man's child. Would Andy have been so gallant? She didn't know. But she sure hadn't been keen on the idea of helping him parent another woman's child. Of course, this was a woman with whom he'd cheated while he and Katie had been in what she'd thought was a committed relationship, so the situations weren't at all the same.

When she opened the door of her room, Katie could smell the tantalizing aromas coming from Sassy Sally's kitchen. Her nose reported the information directly to her stomach, and it grumbled loudly, reminding Katie of how little she'd eaten that day.

She went downstairs to find that Brad was preparing white wine-marinated steak, mashed potatoes with garlic and chives, lemon green beans, and a chocolate brownie pie to be served à la mode.

"This evening is all about comfort," he announced, kissing Katie on the cheek. "Have a glass of wine while I put the finishing touches on the meal."

Katie sat at the dining room table with Nick and Don and joined them in a glass of wine. Because her stomach was empty, Katie's wine was potent enough to loosen her tongue to suspicions she hadn't intended to voice at dinner this evening.

Brad refilled her glass when he served the main course. The steak was tender and juicy, and Katie was ready for comfort—not only in the form of food but in the opinions of her friends.

"You'll never guess what I saw today in Matt Brady's office," she said.

"Who's Matt Brady?" Don asked.

"The photographer who rents space in the Alley." Katie dug her fork into the mashed potatoes. "Brad, you've outdone yourself. This is wonderful."

"Thank you," he said. "But don't leave us hanging. What did you see?"

"A photo of a scantily dressed Erikka Wiley."

"Was it one of those pregnancy photos where the woman is posing holding her rounded belly?" Nick asked.

Katie shook her head. "Nope. Erikka's stomach looked so flat I bet you could've bounced a quarter off it." She frowned. "Is that a thing?"

"Probably not," Brad said. "I have to ask, though, why you find this photo so fascinating."

"Did she have an extra boob or something?" Nick asked and laughed.

Katie glowered at him. "Don't be vulgar and, no. But she didn't have a pregnant belly, even though Matt Brady said the picture was taken about two weeks ago. I wonder if Erikka was faking her pregnancy."

"I can see that." Nick gestured toward Katie with his fork. "Maybe the sexy pics weren't enough to lure Andy away from you, so she upped the ante and said she was pregnant."

"No, no, no." Don sipped his wine before continuing. "A pregnant woman's belly—and her baby—can grow a lot over two weeks. I saw it when my sister was pregnant. Besides, did Matt give you an informal *I took them a couple of weeks ago*, or was he specific about the date?"

"He didn't give me a specific date," Katie said. "But I read online that a woman typically has her first sonogram in her second trimester. When Nick and I saw Erikka the day before yesterday, she didn't appear to be that far along in her pregnancy."

"Still, how could she have altered the sonogram?" Brad asked. "It seems unlikely she could fake that."

Nick waved his hand dismissively. "You can buy practically anything online these days. I'll prove it." He took out his phone to try to find a sonogram for sale but had no luck. "I'll try again later," he said, frowning.

Katie realized her friend was as tipsy as she was. "There are plenty of pictures on Facebook alone. Maybe she just lifted one and printed it," Katie suggested.

"But why would Erikka do something so desperate?" Don asked. "She had to know she'd be found out sooner rather than later."

He was right.

"Hey, my glass is empty," Nick declared and Brad refilled it and Don's, too, but Katie held a hand over hers.

After that, their dinner conversation turned to something lighter, and perhaps it was the wine, because Katie kept getting distracted, asking herself Don's question over and over again: *Why would Erikka do something so desperate?*

* * *

THE DINNER PARTY broke up around eight, and Katie trudged up the stairs to her room. As she removed her makeup, she decided the questions that had been gnawing at her couldn't wait any longer. She phoned Andy.

"Hey, there, Sunshine," he answered brightly—as though he hadn't a care in the world. "Are you all right?"

Katie didn't bother with the niceties. "Did Erikka give you sexy photos of herself in a red lingerie set?"

Other than a sharp intake of breath, Andy was silent.

He's trying to figure out what to say, Katie thought angrily.

"I know she had them made," she said. "I saw them at Matt Brady's studio earlier today."

It took more than ten seconds before Andy replied. "You've got to believe me—I never asked her for any photographs. Katie, I love you. *You*. No one else. I *never* loved Erikka."

"This isn't about love, Andy. I asked you a simple question," Katie said bluntly.

He let out a long breath. "Okay, yes. She gave me the photographs. I didn't ask for them, and I shoved them in my bottom desk drawer," he said. "I told her I was in love with you, and that there would never be a her and me."

"You kept them? You still *have* them?" Katie accused.

Andy groaned. "It's not like that. I put them in the drawer so no one else would see them. And, frankly, I forgot about them until now. I'll get them out and destroy them."

He could say that, but would he actually do it? Considering he and Erikka were just 'friends,' should he have been embarrassed for her and immediately given them back?

"Do you believe Erikka really was pregnant?" Katie demanded.

"Why would she lie about that?" Andy asked, sounding clueless.

"You tell me." But Andy didn't reply. Unable to stand his awkward silence, she said, "I've had a long day."

"Yeah, me, too," he admitted, sounding weary.

"We'll talk tomorrow."

"Okay," Andy said flatly.

"Goodnight."

"Goodnight, Sunshine."

Katie ended the call. For long seconds, she wasn't sure what she felt or what she could do. Then she grabbed her laptop. Although she desperately wanted to give Andy the benefit of doubt and believe his slip-up with Erikka had been a one-time occurrence rather than a full-blown affair, she'd heard the pain in his voice when he'd spoken about how hard it would be for Angelo's employees to work while grieving Erikka's death. Of course, he'd mourn the loss of his coworker and friend—Katie imagined all her coworkers would do the same—but was Andy bereft over a woman he liked or a woman he loved? He claimed to love only Katie and that he'd only slept with Erikka during one night of drunken passion. But had Andy fallen in love with Erikka but denied his feelings because he felt bound to Katie?

She logged onto her favorite social media site and went to

Erikka's profile page. Scrolling through the feed, Katie saw that the sonogram was the last thing Erikka posted. Other people had posted their condolences and memories, but she noted Andy hadn't.

Prior to the sonogram photo, Erikka had posted a photo of a cinnamon bun Andy had made at the pizzeria. It looked delicious —he wasn't called the Cinnamon Bun King of Victoria Square for nothing. She'd captioned the photo: *The second-best thing at Angelo's.* Of course, she could've meant the pizza, but Katie doubted it.

In a post from a few weeks earlier, Erikka made a vague comment about being stalked. That was worth looking into. Katie wrote down the comment and the date it was made.

Erikka had only mentioned "stalking" once. Otherwise, there were memes, inspirational quotes, selfies—the usual social media fodder—but there wasn't anything specifically referencing Andy. Was that telling in itself? Or was Katie looking for damning evidence where there was none and should she ask Andy about it?

When she scrolled past photographs of a newborn baby, Katie stopped and went back to the post. Clicking through to see all the images, she learned that they were of Erikka's nephew. Her sister's name was highlighted, so Katie visited her page. There were posts documenting the baby's growth over the past three months, pictures taken at the time of the child's birth that were similar to those on Erikka's page, and photographs of Erikka's pregnant sister. Katie could definitely see the resemblance between the two women.

And then there it was—the sonogram photo Erikka had posted on her own page. It looked a lot like the picture her sister had posted many months before. Could it have been the same one?

CHAPTER 8

With so much turmoil enveloping her thoughts, Katie found it hard to sleep that night. The next morning, she dragged herself out of bed at seven o'clock, showered, dressed, and headed over to Tealicious to start her day. She let herself in the front door and went into the kitchen to see what Brad was cooking up for the day. Although it was early, Katie could hear the sound of hammering in the apartment above. She and Brad weren't the only early birds.

Standing at the counter creaming butter and sugar in a large mixing bowl, Brad was absorbed in his task. He started when he turned and saw her there. "God, don't scare a guy like that."

Katie laughed. "Sorry."

He smiled. "Good morning. How's your head?"

It took a moment for Katie to remember what he referred to. "Surprisingly enough, it's fine." She was glad she'd stopped at two glasses of wine. "I didn't see Nick taking off for a run this morning, though."

"Neither did I. I'm guessing he slept in."

She peeped over his shoulder and breathed in the scents of vanilla and lime. "What are you making? It smells heavenly."

"Key lime cookies. Once I mix the dough, I'll have to put it in the freezer for half an hour or so to ensure it's properly chilled."

"I'd better let you get to it then. If you don't need me for anything at the moment, I'm going to run upstairs and see how the apartment is coming along."

"Is there anything special you'd like to have for dinner tonight? I don't mind taking over Sassy Sally's kitchen again."

"I'm having dinner with Andy this evening," she said, lowering her eyes.

"All right. If that's what you want."

Katie didn't like the resignation she heard in Brad's voice, but she understood it. "I haven't forgiven him. I only promised to have a meal with him and hear him out."

Raising his hands, Brad said, "I know. I'm not judging. I just don't want you going through what I did with my ex."

Katie felt a pang of sympathy and reached out to pat Brad's shoulder. The heartache his ex-girlfriend had caused led him to end up in rehab for alcohol abuse. "No breakup is ever easy."

Brad raised an eyebrow. "Are you broken up?"

Katie merely shrugged.

Slogging up the stairs to the apartment, she wondered if she and Andy really *were* now over. She hated to think so—they'd been through a lot together, and she thought she loved him. But because of his loyalty to Erikka, he'd been willing to risk their relationship more than once, and that was before Katie even knew about the cheating. Not so long ago, Katie had been livid when Andy had created a full-time position for Erikka so she wouldn't leave Angelo's for another job. He'd been desperate not to lose the woman, no matter how Katie felt about the situation. And then he'd slept with Erikka. Katie's gut tightened. How could their relationship possibly survive that kind of betrayal?

The pounding continued and Katie guessed her contractor, John Healy, was putting down the hardwood flooring today. As she strode into the living room, however, it was Roger, Andy's part-time employee, she saw working diligently.

Katie knew Roger enjoyed apprenticing with Healy and planned to work with him full time as soon as he finished high school.

She waited for a pause in the hammering to call, "Good morning. Brad's making key lime cookies. I'll have him save you some if you're interested."

The young man looked up at her and grinned. "I'd be more interested in chocolate chip cookies."

"I'll see what I can do." She crouched beside him. "This is looking great."

"Thanks. Glad you're happy with it. John had an errand to run this morning and will be here later. He asked me to get started."

Katie wasn't sure how to approach the subject of Erikka's death and finally just decided to come out with it. "I'm so sorry about Erikka," she said softly. "It must be hard on all of you at Angelo's. I think it's good Andy closed the pizzeria for a couple of days."

Roger looked away, nodded, placed another board in line. "You don't..." He didn't finish his thought.

"I don't what?"

Not meeting her gaze, he mumbled, "You don't think *he* did it. Do you?" His last sentence conveyed his uncertainty.

"I don't think who did what?" Katie *thought* Roger was talking about Andy—and Erikka's murder—but she wasn't positive, and she certainly wasn't going to plant that thought in his mind if he'd been asking about something else.

Roger glanced at her. "I don't believe Andy would've ever hurt Erikka. Do you?"

Katie shook her head; but before she could say anything, Roger resumed talking.

"I mean, yeah, they'd begun arguing a lot lately, but that's what people who care about each other do, right? My sister Regan and I fight all the time, but we love each other. I feel like that's how it was between Andy and Erikka." His eyes widened. "Not that they *loved* each other—I know he loves you—but...."

"I understand what you're saying," Katie interrupted, giving him a wan smile. "And, no, I don't think Andy would've hurt Erikka in any way."

Roger let out a breath and looked away. "Yeah, me, either."

Katie remembered Erikka's Instagram post mentioning stalking from a few weeks before. "Did Erikka ever mention having any kind of trouble?"

"What do you mean?"

"Just something she posted on Instagram but it was only the one time."

Roger shook his head. "Nope."

Katie nodded and straightened. "I appreciate all the hard work you're doing. Thanks again."

Roger muttered something about being happy to have the opportunity to make this place her home, but Katie wasn't really paying attention. She was already moving toward the staircase in a daze. Did she truly believe what she'd told Roger—that she didn't think Andy would've hurt Erikka? Or was she lying to him and to herself? She didn't know anymore. But for now, she had to put that possibility out of her mind and get back to work.

Before leaving Tealicious, she returned to the kitchen to tell Brad about Sophie Davenport volunteering to help out at the tea shop over winter break. "I'm sorry I forgot to mention it to you earlier."

"Do we need or want an incompetent in our kitchen during what promises to be our busiest season?" he asked.

"You'll be pleasantly surprised by Sophie," Katie promised. "She's an excellent cook, a smart girl, and she's willing to work hard. *For free.*"

Brad shrugged. "Okay, I'll give her a chance."

"That's all I ask."

"But if she doesn't work out, she goes—deal?"

"Deal." Katie jerked her thumb toward the staircase and smiled. "Somebody hopes you're making something with chocolate chips for today's menu, by the way."

"As it happens, I've already made oatmeal chocolate chip bars with coconut and caramel and have put some aside for Roger," Brad said. "That boy knows I don't take requests, but today he happens to be in luck."

"Uh-huh." Katie knew Brad had a soft spot for the kid or else he wouldn't have already set aside cookies for him. "I'll see you at lunch."

When she stepped out onto the asphalt, Katie saw the lights come on in Ray's shop, Wood U. She hadn't consciously decided to drop in, but she felt herself moving in the shop's direction.

Upon entering the gift store, Katie saw that an older man was standing at the counter yammering at Ray. Whether he was a customer or merely someone shooting the breeze, she didn't know. He must've followed Ray inside as soon as Ray unlocked the shop.

Katie browsed the shop while waiting for the man to leave. It wasn't until she nearly knocked a carved elk off a shelf that she realized her hands were trembling.

This was a bad idea. A very *bad idea.*

Realizing she wasn't going to get to have a private conversation with Ray, Katie headed for the exit.

"Hey, Kate, wait."

She halted and turned to look at Ray. He'd called her *Kate* only one other time that she could recall. They'd been arguing because she wanted to help him prove his innocence of a murder Detective Schuler was trying to pin on him.

Now Ray addressed the man leaning on the counter. "It's been nice talking with you, Walter, but I need to get to work."

"Oh, sure," Walter said. "And I need to get back to my walk.

See you later." He gave Katie an affable nod as he left the building.

"Sorry," she mumbled.

"Don't be." Ray moved to stand in front of her. "I'll put the CLOSED sign on the door if you want me to."

Smiling slightly, she shook her head. "That's all right."

"I don't think *you're* all right." He placed his large, calloused hands on her shoulders. "What's going on?"

"You...you don't think—" She couldn't finish her thought.

"I do once in a while." He gave her a lopsided grin that made her laugh.

Then she was serious again, determined to ask Ray's opinion —his professional opinion—before she lost her nerve. "Do you think Andy could have killed Erikka?"

Ray's mouth drooped. "No."

"Truly? You're answering as a former detective?"

"Yes." He lifted a thumb to caress her jawline. "Don't you realize I'd have told you immediately if I suspected that man for an instant? And do you think I would've let him anywhere near you if I thought he was a murderer?"

Katie closed her eyes and expelled a breath of relief.

"What brought this on?" Ray asked.

"Roger—the young man who works for both Andy and the contractor renovating my apartment. He said Andy and Erikka had been arguing a lot in the past couple of weeks."

Dropping his hands, Ray moved toward the coffee maker. "Care for a cup?"

"No, thanks."

Ray poured himself a cup and added plenty of sugar. "I'd imagine they were arguing over the baby."

"That's the other thing," Katie said. "I don't believe Erikka was pregnant." She explained everything she'd observed—from the photographs to finding Erikka's sister's sonogram and realizing it was the same one Erikka had posted as her own.

Placing his coffee cup on the counter and giving Katie an exaggerated blink, Ray said, "Hold up. Erikka gave Andy sexy pictures of herself, and he *accepted* them?"

She slowly nodded. "And unless he got rid of them since last night, they're still in his desk drawer at the pizzeria."

"That man is an idiot." Ray held up a hand. "I still don't think he's a killer, but he has to be the biggest jerk I've ever known."

"Because he couldn't tell from the photographs that Erikka wasn't pregnant?" Katie asked.

"No. In his defense, he might not have known when the pictures were taken. He's an idiot because he wanted to have you both and thought he could get away with it."

"He told me they were only together—you know—one time."

"You don't believe that, do you?" he asked accusingly.

"Deep down, I guess I don't."

Ray merely shook his head. She could tell there was more he wanted to say, but he restrained himself—and for that, she was glad.

Changing the subject, she said, "There was something else I found on Erikka's social media account. It was only one post, but it might be worth looking into. She indicated someone was stalking her."

"I hate to burst your bubble, but that might've been another ploy for attention." Ray took a sip of his coffee. "But I'll ask around."

"Thanks." Katie nodded at the worktable. "I'd better let you go. You told Walter you needed to get to work, remember?"

"You're the exception." He cleared his throat. "I can't imagine how you're feeling right now. You've got a lot on your plate running two businesses and renovating an apartment, much less finding out about Andy's infidelity and then discovering Erikka's dead body."

She gave him a wry smile. "I'll be all right. I'm tough, remember?"

"I know you are. But at least as far as Andy is concerned, you deserve better; and I hope you realize it."

Did she? Katie wasn't entirely sure.

CHAPTER 9

Katie studied the list of things she needed to do prior to the Harvest Festival when Seth knocked on her door. Smiling, she got up and welcomed him into her office with a hug.

"This is a nice surprise." But then she frowned. "Right? I mean, I hope it is." She peeped behind him, half afraid Detective Schuler was waiting in the vendors' lounge.

"I'm only here to see how you're doing," Seth said, holding up his right hand as if he were being sworn to testify. "I promise."

Katie sat back down behind her desk and invited Seth to take the only other chair. "You haven't heard anything from Schuler?"

He shook his head. "You?"

"No," she replied. "I'd stick with the adage about no news being good news, but I'm afraid he's digging to find something he hopes will incriminate me."

"Too bad. He's not going to find anything."

She wished she felt as confident as Seth seemed to be. Searching his warm blue eyes, she didn't see any evasiveness there.

Seth reached out and took her hand. "Everything is going to be fine."

"Did you find a criminal attorney who'll take my case—you know, if Schuler *does* arrest me?" she asked.

He squeezed her hand before releasing it. "Don't borrow trouble."

Biting her lip, Katie asked, "But you have someone in mind?"

"Yes. Trust me." He smoothly steered the conversation in a different direction. "How are the apartment renovations coming along?"

"Great. I can hardly wait for you and Jamie—" Seth's partner "—and everyone else—to see it."

"I know Nick would be delighted to help you plan a house-warming party," Seth said with a smile.

Nodding, she said, "That's something I can look forward to when there's no suspicion of murder hanging over my head."

"Why don't you join Jamie and me for dinner tonight? I'm making risotto with roasted shrimp."

"Sounds amazing and I truly appreciate the invitation, but I have plans." She examined the flashy nails on her left hand as she spoke. "I hope I can get a rain check."

"Of course." Seth leaned forward, drawing her gaze back to him. "What are you doing this evening?"

"I'm having dinner with Andy."

He regarded her in silence, his expression stony.

Uncomfortable at not knowing what Seth was thinking, Katie blurted, "I have questions I believe I deserve to have answered."

"I'm not judging you," Seth said softly. "You and Andy have been together for a while now. If you can forgive his infidelity and learn to trust him again, then I'll support you in that. And if you can't, I'm behind you in that decision as well."

"Thanks." She swallowed the lump that had formed in her throat. "You're the best big brother I never had."

Seth smiled. "I know."

* * *

After Seth left, Katie resumed work on the Harvest Festival task list. She thought it would be nice for Artisans Alley to host a reception to kick off the event, but she wasn't sure she could manage it with everything else that was going on. Maybe she could enlist the aid of a volunteer or two.

As she mulled over that thought, there was a brisk knock on her door before Janey Ingram strode into the office. Believing Dolly Parton to be her soul sister, Janey wore jeans, cowboy boots, and a pearl-buttoned western shirt that strained to remain buttoned.

"Katie, I'm positively beside myself over this—" She flung herself onto the chair beside the desk. "—this *entanglement* of VJ's."

"I don't think it's anything to be concerned about," Katie said. "They're just kids."

"Exactly." Janey ran a hand heavily adorned with rings across her brow. "I know nothing whatsoever about this girl Izzy, and VJ has almost no dating experience."

Glancing down at her list, Katie had an idea. Even though Janey struggled with multiple sclerosis, she was doing well and serving in a supervisory capacity on behalf of the Alley shouldn't be too taxing for her.

"How would you like to get to know Izzy?" Katie asked.

Perking up, Janey said, "I'm all ears."

"I'd love to have an opening reception for the Harvest Festival." She leaned back in her chair. "It wouldn't have to be anything elaborate—just a nice get-together for the vendors and the Square's merchants showing our appreciation for all their hard work. Unfortunately, I don't have time to organize it myself."

Janey's eyes widened in delight. "Why don't I do it? I'm a whiz at event planning. Why just this summer I acted as a wedding coordinator for my niece, Emma. A heck of a good time was had by all—from the bridal shower to the last dance at the reception."

"So I heard, and I'm thrilled you're willing to help—as long as you don't do too much of the heavy lifting." Katie smiled. "That's where Izzy comes in."

"What a wonderful idea!" Janey exclaimed. "But would she be willing to work with her boyfriend's mom?" She frowned slightly. "I'm guessing she considers VJ her boyfriend…right?"

Katie shrugged, intending for the gesture to encompass both questions. "Let's find out." She picked up her phone and dialed the photography studio. "Hi, Izzy. It's Katie Bonner."

There was a palpable silence before Izzy asked, "Is-is everything all right?"

"Everything is super. I wondered, though, if you could help me with something."

"Of course—anything," Izzy said.

Katie explained her desire to have a reception before the Harvest Festival. "Since I've got too much going on to adequately plan it myself, I'm enlisting a few volunteers for the job."

"I'm glad to pitch in. It'll help me deal with the boredom of finding productive ways to fill my work hours."

Katie frowned. "I encouraged Mr. Brady to give you more to do—such as accounts payable and accounts receivable."

"Yeah, well…he never mentioned it to me. But maybe he will one of these days."

Surmising from the young woman's tone that Izzy didn't hold out much hope of Matthew Brady increasing her responsibilities, Katie said, "Then let's show him how efficient you *can* be."

Izzy laughed. "All right!"

After ending the call, Katie and Janey worked up a budget, made a shopping list, and discussed how to decorate the venue and the entertainment. Finally, Janey headed off to Matt Brady's photography studio.

"Wish me luck!" Janey called.

"You won't need it," Katie assured her. "Just treat Izzy the way you want to be treated, and I guarantee the two of you will hit it off." Beneath her desk, she crossed her fingers.

* * *

IF KATIE DIDN'T MISS Andy, she did miss their every-other-day lunches at Del's Diner. As she'd forgotten to grab a piece of fruit or a muffin from Nick's kitchen, she decided to walk across the Square and visit the Tealicious menu. Of course, she'd need to walk around the Square an extra couple of times, but it was worth it.

Upon opening the teashop's door, Katie immediately spied Nona Fiske. She inwardly groaned; the last thing she needed today was a run-in with Nona who had been a thorn in her side since her first day at Artisans Alley. Outwardly, she smiled and greeted the woman.

"Hello. How are you, Nona?"

She sniffed. "Fine. Someone told me Chef Andrews made some excellent key lime cookies, so I came by to try them."

"And your verdict?"

Nona shrugged. "They're pretty good, I guess."

Katie struggled to avoid looking pointedly at the box of cookies the cantankerous woman carried. "I hope you enjoy the rest of your day."

"By the way—"

Nona's loaded preamble caused Katie to stop and warily turn around. "Yes?" She was barely able to keep the exasperation from her voice.

"When is Andy planning to reopen Angelo's? I understand he must be devastated at losing Erikka, especially under the circumstances," she said, leveling her penetrating gaze directly at Katie. "But I can't imagine he can afford to keep the pizzeria closed for too long. Can he?"

"You'd have to ask him," Katie said, keeping her tone neutral.

Nona arched a brow. "Oh...you don't know?"

"I haven't asked. After all, it's none of my business." She managed a tight smile. "I'm too busy running Artisans Alley and Tealicious to get worked up about the operations and finances of someone else's endeavors. If you'll excuse me, I need to grab a quick lunch and get back to work."

Striding toward the counter, Katie reflected on Nona's comment—*under the circumstances*. She found it hard to imagine Nona on social media. But if Erikka's "pregnancy" was the circumstance to which she'd referred, how else would she have known about it? Did everyone in McKinlay Mill believe Erikka had been pregnant with Andy's child? Even worse, who among them suspected Katie of the woman's murder?

Rather than pausing to the counter, Katie rushed up the stairs, hoping Roger was still working. He was. John Healy was there now as well, but Katie's question was too important to neglect, especially as she'd been so vague earlier that morning. After praising the now nearly completed floor, Katie asked Roger to come downstairs with her to get some lunch for himself and John.

Stopping halfway down the stairs, she turned to Roger. "Earlier I mentioned Erikka having trouble."

"Yeah."

"Did Erikka ever mention being stalked?"

His face brightened as he said, "Oh, that's what you meant. Yeah. Yeah, she did!"

Katie could tell he'd been concerned that Andy could have murdered Erikka—be it accidentally or otherwise and perhaps that was why he hadn't understood what she'd meant—and Roger seemed relieved to have another viable suspect.

"She said something about a stalker more than once," Roger continued. "She'd come into work and say she was afraid she was being followed. At one point, she told us she thought it might be her ex because he'd been trying to get back with her."

"Thanks—that's very interesting. I remember Erikka's ex. From what I observed, he seemed to be an abusive jerk. I'll make sure Detective Schuler knows about him." She resumed the descent to the dining room. "Come on—let's see what Brad has on offer for lunch."

* * *

AFTER A MEAL where she'd forced herself to smile for so long that her cheeks ached, Katie returned to her office at Artisans Alley and immediately called the Sheriff's Office. Detective Schuler was out, so the receptionist put her call through to Captain Spence.

"Good afternoon, Ms. Bonner. How may I help you?" he asked, his tone neutral.

"I spoke with one of Angelo's Pizzeria's employees earlier today, and he told me Erikka Wiley had complained on more than one occasion of being stalked. He said she suspected it might be her ex-boyfriend, Luke Stafford. She also posted about it on social media. I thought that information might be helpful to your investigation."

"Thanks—we'll check it out," he said. "Is there anything else you'd like me to know? Anything you remember from when you discovered the body or from when you saw Ms. Wiley the day before her death?"

Katie's mind flashed to Roger asking, *you don't think he did it. Do you?* He being Andy. "Um…no," she stammered. "But if I remember anything, I'll be sure to let you know."

CHAPTER 10

For the rest of the afternoon, Katie threw herself into her work—even doing the tasks she liked least—anything to keep her mind off Erikka's murder. Still, she kept wondering where Andy had been two nights before. The Andy she knew would never kill anyone. But, then, the Andy she *thought* she knew wasn't a cheater either. By the time she walked across the Square to Sassy Sally's to feed Mason and Della, she'd decided to have Andy meet her at the restaurant rather than allow him to pick her up at the B&B. A gut feeling told her she needed some aspect of control over the situation.

After giving the cats their food and fresh water, Katie called Andy.

"Please tell me you aren't backing out on me." His voice was filled with quiet desperation.

Katie felt a stab of guilt. "Of course not. But I've had a hectic day, and I'm running a little late. Would it be all right if I meet you at the restaurant?" When he didn't respond, she continued. "You could go ahead and get us a table and maybe order an appetizer. I'm starving."

"Okay," he said reluctantly. "As long as you promise me this isn't an elaborate ditch." He barked out a laugh, but it was obvious to Katie that he wasn't joking.

In a tone sharper than she'd intended, she asked, "When have I *ever* lied to you?"

A long silence followed her retort.

"Fair enough. I'll see you at the restaurant." He ended the call without waiting for her response.

She couldn't help it if the truth hurt. His lies had certainly caused her pain.

Katie set her phone aside, stripped, and stepped into the shower. As the hot water sluiced over her skin, her fear and frustration got the better of her and tears filled her eyes. How she wished she could wake up from the nightmare she was now living.

* * *

WITH HER HEAD HELD HIGH, Katie walked into the Texas-themed steakhouse in a royal blue shift and nude heels, knowing she looked her best. Thanks to a depuffing eye mask and skillfully applied makeup, no one would have guessed she'd been weeping half an hour before.

She looked around the noisy, crowded restaurant and spied Andy. He stood and gave a soft whistle of appreciation as she approached the table. "You look amazing." He leaned in to kiss her cheek.

"You clean up well yourself," she replied, as she sat on the chair he pulled out for her.

As he sat back down, Andy said, "I'm happy you agreed to have dinner with me tonight. I-I'm going through a lot, Sunshine...and I don't think I can do it alone."

"You're not the only one," she said and wondered how she could ask him where he was when Erikka was murdered. And how dare he sit across from her asking for her support. She reminded herself that Ray didn't believe Andy to be guilty. *But what if Ray is wrong? Not even Babe Ruth hit the ball out of the park every time he came up to bat.*

"Are you okay, Sunshine?" he asked. "You seem distracted."

"I've had a long day, that's all—apartment renovations, Harvest Festival preparations—lots of minutiae."

"Is there anything I can help with?"

His question was the opening she needed to get some answers. "Actually, I spoke with Roger Mitchell today. Were you aware Erikka had a stalker?"

He shrugged. "She said something about it a time or two, but I figured she was trying to make me jealous. She also told me once that she was seeing someone, but none of us ever met her mystery man."

Before Katie could question him further, a waitress arrived. She brought a beer for Andy and a white wine for Katie.

"I hope you don't mind I went ahead and ordered your drink," Andy said.

"It's fine." She knew her voice was as stiff as her backbone, but she still managed a slight smile and nodded a thank you to the waitress.

"You're welcome!" The girl beamed at them. "Those cheese sticks should be out in a couple of minutes."

Katie sipped her wine and was glad when the waitress scampered off to check on another table. She was suddenly in no mood to deal with someone who could feign such cheery excitement over an appetizer. In fact, she wished she hadn't agreed to come here at all. *Boo-hoo, poor Andy needs some support and encouragement. Well, guess what? So do I.*

"Why do you believe Erikka made up her stalker and so-called mystery man to make you jealous?" she asked.

"Look, I knew she had a crush on me. But she knew I was with you."

"Except when you weren't."

Ignoring her statement, Andy swigged his beer. He seemed to be pondering how to get Katie onto a different subject when an older couple stopped at their table.

"Andy, dear, we're sorry to interrupt, but we wanted to offer our condolences." The woman patted Andy's shoulder.

"If there's anything we can do, you only have to ask," the man added.

"Thank you," Andy said. "Your sympathy and encouragement mean a lot."

The woman looked at Katie. "We're Judy and Bob Mills. Andy and Erikka visited our bed and breakfast in Rochester once." She smiled sadly. "Such a lovely couple."

"Is this fetching young lady your sister, Andy?" the man asked.

Katie had no idea how Andy replied. The blood in her veins had turned to ice and all she could hear was her heart pounding in her ears while Judy Mills' voice repeated over and over: *Andy and Erikka visited our bed and breakfast in Rochester....*

Andy had already admitted to sleeping with Erikka once. To learn they'd visited a B&B in Rochester proved it wasn't just a one-time slip. It was a full-blown affair!

Too stunned to move, Katie was jolted back to reality when the waitress brought their appetizer. Judy and Bob said their goodbyes and retreated. Feeling suddenly nauseous Katie sat contemplating the platter of cheese sticks in the center of the table.

Andy reached out and took one of her hands in both of his. "Katie, please—"

"When?" She jerked her hand away and slowly raised her eyes to his. "When were the two of you in Rochester?"

"It was the night you stayed with Ray's daughters. He'd been arrested, and I was angry that you were going above and beyond for him."

"So, your affair with Erikka was *my* fault?" she asked angrily.

"You actually have the gall to blame *me*? Don't you have to make reservations at B&Bs well in advance?"

"Not when you know someone. After all, *you* were able to stay at Sassy Sally's at a moment's notice." He took a gulp of beer. "Erikka's family are friends of the Mills. That's how we got in on such short notice."

Katie was beginning to suspect this wasn't Andy's first beer of the evening. "And why *wouldn't* they welcome such a lovely couple to their B&B?"

"I'm sorry." He took a cheese stick and put it on the small white plate in front of him. "By the way, I appreciate your not telling the Mills the truth about our relationship. I wouldn't want Erikka's family to be humiliated."

The numbness was wearing off now, and Katie gave a harsh laugh. "Goodness, no! It would be such a tragedy for anyone to know the truth about Erikka…for the Wiley clan to be *humiliated*. But go ahead and heap one mortification after another onto Katie's head—she can take it!" She scraped back her chair, tossed her napkin onto the table, and stormed out of the restaurant. She expected Andy to hurry after her but—for whatever reason—he didn't.

A far cry from the weepy woman in the shower, Katie was now livid. Although she knew better than to get behind the wheel of her car in her emotional state, she did. Pushing her pedal to the metal, Katie drove far too fast.

It wasn't but a minute before a car pulled up behind her and the driver put on his four-way flashers. She knew it wasn't Andy. He hadn't even tried to stop her when she'd left the restaurant.

Peering into the rearview mirror, she recognized Ray's junker. She swerved onto the shoulder of the road and slammed her gearshift into park. Ray pulled his vehicle up behind her. Katie jumped out of her own and stalked over to intercept the former detective.

"What's the matter with you?" she shouted.

Exiting his car, Ray yelled, "*Me*? You're the one trying to get yourself killed!"

She anchored her hands to her hips, refusing to back down from any fight that came her way this evening. "Why are you following me?"

"I wasn't following *you*."

She gasped. "Then you were tailing Andy? You lied to me—you do think he's guilty of murder!"

"Don't put words in my mouth, woman," Ray retorted.

"Then explain to me what you're doing standing on the side of the road with me," she accused as traffic zoomed by them.

"I'm here because you left the steakhouse in a rage and were driving recklessly." His lips twitched. "I'd turn you over my knee and give you a spanking, but I'm afraid we'd both enjoy it too much."

"You'd die trying!" she shouted.

He laughed. "There's my little spitfire."

Katie's eyes narrowed. "You think you're funny, huh?"

"I'm a regular Jerry Seinfeld."

"Then answer my question, Jerry. Do you think Andy could be guilty of murdering Erikka?"

Shifting from one foot to the other, Ray said, "I still think the only thing Andy Rust is guilty of is of being a damned fool. But after you came to me this morning and asked, I wanted to be certain."

She nodded. "Fair enough." Her shoulders slumped and she let out a heavy breath, feeling more than a little chagrined. "I suppose I should thank you for pulling me over. Once a cop, always a cop, huh?"

"Something like that. What made you come storming out of the restaurant like a whirling dervish?" Ray asked.

Katie turned and leaned against her driver's side door, which felt cool on her backside. "A couple who owned a B&B wanted to offer Andy their condolences on Erikka's death."

"That was nice of them."

"A B&B that Andy and Erikka visited for an overnight stay back in June?"

Ray grimaced and let out a breath. "I'll bet that didn't go over well."

"I thought about shoving a couple of cheese straws up his nose."

Ray winced.

Katie crossed her arms across her chest and let out a breath, every muscle in her body tensed. Fight or flight—and she'd flown.

"Would you like me to drive you home?" Ray offered.

"Home? I don't have a home—at least not right now. And I sure as hell am going to empty everything I own out of the apartment over Angelo's as soon as possible. If I can't move in right away, I suppose I'll have to rent a self-store unit."

"I've got some room in my garage."

Ray was still in the rental house, and Katie knew he hadn't totally unpacked from his move the previous year. The garage was still filled with boxes. His house-hunting efforts seemed to have come to a standstill.

"That's very nice of you, but I can manage. I've already called a mover."

"Why don't you take the rest of the evening to figure out your next move. Your apartment over the tea shop will be ready pretty soon. Now's not the time to rush into things."

"I'd say I've waited far too long to make the break." She glanced askance to see that Ray was trying to stifle a smile. "Don't get any ideas, Ray," she warned.

"About what?"

"About anything."

He sobered. "Katie, I'm your friend. I'll always be your friend, and if that's all I'll ever be, I'm okay with that."

Sure, now even Ray didn't want her.

Katie shook her head. “I’m going back to Sassy Sally’s and hope Brad made enough dinner for four.”

“I’d be happy to take you to dinner.”

“Thanks, but ... I’m good.”

She had already said far too much. If she was going to commiserate with anyone, it would be Nick...or Seth, or Don, or Brad.

It was then Katie realized there were far, far too many men in her life.

CHAPTER 11

Hungry and not wanting to invade Sassy Sally's kitchen, Katie parked her car in front of Tealicious. Upon unlocking the door and entering, she ventured to the kitchen where she peered into the refrigerator to see what she had to work with. Ham, herbed butter, watercress, mayo, roast beef—she took all of it out and placed it onto the counter. Next, she retrieved a slice of rye bread, a slice of wheat, and a slice of white. Cutting the rye bread in half, she spread some mayo on it and then stacked the ham. On the wheat, she piled on roast beef and light horseradish. The white bread was reserved for the herbed butter and watercress. Now if she only had a bottle of wine—or two—to wash it all down.

After arranging the tea sandwiches on a plate, she put on a pot of kava tea to soothe her nerves and looked to see what left-over pastries remained after the teashop had closed for the day. Sadly, the oatmeal chocolate chip bars were all gone, but a few of the key lime cookies and some almond butter shortbread remained. She piled a few of each on another plate and took them to her favorite table in the empty, dimly lit dining room.

Katie sat and studied her repast wondering, after what she'd learned about Andy and Erikka, how she managed to retain an appetite. Maybe she was in shock. Yeah, that sounded right. Except...if she was honest with herself, she'd suspected Andy had lied to her about his relationship with Erikka. She'd seen them together too many times through the pizzeria's big front window, laughing, looking at each other with eyes that sparkled—yes, sparkled—like in a Hallmark movie! And now she felt like a damn fool for trusting him.

A noise at the shop's door caused her to look up. Key in hand, Brad entered the shop. He looked around the room with concern, having not yet seen her, and Katie called to him: "Over here!"

"Oh!" He let out a breath as he strode toward her table. "What are you doing here so late? Are you all right?"

Katie shrugged. "Pretty much."

"I didn't intend to intrude," he said. "I was concerned when I saw lights on in the dining room. I'm accustomed to seeing them upstairs in the apartment after closing but not down here."

"You aren't intruding in the least. I appreciate your concern and diligence." She nodded toward a chair. "Care to join me?"

He sat. "I take it your evening with Andy didn't go well then."

"It was practically over before it started." She told him about the Rochester inn owners who'd stopped by the table to express their condolences to Andy on his loss. "That would've been fine had they been consoling him on the loss of his friend-slash-assistant manager. But, no! They thought I was Andy's *sister*! And they told me what a lovely couple they found Andy and Erikka to be when they stayed at the inn!"

"Oh, wow. That really sucks." He snagged a piece of the almond butter shortbread. "Want me to punch Andy for you?"

"If anybody punches Andy, it's gonna be *me*. I wouldn't deprive myself of the satisfaction." She sipped her tea, feeling heartsick. "But violence isn't the answer. I've been such a fool, and I'm not wasting another minute on Andy Rust wondering why he did what he did, why I wasn't enough for him, and if I could ever forgive and trust him again. All I want now is to clear myself of suspicion in Erikka's death and move on with my life."

"Hear, hear. You do realize I'll help in any way I can, don't you?"

"I do," she said and even managed a weak smile. "And your support means a lot to me."

After eating in silence for a moment, Katie added, "I'm sorry I wasn't around to help you through your breakup with Julia."

"That would have been difficult, since we hadn't yet met," he said and laughed. "Still, I'm kinda glad you weren't." He gave her a wry grin. "I was such a horrible friend to everyone who tried to help me that I managed to alienate almost all of them. Thankfully, Nick remained a true friend and refused to budge—it was he who was finally able to talk me into going to rehab."

"How long did it take you to get over her?" Katie asked before popping the rest of the watercress sandwich into her mouth.

"Not long once I dealt with my anger and got sober," he said. "I accepted the fact that she didn't want me and realized that if she didn't love me I didn't want her either. And, eventually, my love for her dimmed and made it possible for me to move on. You'll get to that point, too."

Katie managed a wan smile. "Promise?"

He nodded. "Cross my heart."

They finished eating, and Brad insisted on helping Katie with the dishes and buttoning up the kitchen for the night.

"Are you going to drive back to Sassy Sally's?" he asked, as he locked the door.

"No. I can move my car tomorrow. Then again, I'll be parking behind Tealicious from now on anyway."

"Great, then I'll walk you home."

Home? Not quite.

At that moment, they heard a slam from somewhere on the darkened Square. Brad stepped protectively in front of Katie.

"What was that?" she asked.

"Probably just one of the merchants closing up shop. Come on."

He started walking, and Katie hurried to catch up. Although she wasn't superstitious, Katie was oddly glad she had the crystal from The Flower Child in her purse.

* * *

WHEN KATIE RETURNED to her room at Sassy Sally's, she cuddled with Mason and Della on the bed. She told the cats all about how rotten her so-called date had been, and then she promised them they would be moving into their new home soon.

Seeing that it wasn't terribly late, she picked up her phone and called John Healy.

"Good evening, Katie," Healy answered brightly. "I hope nothing's wrong."

She gave a weary laugh. "You're hoping I'm not calling to complain about anything."

"Well, sure, but your satisfaction is my top priority. What's up?"

"I'm actually calling to see if I can move my furniture into the apartment sooner than I'd anticipated. I know I told you I was planning to do it at the end of the week, but I'd like to go ahead and move some of it in if I can. I'm eager to establish my new home for myself and my cats."

"I don't see why you couldn't," he said. "It's close enough to the end of the week that I believe it'll be fine. We're just doing the final touches now—we're almost ready for you to do your walk-through. Would you like to do that before moving the furniture in?"

"Sure. Thanks, John."

"That's what I'm here for. Let me know when to expect the movers."

"I will, thanks."

Katie ended the call. Saying she was eager to move in was putting it mildly. While her new home would be smaller than even the apartment over Angelo's Pizzeria, it would be hers—*all* hers. Well, except for her being beholden to her ex-mother-in-law, Margo for the loan to do the work. But she had a plan to pay off that debt and she'd make that self-imposed deadline on time, if not before.

After reaching to turn off the light by the side of the bed, she sank back into the mattress. As she did so, her cats moved to nestle against her. It was then that she finally gave into the tears that had been threatening for hours. And she cried herself to sleep.

* * *

BY THE NEXT MORNING, Katie had not only regained her composure, but her resolve, as well. She dressed and ventured out to power walk around Victoria Square. When she saw Moonbeam unlocking the door to The Flower Child, she called, "Good morning!"

Moonbeam turned and said, "Hey, Katie! That looks fun. I really should exercise more often." She pushed open the door and stood on the threshold. "Would you like to come in?"

"I would actually." Katie paused. "What does my aura look like today?"

Moonbeam waffled her hand back and forth. "No way near as bad as it was, but still not in the most optimum place. Have you suffered another shock recently?"

Katie didn't want to confide too much to Moonbeam, since she still didn't know the woman well. So, she gave a humorless laugh and said, "I feel as if lately my life has turned into a B-list horror movie—one scare after another. But that's not why I'm here—I'm here to make sure you know about the Harvest Festival."

"I hadn't heard about it," Moonbeam said, so Katie explained that it was an annual, highly publicized event that Victoria Square merchants participated in to offer sales and to get their name in front of customers.

"I hope you'll participate," Katie said. "People need to know about The Flower Child." She smiled. "Also, this year, Artisans Alley is hosting a vendor appreciation reception. The arrangements are still being made, but I wanted to extend an invitation to you while it was on my mind. It would give you a chance to meet your fellow merchants—or, you know, the ones you haven't met yet."

"Awesome! I'll look forward to it."

Katie took some money from the wristband wallet she wore. "Thank you again for the massage and the crystal." She slid the money across the counter.

Moonbeam held up a hand. "You put that right back where you got it. The massage and the crystal were gifts. I'm happy they made you feel better."

"They sure did," Katie said. "I apologize again that I didn't come by to check on you sooner."

"Nonsense. You've had a lot on your mind. Do you have a few minutes to chat? I don't want to keep you from your walk."

"Trust me—I'd much rather chat."

"Super. Let me fill the kettle with water, and in a couple of minutes, we can have tea while we *spill* tea." She giggled at her own joke as she took the kettle into the tiny kitchenette.

Katie looked around the shop. She hadn't paid much attention to it when she'd been there before—she'd been too relaxed by her massage and then mildly unsettled by Moonbeam's talk of Erika's negative energy and where it might go.

The Flower Child was a charming little shop. In addition to the crystals, herbal teas, and eclectic jewelry, Moonbeam's inventory also consisted of dream catchers, scented soaps, lotions, candles, CBD oil products, incense, and new-age books lining her shelves and display cases.

Moonbeam returned and attached the kettle to the heating element, plugging it in. After flipping on the device, she returned to the kitchen for two mugs and a variety of tea blends. "What's your pleasure?"

Katie chose a maple oolong. "Tell me—what was it like growing up with the name *Moonbeam*?"

Laughing as she plucked a white pear tea from the platter, she said, "Surprisingly, it wasn't that big a deal. My parents taught me to embrace my uniqueness and to ignore any negativity that tried to worm its way into my life. So I ignored the bullies, and everyone else accepted me as the girl with the quirky name."

"What are your parents' names?" Katie asked, as she placed the tea bag into her mug.

"Mary and John." At Katie's surprised expression, Moonbeam added, "If I'm lying, I'm dying."

Both women laughed.

"I'm really glad you made your way to Victoria Square," Katie said.

"Me, too." Moonbeam poured hot water into both their mugs, and the teas' soothing aromas filled the air. "By the way, your prediction came true—a couple of detectives stopped by yesterday to ask me if I'd seen or heard anything unusual on the night prior to or the morning of Erikka Wiley's death."

Katie stirred a packet of stevia into her tea. "What did you tell them?"

"The truth. I didn't see or hear anything. I did wonder, though, if either of those policemen was the one Erikka had dated."

Her spoon clattered onto the countertop. "Wh-what?"

"You didn't know?" Moonbeam lifted one shoulder in a half-shrug. "Of course, she could've been lying—who's to say?"

"Wait. Erikka *told* you she was dating a police officer? When?"

"One night, I went into Angelo's right around closing time for one of those yummy cinnamon rolls. Erikka was getting ready to leave, and I offered to walk out with her. You know, safety in numbers and all?" She took a sip of her tea. "Anyway, she said something along the lines of, "Don't worry about me. I'm dating a cop. He always makes sure I'm safe."

"How weird," Katie murmured.

"Right? I was a little affronted that she didn't care about *my* safety in the least. Of course, I've already told you what shape that woman's aura was in." Giving a slight shake of her head, Moonbeam added, "I suppose I shouldn't have been surprised at her complete self-absorption."

"Did she make her comment loudly—possibly for the benefit of anyone else who might be listening?" Katie asked.

"I don't think so. The only other person I saw was a kid mopping the floor...and he was wearing earbuds."

Was that kid Roger?

Erikka was dating a cop? Had Andy known that? And, if so, could he have been jealous?

Unfortunately, now that she and Andy were officially through, Katie wasn't in a position to ask.

A cop? Who could that have been? McKinlay Mill had no police force. As a village, they depended on the county mounties for protection, but the next town over had its own force, as did the city of Rochester. The word "cop" covered a lot of territory. Was the man from Erikka's past? Where could she have met him?

Those were questions Katie feared she'd never have answered.

CHAPTER 12

Finishing her three-circuit power walk around the Square and returning to Sassy Sally's, Katie decided to follow up on Moonbeam's assertion that Erikka claimed to be dating a police officer. She was glad she didn't bump into anyone on her way to her room. She wanted to shower, change, and investigate this rumor on her own.

For one thing, why would Erikka still be obsessed enough with Andy to pay a professional to photograph her in skimpy lingerie—and present those photos to Andy—if she was involved with someone else? Had she merely dated the other man—the officer—in an attempt to make Andy jealous? Or had Erikka been in some sort of love triangle with Andy *and* the policeman?

Katie guessed that since she and Andy had been together at the time, it was more fitting to deduce that—if Erikka was, in fact, involved with another man—the four of them had made up a love square.

More like some sort of freakish love merry-go-round. Why hadn't I seen what was going on right under my nose? Had I been too involved in my businesses, my new apartment, and Ray's plight that I hadn't paid enough attention to the dynamic between Andy and Erikka? Had I simply closed my eyes to what I hadn't wanted to believe? Or had I believed that Andy and Erikka were merely friends, like Ray and me?

Remembering the passionate kiss she and Ray had shared, Katie felt a stab of guilt.

But that was different! Andy and I were broken up when Ray and I kissed. Okay, maybe not officially, but... I'd have never acted on my feelings for Ray if—

The thought stopped her in her tracks. Her *feelings* for Ray? Did she *have* feelings for Ray that went beyond friendship? Obviously, that kiss said she did. Of course, the embrace had occurred at a time when she was feeling alone, vulnerable, and betrayed.

Shaking her head, Katie stepped into the shower's spray. Whether she had feelings for Ray Davenport—or anyone else—at this time was a distraction she didn't need in her life. It was taking every ounce of her mental capacity to run Artisans Alley and Tealicious, get ready to move into her new apartment, oversee the preparations for the Harvest Festival, and discover who'd murdered Erikka Wiley—or, at least, provide Detective Schuler with another viable suspect. All of this in addition to dealing with her breakup with Andy. Because one thing had become crystal clear to her the night before when Bob and Judy Mills stopped by their table to console Andy—her relationship with him was now irrevocably broken.

The water pounded down on her head, washing away the shampoo's lather. Too bad it couldn't wash away the profound sense of loss she felt.

* * *

UPON ARRIVING AT ARTISANS ALLEY, Katie scrounged a cup of coffee in the vendors' lounge and hid away in her office with her computer. According to Erikka's social media accounts, it didn't appear that any of the woman's friends or followers were police officers. Of course, Katie could only see the profile pictures and names of Erikka's friends—and not many officers used their uniform portrait for a profile pic—but none of the images leapt out at Katie as anyone she'd ever seen before. And since taking over the running of Artisans Alley, Katie had interacted with a *lot* of the county's finest.

Finding nothing helpful on Erikka's social media pages, she combed through both Erikka's sister's and her former boyfriend's pages. Nothing on either of those accounts provided the information Katie sought, but she did learn that Luke Stafford was working at a grocery store on the outskirts of town now. She decided to drop in there at lunchtime and see if she could talk with him.

Katie logged off social media and was determined to knuckle down and get some work done when Janey Ingram barreled through her door after giving the briefest of knocks.

"Good morning!" Smiling broadly as she plunked down in Katie's only guest chair, Janey clapped her hands together. "Thank you for teaming me up with Izzy. What a little dynamo! After speaking with her, I believe she'll be a wonderful influence on VJ."

"I'm glad everything's going so well," Katie said. "How are the reception preparations going?"

"Just fine. I'm planning on talking with Chef Brad this afternoon about providing a few items for the buffet, and I thought I'd see if any of the other merchants want to showcase any of their specialties as well."

Frowning slightly, Katie said, "This event is *for* the merchants. I don't want them to feel obligated to provide the food."

"True. But hear me out." Janey leaned forward in her chair. "I'm having the majority of the food catered by Del's. The items provided by the merchants—*if they so choose*—are merely to promote their businesses to their peers."

"Okay. I can understand that, especially for us newbies like Tealicious."

There weren't any other "newbies" in Victoria Square, as far as eating establishments went, but perhaps the other merchants might have some new recipes they'd like to test out.

"Izzy is working on the entertainment," Janey said. "She's checking with some groups she and VJ know from their schools, and she might even be able to get the university's acapella choir to perform." Smiling, she added, "I'm looking forward to seeing what she comes back to me with."

"Great." Katie tasted her coffee and was disappointed to find it had grown cold. She stood. "Would you like a cup of coffee?"

Janey got to her feet and stepped toward the door. "No, thanks. I need to be going—I have a hundred things to do."

"Thanks for all your hard work," Katie said, opening the door with a pronounced bounce to her step. "Keep me posted."

She took her cup into the vendors' lounge, emptied it, and refilled it with fresh hot coffee that would, hopefully, help restart her brain. But first things first; she needed to call the moving company.

IT WAS NEARLY eleven that morning when Seth Landers made an unexpected appearance at Artisans Alley. Delighted, Katie stood and gave him a hug.

"I was in the neighborhood and thought I'd drop by," he said, lowering his lanky frame into the chair by Katie's desk.

She arched a brow and grinned. "Really? That old cliché?"

He laughed. "Clichés are still around because they're based in truth. Or, at least, some of them are."

"Speaking of truth..." She left the prompt open-ended.

Seth's smile faded. "I spoke with Nick, and he told me you were pretty upset when you came in last night."

"I wasn't as upset as I had been *before* I came in, but no—" She sighed— "it wasn't one of my better dates." She told Seth what had happened at the restaurant the night before. "So, anyway, I called the movers and they rescheduled me for tomorrow afternoon for no extra charge."

"Is the apartment ready then?" Seth asked.

She shrugged. "John Healy is putting the finishing touches on it. I spoke with him last night, and he said that bringing in the furniture now won't hinder the work that remains. He just wants me to do a walk-through before we do that. It'll happen later today."

"That's excellent news. I know you must feel relieved."

Katie gave a slow nod. "I am. The sooner I get my stuff out of Andy's building and into my own, the better. Now if I could only learn who killed Erikka Wiley."

"Your suspicions about her were correct, by the way. I'm telling you this in the strictest of confidences, but Jamie confirmed to me that Erikka wasn't pregnant."

Seth's partner, Jamie Siefert, worked in the medical examiner's office.

"That's not a surprise to me," Katie said. "You know what *is* though? Moonbeam Carruthers said this morning that Erikka told her she was dating a police officer. I've been trying to follow that lead, but I haven't had any luck."

"You know whose help you need with that, don't you?"

Of course, she did. She'd have to swallow her pride and talk to Ray.

Katie sidestepped Seth's observation. "The only other lead I have is Erikka's assertion that she had a stalker. I'm thinking it might've been her ex-boyfriend, Luke Stafford. He's working at a grocery store in Greece, and I plan to go there on my lunchbreak to talk with him."

"Not alone, you aren't. If I remember correctly, that guy is dangerous." Setting his mouth in a firm line, he said, "I'm coming with you."

Katie managed a wry grin. "I'd welcome the company."

“Great. I hear they have a market café.”

“They do indeed.”

“Then would you do me the honor of having lunch with me there?”

Katie’s smile softened. “I’d be delighted.”

CHAPTER 13

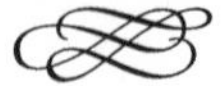

Seth insisted on driving them to the grocery store where Luke Stafford was a full-time, day-shift manager. As she got out of Seth's sleek black Mercedes, Katie felt under-dressed in her jeans and T-shirt. She'd rather talk to Luke without the impeccably dressed attorney at her side, but that wasn't going to happen. She strode toward the entrance with Seth matching her stride for stride.

"What's your game plan once we get in here?" he asked.

"If I don't see him right away, I'll ask for him at the service desk."

Seth took her arm, "You can't just storm in there, ask to see Stafford, and start firing questions at him."

"Please," she said and glowered. "I have more diplomacy than that."

Seth still looked wary as he accompanied her into the store where the aromas of pizza and other hot entrees from the café filled the air, making Katie's stomach rumble. Rather than approaching the customer service counter, Katie wandered into the produce section. "What beautiful apples!" she exclaimed, plucking an Empire apple from a bin. "Aren't these gorgeous, Seth?"

His eyebrows came together. "Sure." It was evident he hadn't a clue as to what she was doing.

A tall, slightly stooped older gentleman was adding Vidalia onions to an already ponderous pile.

Katie approached the man. "Hi. Is there any chance I could speak with the store manager?"

Noticing the apple in her hand, he asked, "Is there something wrong with that apple?"

"On the contrary, I think this is a fantastic apple," Katie said. "I want to know what farm it came from. Are these apples locally grown?"

"Yep. They're from Foster Farms." At Katie's squint, he added, "It's an orchard in Wayne County."

"Cool. Is the produce there organic?" she asked.

"Some of it is."

At the older man's succinct response, Seth crossed his arms and smirked at Katie.

Raising her chin, Katie said, "You certainly are knowledgeable about your produce."

"I have to be," the man said. "It's my job."

"Marvelous." Katie gave the man a broad smile. "I think it's wonderful when people take such pride in their work. In fact, I would love to speak with your manager to tell him of your superior knowledge." She gave him a wink.

The man's cheeks reddened. "That's not necessary. I'm happy I could help."

"But I really would like to talk with your manager," Katie said.

A deep, irritated voice came from behind her. "Is there a problem here, Duncan?"

"N-no sir," the older man stammered. "No p-problem."

"No problem at all." Katie turned and found herself face to

chest with Luke Stafford. She'd forgotten how tall, muscular, and scary the man was.

Looking up into Luke's face, Katie feigned surprise at seeing him there. "Luke? Luke Stafford? It's me—Katie Bonner."

He scrutinized her face, his expression stony. "I remember you."

"And Seth?" Taking Seth's elbow, she pulled him closer. "You remember Seth Landers, don't you?" she asked, knowing Luke had never met him.

"Can't say as I do."

"That's okay," Seth said. "I'm not that memorable."

Katie gave his arm a playful tap. "Of course, you are! But where are my manners? Luke, I'm so sorry for your loss."

Luke's almost black eyes narrowed. "What loss?"

"Well...Erikka Wiley. You *did* hear about her death, didn't you?"

"Sure, I heard about it. It's no skin off my nose, though. She and I were over long ago. In fact, I'm engaged to a much prettier woman now."

Was he kidding? Erikka was a stunning brunette.

"Congratulations." Katie's brain raced for something else to ask him—a way to find out where he was when Erikka was killed.

"Thanks. But you aren't here to ask about my love life. Why were you giving Duncan a hard time?"

"She wasn't," Seth said. "She wanted to tell his boss what a fine job he's is doing."

Duncan nodded emphatically.

"Fine." Luke jerked his head toward the cart of vegetables that needed to be added to the shelves and tubs. "Please get back to work. I'll handle this," he told the older man. Turning back to Katie, he snapped, "Is there anything else?"

"Had you seen Erikka lately?" she asked, trying to sound casual.

He anchored his fists to his hips, scowling. "That's none of your business." "Now, if there's nothing else I can help you with, I have a department to run," he said pointedly.

"No, thank you. It was so nice to see you again," Katie lied sweetly. "Have a good life." Without a backward glance, Katie flounced out of the produce department with Seth by her side.

He waited until they were closer to the café's hot food trays to speak, looking over his shoulder to see if Luke was watching them. He wasn't. "So, I suppose he's off our suspect list for Erikka's stalker."

"Not necessarily. He wouldn't tell me when he'd seen her last, especially not if he'd been stalking her. And how do we know his story about being engaged is even true?" She took out her phone, planning to check out Luke's social media pages once more.

"You need to ask Andy," Seth said. "He's your best chance of finding out who might have been stalking Erikka."

She sighed, slipped her phone back into her purse and kept walking. "I know. And he's left a dozen messages on my phone since last night but I'm not ready to face him yet."

"It's something you're going to have to do sooner or later. Personally, I think you should get it over with if you really want insights into Erikka's murder. Besides, if nothing else, you need to get closure with Andy."

Katie felt herself deflate more than just a little. "You're right, of course. I was planning on talking with him when I dropped off the keys to the apartment, but I suppose this can't wait." She looked up and frowned at Seth. "Can it?"

"If it were me, I'd want answers—and the sooner, the better."

Katie stopped walking. "Wait. You know something, don't you?" she accused.

Expelling a breath, he said, "Not really, but Jamie has heard rumors floating around. Schuler is really gunning for you—and Andy—on this."

Katie's brow furrowed. "You mean, he thinks we conspired to kill Erikka?"

Seth spread his hands. "Again, it's just a rumor. But if you can, you need to find a more viable suspect and concentrate on him or her."

What he said resonated with her.

Katie's stomach growled once again. She inhaled the aroma of various Chinese entrees that sat in the hot-food trays.

"Lunch?" Seth suggested.

"Lunch," Katie whole-heartedly agreed, and hang the calories.

* * *

LATER THAT AFTERNOON, Katie sat at her desk at Artisans Alley and debated about what was the lesser of two evils: to contact Ray or Andy. She chose Ray.

She pulled up the contacts list on her phone, pressed Ray's number, and waited for him to answer.

"Still mad at me?" he asked brusquely, apparently recognizing her number.

"Wow, that's some greeting. You're obviously not vying for the title of most congenial phone recipient."

"Answer my question, Bonner. If you're still miffed, I don't have time to be berated," he growled.

"I'm not going to berate you, *Davenport*." Was that what they were doing now—addressing each other by last names as if they were hockey teammates? "I called to ask you a question about Erikka."

He let out what seemed to be an exasperated breath before answering, "All right, let's hear it."

"This morning, I had an interesting conversation with Moonbeam Carruthers over at The Flower Child. Apparently, Erikka told Moonbeam she was dating a police officer," Katie said. "She didn't give her a name, though, and—"

"Isn't she supposed to be psychic or something?" he interrupted. "She strikes me as a real woo-woo type. Can't she look into a crystal ball or something else to find out who Erikka was dating? Better yet, why doesn't she conduct a séance and get Erikka to tell her the identity of her murderer?"

It seemed like the previous year of friendship and trust had suddenly evaporated, and Ray sounded like the curmudgeonly detective Katie had initially met two years before.

"Calling you was obviously a mistake. I'm sorry I interrupted your work." She ended the call, stabbing the end-call icon—the equivalent of hanging up on him.

She sat there, fuming, still not ready to talk with Andy, and decided she might as well go to Tealicious and do the walk-through of the apartment. She'd no more than gotten up from her desk when Ray stormed into her office.

"Don't ever hang up on me again," he said angrily.

Katie's cheeks flushed with irritation. "Then don't be such an ass. If you were still angry with me, you shouldn't have answered my call."

"If I recall correctly, *you're* the one who gave me a dressing down on the side of the road last night."

"Because you were spying on me!"

"We've already been over this, and I have no intention of repeating myself," he asserted.

Katie glowered at the man. "How'd you get here so fast anyway?"

Ray shrugged. "I was in the building talking with Vance."

She wondered what would bring him to the Alley in the middle of the day but figured it was probably none of her business. "I'm sorry I hung up on you," she lied, "but if you'll excuse me, I need to be somewhere else right now."

"Where?" he demanded.

Pursing her lips, she debated not telling him, but at last she said, "If you must know, I'm going to do a walk-through of my new apartment."

"Fine. I'll come with you," he said.

Katie glowered. "I don't *need* your input."

"Oh, yeah?" He raised a bushy eyebrow. "Then why did you call me?"

"I called to see if you'd ask some of your police friends if they knew of anyone who was seeing Erikka," she said. "Maybe the comment she made to Moonbeam was a lie, but I'd like to know for sure. Seth told me Jamie, his partner, heard a rumor that Schuler is determined to pin Erikka's murder on Andy and me."

Ray swore under his breath. "Okay," he said grudgingly. "I'll look into it."

"Thank you."

"And I *would* like to go do the walk-through with you," he said more kindly. "I might catch something that you don't. That is unless you're planning on having *Brad* walk through the place with you."

"Why would I do that?" Katie frowned. "He's probably too busy to bother with it. Plus, he's a chef. What would he know about apartment renovation that I wouldn't?"

Shrugging, Ray said, "Well, I imagine he'll be spending a lot of time there..."

"Downstairs in the tearoom." Her eyes widened. "You *were* still spying on me last night, and you saw Brad and me leaving Tealicious!"

"I saw you, but it wasn't because I was spying on anyone. I'd stopped by Wood U. Trust me—I couldn't care less what you were doing last night."

Katie stood on her tiptoes and got almost nose to nose to Ray. "Is that right?"

"Don't strike that match unless you're ready for it to burn," he warned.

The intensity in his eyes disarmed her and the electricity

between them crackled. She lowered herself back to her normal height. "Brad saw a light on at Tealicious and stopped to make sure everything was all right. I hadn't eaten at the restaurant and didn't want to invade Nick and Don's kitchen, so I stopped at the tea shop. No big deal."

He nodded.

Was that a smile? If so, he hid it too quickly to be sure.

"You're more than welcome to come do the walk-through with me," she said.

"Fine," he said and offered his hand, but Katie was perfectly capable of making her way through the Alley and onto the tarmac outside without the help of a man—*any* man. And she was damned if she was about to let Ray bully her into feeling like a damsel waiting for rescue.

"Follow me," she said and strode past him and into the vendors' lounge.

Ray obediently traveled in her wake.

CHAPTER 14

Katie and Ray headed up the covered stairwell to the private entrance to her new apartment positioned at the side of the building. While John and his team had done a wonderful job building the staircase, he hadn't yet put up the handrail. Naturally, Ray immediately complained about it.

"I hope you never suffer vertigo," he grumbled. "And what about these steps in the winter or when you're carrying groceries in? They need treads."

Katie blew out a breath, resisting the urge to smack him in the head. "Mr. Healy is working as quickly as he can. He'll have the handrail installed by the time I move in."

"I'd hold up my crossed fingers, but I'm afraid I might fall."

"Is your balance that bad?" Katie challenged. "Rose might know of some senior exercise classes you could take."

"Ha, ha," Ray deadpanned.

The door at the top of the landing was open and Katie greeted the contractor upon entering the apartment.

"Hey, Katie."

"John, this is my friend Ray Davenport. He wanted to do the walk-through with me," she said. "Is that all right?"

"Fine by me." Healy shook Ray's hand. "Where would you like to start?"

"You *do* have the handrails for the staircase made, don't you?" Ray asked.

"I sure do. We'll be putting them up as soon as Roger gets back."

"I didn't have a chance to inspect the latest improvements in the kitchen when I was here yesterday," Katie said.

Healy extended an arm toward the galley kitchen. "After you, m'lady."

Katie advanced to her galley kitchen. "The tile in here is beautiful," she said, admiring the blue-and-white flooring. "It looks even better than I'd imagined."

Healy smiled at her appreciation of his work. "Thank you."

Ray went to the refrigerator and opened the door. He checked the temperature in both the refrigerator and the freezer. He then turned on the faucets in the kitchen.

"What're you doing?" Katie asked.

"Checking the water pressure and how long it takes the water to get warm." He plugged the sink, filled it with water, and then let the water go down the drain. Nodding, he said, "Drains quickly—that's good. John, have you got a phone charger?"

"I do. I'll get it for you."

When John left the room to get the charger, Katie hissed, "Can't you wait until you get back to Wood U to charge your phone?"

"I'm not charging my phone," he said.

"Then what are you doing?"

"Here you go," Healy said, returning to the kitchen with the charger.

Ray took out his phone. "I'm afraid this charger won't fit my phone. Could I borrow yours?"

"Of course." John handed over his phone.

"I'm sorry," Katie said to John. "I have no idea what he's doing."

John grinned. "He's checking the power outlets. You should be happy he's looking out for you. I'd do the same thing for *my* daughter."

Ray's cheeks flushed, but he ignored the comment. Katie couldn't suppress a smile and impishly chose not to correct Healy's assumption.

Thirty minutes later, after Ray had flushed the toilet, made sure the smoke and carbon monoxide detectors worked properly, checked the windows for drafts, and inspected the locks, the walk-through was complete.

As Healy escorted Ray to the apartment door, Katie glimpsed something gleaming in the corner of the living room windowsill. Looking down, she saw it was a gold butterfly ring. A chill ran through her as she picked it up and slipped it into her pocket. She'd seen it before on Erikka Wiley's hand. What was it doing in her newly renovated apartment?

"Katie?" Ray called.

"Coming." She paused on the landing as Healy outlined the rest of the minor jobs that still needed his attention. "We'll make your timeline with no problem," he assured Katie.

"Thanks. I can't tell you how happy I am with your work and how beautiful it turned out. I can't wait to move in."

"It's been my pleasure," Healy said, nodded, and went back inside.

Katie followed Ray down the stars. They walked onto the tarmac and paused to gaze up at the building's second floor that Katie would soon call home.

"Do you wanna tell me what you slipped into your pocket up there?" Ray asked.

"Not particularly." Katie sighed and jerked her head toward Artisans Alley. "At least not here. Let's talk about it in my office."

Ray shrugged. "Fair enough."

She should've known Ray's eagle eyes would've caught her palming the ring. Once they were seated in her office and Katie was munching on a peppermint, she removed the ring from her pocket and placed it on the desk between them.

"I'm guessing this isn't yours," he said, picking up the ring and examining it more closely.

"No. And I don't think it belonged to the teashop's previous owners either." She swallowed. "I believe it was Erikka's. I recall seeing her wear one like it."

"Erikka's?" He frowned. "When—and *why*—would she have been in your apartment?"

"That's just it. I can't think of a reason she would have been."

"Then who *has* been in your apartment who could've had access to this ring?" Ray asked.

Katie shook her head. "I suppose it's possible Roger found it at Angelo's and took it with him to return to Erikka later..."

"What about Andy?"

"He hasn't been there." She rubbed her forehead. "Knowing what I now know, I wouldn't have put it past him to have a tryst with Erikka there, but John Healy and his crew have been working here since before I left the apartment over Angelo's."

"I'm sorry."

He'd spoken so softly Katie hadn't understood what he'd said.

She looked up into his eyes. "Excuse me?"

"I said I'm sorry. I never dreamed Andy would hurt you the way he has. You deserve better."

"Thank you." She blinked back the tears that threatened, embarrassed to be so weepy. "I'll survive."

"I know. We just need to keep you on this side of a jail cell." He held up the ring. "I'm betting this ring is a deliberate plant."

"You think so?"

Ray nodded. "And as such, you don't need to be found with it in your possession. Why don't I hang onto it?"

"That's not a bad idea. It would be just my luck for Schuler to find a murdered woman's ring in my apartment." She drew in a breath. "But, wait, what about you?"

"He isn't looking at me for this one," Ray said. "I'll put the ring somewhere safe."

"You mean, you'll hide it."

He grinned. "Well, I'm not going to go waving it around the Square."

"But how do I find out why the ring was in my apartment?"

"If it's important, someone will ask you about it. Trust me. That's why investigators always keep something about a crime scene from the public."

That sentiment didn't bring Katie any comfort.

* * *

AFTER RAY LEFT her new apartment, Katie sat at her shabby, ancient desk and wished she had a nice one for her new apartment. Francine, from whom she'd bought the tea shop, had left a desk upstairs—the space had served as her office—but it was small and chipped and ugly. Katie had instructed Healy to dispose of it when he began the renovations. He'd yet to do so.

Knowing she wouldn't get anything done the rest of the day for thinking about finding Erikka's ring, Katie took her small tape measure and informed Vance that she was going to the big antique arcade in the next town.

"Call me if you need me for anything," she told him.

"Will do."

Was it her imagination, or did Vance's spine stiffen ever so slightly and his chin come up a fraction at being left in charge? She smiled to herself. He was an excellent assistant manager. Sure, he'd been known to throw his weight around on occasion, but he really was indispensable.

As Katie drove the four or five miles along the back roads, her anxieties began to lessen, and she heaved a sigh of relief upon entering the store. She'd loved vintage furniture for as long as she could remember. Even as a little girl, she'd preferred to read on Aunt Liz's Victorian fainting couch as opposed to the well-worn easy chair. This store, with more than ninety vendors, was chock full of unique items.

As Katie wandered around the store, she wished her new apartment was bigger so that she could decorate it the way she truly wanted.

One day.

For now, a pretty little desk would have to suffice. She rounded a corner, and there it was—a secretary made of meranti wood and featuring a top door that folded down to create a desktop.

She walked over and gingerly lowered the door. Behind it, there were four cubbies and two adjustable shelves. Below the drawer were three doors.

Perfect. Absolutely perfect.

She could imagine the desk set she'd store on one of the shelves, the stamps and stationery she could tuck into a cubby... But would it fit into the space she'd allotted?

Biting her lower lip, she measured the length. It was thirty-six inches long. And now, the width. She measured twice to ensure the desk wasn't more than eighteen inches wide.

Yes! It would fit in the space she had in mind. And she could use one of the chairs from the breakfast set when she sat at the new-to-her desk.

Katie couldn't keep the smile off her face. This desk was so beautiful. It would serve several practical purposes—the least of which was additional storage space—and it was one new piece of furniture that held no memories of Chad, Andy, or anyone else.

She started when she heard a voice behind her ask, "Have you found something you like?"

Turning, Katie saw one of the apron-clad workers standing nearby. "Yes. I'll take it."

After paying for the desk and giving the shop her address for delivery, Katie was about to leave when she spotted a young woman with a baby in a carriage heading toward the building. She hurried to open the door.

"Thank you!" The woman looked up at Katie with a smile of relief. "I—" Whatever she'd been about to say died on her lips as her smile faded. "You!"

At that moment, Katie recognized her as well. Though she'd never met the woman, she'd seen Erryn's profile picture...and the sonogram her sister Erikka had used to trick Andy into thinking she was pregnant.

"I'm—I'm so sorry for your loss," Katie said softly.

"Are you?" Erryn demanded.

"Yes, I truly am."

"Detective Schuler seems to think *you* had the motive, means, and opportunity to...to—" She broke off, looking down at her baby boy, who'd started to whimper. "I can't do this right now."

"I assure you that I did not harm your sister in any way. I wasn't her biggest fan, but—"

"No, because you just couldn't let go of Andy Rust, could you? How pathetic that you kept hanging on when he was obviously in love with *my* sister?" She picked the baby up out of the stroller and bounced him on her hip.

"It wasn't like that," Katie said. "Andy never tried to break things off with me. He told me he still loved me, not Erikka."

Erryn's black eyes narrowed to slits. "You got rid of her so you could have him back. Admit it!" She practically spat the words in Katie's face.

"You've got it all wrong." Katie's voice was soft but firm. She could understand why Erryn was directing this venom in her direction, but she certainly didn't deserve it. Still, Katie had compassion for a grieving sister. "Excuse me."

Erryn didn't move. "Admit it!" she screamed.

When his mother lost it, the baby did, too. His face crumpled, and in seconds he was red-faced and wailing. His mother began to sob as well. The saleslady who'd handled the desk transaction for Katie was headed in their direction to see what the commotion was about. Katie merely brushed past Erryn and the child and left the shop. The desk was paid for. The store would deliver it, even if they now suspected Katie of murder.

As soon as she got into her car, she took out her phone. Hands shaking, she punched in Andy's number. He answered on the first ring.

"We have to meet and talk," she said, "and right now!"

CHAPTER 15

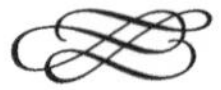

Katie and Andy agreed to meet at the apartment over Angelo's. Despite him working directly beneath in the pizzeria, Katie arrived before he did and was doing a final walk-through of the apartment to ensure that she had everything packed and ready to be moved. It was strange seeing the large cardboard boxes marked *Kitchen* and *Living Room*. She'd been eager to start on this new chapter of her life for months—but she'd never dreamed her leaving would include closing the book on her relationship with Andy.

Well…that wasn't entirely true.

As if conjured by her thoughts, her former "beloved" walked through the kitchen door and immediately put his arms around her.

"Sunshine, are you all right? You sounded so upset over the phone."

She wriggled out of his embrace. "I was upset. I *am* upset!" She explained about seeing Erikka's sister and the scene she'd made. "Apparently, Detective Schuler has convinced her that I killed Erikka."

Andy raked a hand through his hair and paced through the

kitchen into the living room. "That's utter nonsense. The man is grasping at straws, and he knows it. I'm going to talk with him."

"And say what?" Katie demanded. "Are you going to tell him you know I didn't do it because I'm such a great person? Like *that'll* sway him."

"I'll tell him you were with me that night—all night."

"But it's not true, and it contradicts what we've both previously told the man. That will just make it appear that we're both guilty and that we're using each other as alibis." Katie stalked into the living room and sat on the love seat. "We have to be rational."

He sat beside her and reached out as though he wanted to touch her but then dropped his hands onto his lap. "Tell me what to do, babe. I'll do anything to make this right."

She wasn't sure whether he was talking about solving Erikka's murder or repairing their relationship, but she wanted to avoid the latter. As far as she was concerned, their relationship was irrevocably broken. Their main, shared concern should be to prove themselves innocent of Erikka's murder.

"We know Schuler is either convinced of our guilt, or he merely wants to pin this murder on the two of us," Katie said. "The fact that Erikka lied about being pregnant dampens our motive, but I doubt that either Schuler or a jury would see it that way."

"Wait." Andy's jaw dropped. "Erikka *wasn't* pregnant? A-are... are you sure?"

She hadn't meant to blurt out the news about Erikka's *misconception*—at least, not now...not like this—but she had. And it was best that Andy knew the truth. He'd hurt her and she was furious with him, but she still cared enough about him not to want him possibly grieving for an unborn child who'd only been a fantasy in Erikka's twisted mind.

"I'm positive," she said softly. "Erikka used her sister's sonogram for her social media announcement."

Andy slumped against the love seat in obvious relief. "Thank

God. It was breaking my heart to think my son had been murdered. I-I mean, I didn't intend to get Erikka pregnant—and obviously, I didn't. It's just...I do want kids someday—*our* kids." He squeezed Katie's hand.

She pulled her hand back. "Please, let's get back on track. Neither of us will have a future to worry about if Schuler has his way. Now focus, Andy—we have to determine who killed Erikka...and why."

He merely nodded, probably too relieved that Erikka wasn't pregnant to think about much else at the moment. But Katie had to get through to him. She had to persuade him to help her.

"Moonbeam Carruthers told me that Erikka told her she was dating a cop," Katie said. "Did you notice any cops coming into Angelo's on a regular basis?"

"Sure." He shrugged. "Sheriff's deputies come into the pizzeria all the time—I give them a discount."

"Were any of them particularly friendly with Erikka?"

"They all were—she was..." He faltered before ending the sentence with "nice to them."

Katie wasn't fooled. The officers were friendly and flirty with Erikka because she was gorgeous.

"I'll ask the staff to see if any of them know anything about who Erikka might've been dating," Andy said.

"Thank you," Katie said. "I'm following up on every lead I can find. I mean, Erikka indicated on social media that she was being stalked and told Moonbeam she was dating a cop—I'm trying to find anything or anyone who'll make us appear less likely to have killed Erikka. I even went to Greece to talk with Luke Stafford."

He blinked. "You did what? You know what a hot head that guy is! Erikka said he was physically abusive to her when they dated. Why in the world would you go see him?"

"Because I'm trying to save our butts," Katie said. "Luke denies any knowledge of Erikka's recent activities. He says he's engaged to someone else and hadn't seen Erikka in ages. Still, while you're talking with your employees, would you mind checking to see if anyone might've seen a guy matching Luke's description hanging around?"

Andy nodded. "Of course. It would certainly make our lives a lot easier if Schuler could arrest Luke Stafford for Erikka's murder."

"Only if Luke is guilty," Katie pointed out.

"Yeah, but who would have more motive to kill Erikka than a jealous ex-lover?" he asked.

She grimaced. "According to Schuler, *we* do."

* * *

AFTER ANDY WENT BACK to work, Katie stayed behind to finish packing up a few things she'd left in the bedroom. On the nightstand was a photo of her and Andy in happier times. She couldn't even remember who'd snapped the photo—Rose, maybe?—but Katie and Andy were lovingly gazing into each other's eyes. It had been taken during the Square's Independence Day celebration the year before—a bright, beautiful summer's day filled with laughter, good food, and afterward sailing on Seth's boat on the lake, and fireworks. Lots of fireworks.

Andy spoke from the doorway, startling her so badly that she dropped the photograph. Luckily, the frame didn't break.

"I'm sorry," he said. "I thought you heard me come back in." He held up a box. "Thought you might need this."

"Yeah...thanks." She tried to wipe her eyes without his noticing, but that was impossible.

He came over and picked the photo up off the floor. He smiled. "I remember this. It was a terrific day."

"It was."

Placing the photograph back onto the nightstand, Andy asked, "So...will you be displaying this picture in your new apartment?"

"No. Right now it's a painful reminder of what we've lost."

"We could have it back again," he said. "And maybe even be stronger for weathering this storm."

Did he honestly believe she could ever trust him knowing how many times he'd lied to her? Betrayed her? Not wanting to argue, she said nothing and began packing items into the box.

Andy kissed the top of her head and left.

She resumed packing, including the photograph from the Independence Day celebration but placing it face-down in the box.

Within minutes, she heard a knock on the door. She sighed. Couldn't Andy just leave her in peace to finish packing away the remnants of their life together? She didn't move to answer it. After all, he had a key. Why didn't he simply come on back in as he had earlier?

The pounding became louder and more insistent. Maybe it wasn't Andy after all. But, who? The movers? No, they weren't expected until the next day.

Katie went to the door and looked through the peephole.

Schuler. Great. That's just who I needed to brighten up my day.

Opening the door, Katie said, "Good afternoon, Detective. How can I help you?"

He held up a piece of paper. "We have a warrant to search these premises, your office at Artisans Alley, and your residence above Tealicious."

"Wh-what?" It was only then that she noticed the other deputies standing behind Schuler.

Shoving the paper toward her, he said, "Here. It's all in there. Read it. Now, move aside."

Before Katie could adequately move out of Schuler's and the other deputies' way, Andy was muscling his way inside.

"What the hell is going on here?" he thundered, putting his body between Katie and the advancing herd of law enforcement officers.

"Ask your girlfriend." Schuler looked around Andy to Katie, a sneer curling his lip. "That is if you can still call her that. She's got the search warrant. It's up to her whether or not she lets you read it. But, for now, I need to ask you both to step outside."

"B-but what—? What are you looking for?" Katie asked.

"Evidence to prove your connection to the murder of Erikka Wiley." Schuler's tone was smug. Katie wouldn't have been surprised if he'd smiled at her when he said it. He must've practiced saying that with a straight face in the mirror before he drove there.

"I need my phone," she said. "It's in the bedroom."

"I'll go with you to ensure that's all you take," Schuler said.

"I'll go, too." Andy drew himself up to his full height, shaking with rage. Schuler looked much less intimidating when compared to Andy...or he *would* have had he not had the authority—and the obvious desire—to throw Katie in jail.

"This is ridiculous," Katie said as she strode to her bedroom with both the men in tow. "You know I didn't hurt anyone."

"Let's hope the evidence bears that out, Ms. Bonner." And then Schuler *did* have the nerve to give her that smug smile he'd been repressing.

"What exactly are you looking for?" she asked.

"Evidence—that's all I can tell you." He nodded toward the bed. "There's your phone. You may take it with you outside, but do not go farther than the parking area around this building and attempt to go to Artisans Alley or Tealicious. Officers have been placed on those premises to ensure you don't enter and try to destroy evidence."

"There's no evidence to find, much less destroy!" Andy shouted.

"I must warn you, Mr. Rust, you *will* keep your voice down and won't impede my investigation, or I will have you removed from the building—and that includes the pizza parlor."

Katie put her hand on Andy's arm. "Come on. Let's go downstairs and call Seth."

As soon as they got to the bottom of the stairs, Andy let out a growl of frustration. “It was all I could do not to punch that self-satisfied smirk right off that bastard’s face.”

“I can’t imagine what he hopes to find.” Katie’s knees felt weak. “Could we sit down somewhere please?”

“Yeah. Let’s go into my office.”

Trying to ignore the curious stares of staff and patrons alike, Andy and Katie went into his office at Angelo’s. By the time he’d closed the door behind him, Katie had Seth on the phone.

“Seth, Schuler is in the apartment over Angelo’s, and he has a search warrant for Artisans Alley and Tealicious too. What do I need to do?”

“Sit tight,” Seth said. “I’m on my way.”

CHAPTER 16

As they sat in the two chairs in front of Andy's desk—they heard the bell over the pizzeria door ring.

"I'll see if that's Seth," Andy said, giving Katie's hand a squeeze before leaving the office.

Katie's mind was whirling. Thank goodness she and Ray had found Erikka's ring earlier that day and that she'd given it to him for safekeeping. But how had it gotten into her apartment over Tealicious? She didn't want anyone—besides Ray—to know about the ring just yet. Seth, probably, but not Andy. She'd tell Seth later, when it was just the two of them. She wasn't quite ready to examine her reasons for not wanting Andy to know she'd found the ring.

Andy returned to the office with Seth in tow. Katie stood when the men entered the room, and the attorney gave her a quick, reassuring hug. Unfortunately, it did little to comfort her under the circumstances.

Stepping back, Seth said, "Let's see that search warrant."

Katie handed it over, and Seth sat at Andy's desk to examine it. Andy tried to take Katie's hand as they took their seats in the guest chairs, but she shook him off.

"Well?" Katie asked when she couldn't handle the suspense any longer. "Is what Schuler's doing legal? Is the search warrant valid?"

"I'm afraid so." Seth sighed and lowered the document. "It says that an anonymous source provided information to Detective Schuler and that the source's name has been made available to the judge privately in order to protect the informant's safety. Do either of you have any idea who or what this could be referencing?"

Katie shook her head before looking at Andy.

"No," he said. "I have no clue."

Seth took his cell phone from his jacket pocket and called his secretary. "Hey. Could you please reschedule my remaining appointments for this afternoon and then call J. P. Trammel's office to see when Katie and I can get in to see him? Thanks. Yeah, that's fine. I'll be back as soon as I can."

After ending the call, Seth assured Katie that he'd stay with her until after Schuler had completed his searches.

"You don't have to do that," Katie said. "I don't want to ruin your entire day."

"You're not ruining anything, and I want to be here. Once the searches have been concluded, we'll know what we need to do next," Seth said.

"You don't think… I mean, they're not going to arrest Katie, are they?" Andy asked.

"We won't know that until after the searches have been completed." Seth had spoken quietly, but his voice seemed to echo in Katie's ears.

She swallowed hard. *I could actually be arrested today! For* murder*!*

"But why is Schuler targeting Katie?" Andy demanded. "She'd never hurt anyone."

Seth merely shrugged.

Andy's expression darkened. "What if…what if I confess? Tell

Schuler I did it just long enough to get him off Katie's back," Andy said. "I can take it back later, right?"

"That's the stupidest thing I've ever heard," Katie said. "Who knows what Schuler would do with a false confession? It might wind up making me look even worse! It would appear that you were so worried about my being convicted that you tried to throw law enforcement off the track."

"I didn't think of that," Andy mumbled.

"She's right." Seth leaned forward. "It's better to stick with the original stories you gave the police—that is," he said and eyed Andy critically, "if those accounts were factual."

"Absolutely," Katie said. She turned her gaze back to Andy. "What we need to do is discover what evidence Schuler has—or thinks he has—against us."

Andy wouldn't meet her gaze. "I guess."

Katie was feeling increasingly annoyed with Andy. He'd glibly lied to her about his relationship with Erikka, and now he was willing to lie again. Who was this man she'd given her heart to? Yes, he had many good qualities. He'd help rehabilitate a score of teenage boys at risk...but did he lie to them as well? Was he as good a role model as everyone seemed to think?

Ezra Hilton had not trusted Andy because he'd stolen and destroyed his painstakingly restored prize Porsche. He'd never forgiven Andy for it. When Katie had learned of Ezra's prejudice, she had judged the old man harshly. Now she wondered if she'd been wrong with that assessment. Andy claimed to love her...but had he told Erikka the same thing? And even if he hadn't, he'd had sex with the woman—a second time—in a fit of pique when Katie had promised to stay with Ray's daughters when he'd been tossed in jail for a crime he hadn't committed. Talk about a childish reaction on Andy's part.

Seth reached to touch Katie's arm. "What are you thinking about, love?"

There was no way Katie would voice her thoughts—not in

front of Andy. Not at that moment. Would she have to do so in the not-too-distant future?

Yes. And she wasn't looking forward to the conversation.

CHAPTER 17

After a round of Andy's cinnamon buns, a copious amount of coffee, and a distinct lack of conversation later, a brisk knock sounded on the office door. Captain Robert Spence swung it open, stepped into the room, and closed the door behind him. His eyes swept the room. "Hey, Seth Landers! Nice to see you...although I'm surprised to see you here. I didn't think criminal law was your forte."

"Katie's a friend," Seth explained. "I'm here to help until we can get her more suitable representation...should she need it."

Captain Spence nodded. He then addressed Katie. "Our searches have concluded. I'm sorry, but you'll have to repack most of the belongings you had boxed up in the apartment upstairs. We tried not to leave your office at Artisans Alley and your residence at Tealicious a mess, but you'll have some straightening up to do at those places too."

"I'm not concerned about that, Captain," Katie said. "Am I going to be put under arrest?"

"No, ma'am...not at this time. We found nothing connecting you to the murder of Erikka Wiley." He spread his hands. "That doesn't mean you won't be charged if and when sufficient evidence comes to light."

Seth cleared his throat. "Do you feel Katie should retain a criminal attorney at this time?"

"It wouldn't hurt," Spence replied. "And that sentiment applies to both Ms. Bonner and to Mr. Rust. Obviously, you're the legal expert here, but if it were me, I would…and I'd do it today."

Seth thanked him, and Spence nodded to the trio respectfully before leaving the room.

After sitting in shocked silence for a moment, Katie stood. "Well, I suppose I'd better get back upstairs and repack before the movers get here."

"I'll help you," Andy offered.

"No, thank you. You have your own business to attend to." She managed a shaky smile at Seth. "Please let me know when Mr. Trammel can work me in."

"I will. Call me if you need anything." With a quick hug and a peck on the cheek, he left.

"Are you sure you don't need my help?" Andy asked. "I could leave Roger in charge."

"No. I think it's more important for you to find out if anyone on your staff knows who—or, rather, who *else*—Erikka might've been dating." She narrowed her eyes. "Did you ever take her to my apartment—either of them—for a tryst?"

"Of course not! I'd never disrespect you like that!"

But you'd disrespect me by cheating on me.

She blew out a breath. "I'm just trying to figure out why the police would think I have anything in my possession that would lead them to believe I murdered her." She wasn't about to mention the ring she'd found in her new apartment. After all, she could no longer count on Andy as someone she trusted. Someone had placed it there for Schuler and his team to find. She was not about to mention it to anyone…at least, not yet. Would that make her look even more guilty? It was a gamble she was willing to take—for now.

"Yeah, I don't know either." Andy ran a hand through his hair. "I'll let you know what I find out about any officers or anyone else Erikka might've been involved with." He brightened. "And, hey, if any law enforcement officer Erikka might've been dating is taking part in the investigation into her murder, his involvement would be a conflict of interest and render the whole thing void, right? The court would have to throw out any evidence found!"

"Maybe...I'm not sure how that works."

Andy obviously read the concern etched on Katie's face. "No, I mean...you know...if Schuler is trying to skew the evidence to implicate us, then this officer could be his downfall."

"Yeah, right." She jerked her head toward the door. "I'd better hop to it. I dread seeing what kind of mess Schuler has left me upstairs."

Andy reached for her, but she brushed him aside and exited the pizzeria. As she climbed the stairs to the apartment, she tried to deny the mammoth seed of doubt that had been planted in her mind about Andy's innocence. She didn't think he would have killed Erikka on purpose, but could he have done it accidentally?

Katie opened the door to her apartment and her heart sank at the devastation before her. The boxes she'd so neatly stacked for the movers had been dumped onto the floor with her belongings scattered everywhere. How would she ever get the boxes filled again—much less, tidily—before the movers arrived?

As she was going through her dishes to ensure none had been broken, someone knocked on her door. She'd been so distracted she hadn't heard footsteps on the stairs. Ray looked past her as she opened the door.

"Yup," he said. "I figured this place would be a disaster area and that you could use some help tidying up."

"Thank you, but I've got this," she said, dispirited.

"Didn't you say the movers would be here this afternoon?" He looked pointedly at his watch.

"Yeah, they will." She sighed. "I guess I could use the help, if you don't mind. Besides, we need to talk—"

He quickly placed an index finger over her lips and mouthed, *Not here*. "I agree. We *do* need to talk. Let me buy you dinner this evening."

She frowned. "Okay."

"Trust me," he whispered.

Katie swallowed, considering how in just a short space of time the pool of people she had considered trustworthy had shrunk. She answered truthfully. "I do."

BY THE TIME Katie had time to take a breath and look up at the clock that evening, it was after six p.m. She was supposed to meet Ray at a restaurant outside of McKinlay Mill at six-thirty. There was no way. In just a few hours, she had repacked her belongings at the apartment over Angelo's; tidied her office at Artisans Alley; gathered what few things she had at Sassy Sally's—including, of course, Mason and Della; and moved into her new apartment. All she wanted was to ease her aching body into a tub of hot water and Epsom salts and soothe away the day. Talking with Ray would have to wait.

As she filled the tub, she called Ray.

"Hey, Katie," he answered. "I'm just getting ready to leave."

"I'm sorry, but I simply can't. I'm too exhausted. Could I have a raincheck for tomorrow?"

"No." His voice was firm and serious.

"Why not?" she asked.

"Look, it's imperative that we meet tonight. I just...I really need to see you." He paused. "Sophie left some casseroles in the freezer for us when she took off for school yesterday, and Sasha and Sadie are doing a sleepover with friends. Why don't you come here for dinner?"

"Do you really need to see me? I mean, what's the rush?" Then realization clawed its way through her foggy brain. "Oh! Do you have information about the—"

"Nope, nope, nope," he interrupted. "We won't discuss anything over the phone. Come here, and we'll talk over everything."

She sighed. "Oh, Ray, I'm really tired."

"But are you also hungry?" he asked rather playfully.

Katie's stomach responded with a resounding growl. "Yeah…I am."

"Then come here for dinner," Ray said. "I won't even get offended if you fall asleep on me."

"Oh, all right. I'll be there soon." She imagined herself falling asleep in the tub. "But if I'm not, send out a search party."

"Damn straight I will."

* * *

HALF AN HOUR LATER, Katie pulled into Ray's driveway, got out of her car, and slogged up the walk. He met her at the front door.

Looking over her shoulder, Katie said, "I really wish we could've waited until tomorrow to talk. If anyone sees me here, they'll think—"

"Who cares what they think?" he asked, stepping aside for her to come in. "I'm trying to keep you from going to prison for a murder you didn't commit. If I recall, you did the same for me not too long ago."

"Yeah, well…I appreciate that." She was struck by the tantalizing aroma coming from the kitchen. "Dinner smells wonderful."

"Thanks. It's some chicken, cheese, and broccoli concoction Sophie fixed up. All I had to do was heat it and warm up a pan of rolls." He led her through to the homey kitchen. "As for your concern about what people might think, who's to say the girls aren't here? You could be helping them with one of their projects, for all anybody knows." He grinned and pulled out a chair for her. "On the other hand, screw what other people think. What're you drinking?"

"I'd say hard liquor, but I'm driving, so you'd better make it water," Katie said.

"Water, it is. Besides, you need to keep a clear head about you." He poured them both a glass of water over ice, pulled the casserole from the oven, and set it down on a trivet on the table. He brought out the rolls and butter and then sat down at the table.

As they filled their plates, Katie asked, "Why wouldn't you talk with me at the apartment today? Or over the phone earlier?"

"You're in a precarious position." Looking down as he put his napkin on his lap, he said, "That search warrant might carry more weight than you realize."

"What do you mean?" It seemed to Katie that Ray was reluctant to look at her. "Come on, tell me, Ray."

"The fact that the search warrant included testimony from an anonymous source and that it encompassed your two residences and your office at Artisans Alley means that they have some compelling evidence or testimony against you," he said, leveling his gaze at her.

"The planted ring in my new apartment?"

He nodded.

Katie spread her hands. "I know—this is serious. I realized that the instant Schuler and his deputies barged into the apartment over Angelo's today."

"You don't understand. The search warrant Schuler showed you might not be the only search warrant he has."

As Ray spoke, Katie's stomach plummeted. "Meaning?"

"Meaning he might have placed listening devices in the areas he searched. Until this investigation is concluded—and you're cleared of suspicion—you need to be extremely careful about what you say, to whom you say it, and where you're speaking."

Katie ran a hand over her forehead before pushing her plate away. She'd lost her appetite. "I just want this nightmare to end already."

"I know," he said. "So do I."

"Is there any chance you're merely being paranoid about the listening devices?" she asked.

He raised his bushy eyebrows. "Sure, there's a *chance*."

She understood what he wasn't saying. He'd been a county Sheriff's detective for a very long time. If he believed there to be listening devices in the places Schuler had searched, Katie was wise to accept that there probably were. "What about Andy?"

"What about him?" Ray asked.

"Should I warn him about the bugs? I mean, if there's one in the apartment over Angelo's…" She trailed off.

Ray shook his head. "Let Andy worry about Andy. You concentrate on taking care of yourself."

CHAPTER 18

Katie's mind was awhirl as she drove back home. *Home*. The apartment over Tealicious didn't even feel like home yet...especially now that she knew Schuler and his deputies were likely listening to everything she said there.

Climbing the steps to the apartment, she was glad John had put up the handrail. She was bone tired and thought she might need to use it to pull herself up the stairs.

She opened the door, walked inside, and was immediately greeted by an obviously stressed Mason and Della. She sank to the floor and cuddled them both in her arms. As they nuzzled against her with their purrs and kitty kisses, the apartment began to feel more like home. If only she could find and destroy those listening devices.

Thirty minutes into exhaustively searching the apartment, Katie realized she didn't even know what she was looking for. She got her laptop, settled onto the sofa, and did a search for police listening devices. Within seconds, Della and Mason had cuddled on either side of her and had begun their comforting, rhythmic purring. It didn't take long for her to realize that Schuler's listening devices—if there were, in fact, any in the apartment—could look like anything from an ordinary ink pen to a tiny black box affixed anywhere in the small apartment. But she could also buy a bug detector online. She immediately ordered one–hang the cost. Her life and freedom were at stake. And yet, she also learned that law enforcement could just as easily be listening in on her from *outside* the apartment. She couldn't find a gadget for that.

Well, good luck, Schuler, Katie thought. *All you'll be hearing tonight is the purrs of two sweet cats...and maybe a little snoring....*

* * *

KATIE AWOKE to find that she was still half-lying on the love seat. She had, at some time during the night, closed the laptop and moved it over to the coffee table, wishing she'd put sheets and blankets on the Murphy bed. Stretching and trying to work the kinks out of her neck, she disturbed Mason and Della, who'd been plastered against her. Mason decided it was time for Katie to give him his breakfast, while Della decided it was pertinent to sit on Katie's chest and headbutt her chin. Katie gave Della a hug and then sat her onto the floor. Reluctantly standing, she went into the kitchen and filled the cats' food and water bowls. As she staggered through to the bathroom, she looked longingly at the bed. How she'd love to climb into it and simply stay there for the rest of the day.

After taking a hot shower and having a cup of coffee, Katie felt slightly better. While she still would have liked nothing more than to hide in the cozy apartment all day, she had too much to do. Deciding a cinnamon coffee cake would be not only an excellent addition to the Tealicious menu but a balm to her weary soul, Katie set off down the stairs to the tea shop's kitchen, where Brad was already hard at work.

"Good morning," he greeted her cheerily. "How was your first night in the new apartment?"

"Uncomfortable," she admitted sourly. "I fell asleep on the love seat."

He smiled. "You were likely exhausted from the move. Did you get everything set up?"

"I did. Sort of. There are still a few odds and ends that John will be by to finish up later today, but for the most part, everything is settled." She grabbed an apron off a hook near the kitchen's entrance.

"What're you doing?" Brad asked. "You should take the day off. Given everything you've been through—you deserve it."

"Thank you." She moved around him to the counter and took out a mixing bowl. "As much as I appreciate your concern, I really want some coffee cake."

"All right. Let me make you one."

Tilting her chin up at him, she said, "Come on. You know better than anyone how therapeutic baking can be."

"Excellent point." He slid the bag of cake flour across the counter to her. "Be my guest."

Once the cake was in the oven, Katie helped Brad with other tasks while they waited for it to bake.

"Did you ever see Erikka Wiley here in the shop?" she asked, as she mixed the ingredients for cinnamon walnut scones.

"She might've stopped in once or twice since I began working here, but she wasn't a regular. Why?"

She shrugged. "I just wondered if you'd ever seen her here with someone who might've been a date. I know I'm grasping at straws, but if I could only find another person of interest in Erikka's murder, then maybe the police would get off my back."

"Understandable," Brad said. "Thankfully, the officers didn't come through here yesterday when they conducted their search—they used the private entrance to the apartment."

"Still, everyone saw them. I'm afraid business at both Tealicious and Artisans Alley may suffer thanks to Schuler's actions yesterday."

He shook his head. "Are you kidding me? We'll be slammed today with people wondering what was going on."

"I hope you're right," Katie said.

For the next twenty minutes or so, they chatted about the various promotions the Merchants Association had planned for the coming months and how Tealicious could participate.

Katie was about to take the coffee cake out of the oven when Brad spoke. "You know what? Now that I think about it, I *did* see Erikka here in the dining room with someone once—that photographer who has an office at the Alley…Matt somebody or other."

"Matt Brady?" she asked.

He nodded. "Yeah…the one who took those photos you were telling us about. They seemed pretty chummy."

"In what way?"

He shrugged. "I don't know. Looking across the table, leaning close to each other, whispering."

"That's interesting," Katie said. And intriguing. It looked like she needed to have another little chat with the Square's photographer.

* * *

RIGHT AFTER ENJOYING a warm slice of coffee cake with Brad, Katie hurried to Matt Brady's studio. If he had a relationship with Erikka, he might've believed those photos were made just for him. What if he found out she'd taken them to a photofinisher, had a set made and had given them to Andy and then Brady killed her in a jealous rage? Not that he'd confess that to *her*, of course, but she was a good enough judge of character to get a read on him when she confronted him.

Upon walking into the studio, the first thing Katie heard was sniffling. "Izzy?" she called.

The young woman came out from behind a screen. She held a soggy tissue in one hand, and tears streamed down her cheeks.

Katie stepped forward and offered her arms for a hug. Izzy leapt forward to accept her embrace. "What's happened?" Katie asked and pulled back.

"V-V-VJ b-broke up with me," Izzy wailed.

"Oh, no." Katie hugged her again. "I'm so sorry."

"H-he's m-mad because his m-mom likes me too much!"

What? That made no sense at all.

Katie led Izzy over to the client's couch. "I'm sure he'll come to his senses." *I'm sure? How could I be sure of anything? The man I thought loved me cheated on me and thought he got the other woman pregnant! What am I even doing trying to console this kid? I should be telling her to run away—not only from VJ but from everybody. Guard your heart, Izzy. Wrap it in steel and never let anyone get close to it again!*

Realizing the girl was saying something, Katie asked, "What's that?"

"I thought he *wanted* me to get along with his mom!"

Before Katie could respond, Matt Brady bustled into the office with a camera bag over his shoulder. Looking from one to the other, he focused on Katie. "What did you do to Izzy? If you're harassing her about—"

"I'm not harassing her about anything," Katie said, exasperated. "I'm trying to console her."

He dropped the bag onto the floor by the couch. "What are you doing here, anyway? I know the rent isn't due again already…unless you're going to start wanting it in advance."

"Well, that's how it works," Katie stated, "but my being here has nothing to do with the rent. I need to speak with you privately." She looked at Izzy as she stood. "Don't worry, Izzy, I'm sure everything will work out." *And it would—one way or another.*

"You all right, kid?" Matt asked Izzy.

She nodded. "W-we'll talk l-later."

"Okay." He squinted at her. "If anybody needs a butt-kicking, you let me know."

Izzy tried to smile and nodded, dabbing at her watery eyes.

"Sorry," Matt half-heartedly apologized as he ushered Katie into his office and closed the door. "I thought you made her cry." He gestured toward one of the client chairs in front of his desk. "What's up?"

Now that she was sitting across from the man, Katie didn't quite know what to say. She didn't want to flat-out accuse him of anything, but she didn't have time to dawdle.

"Were you and Erikka involved?" she asked.

Brady blinked. "Involved? What's that supposed to mean? She was my customer—you know that—you saw the photos."

"Right, but one of my friends saw the two of you together and thought you might be dating," Katie said.

Matt gave a derisive snort. "Dating? No. Okay, we hooked up a few times, but it was nothing serious."

She frowned. "You...you *hooked up*?"

Brady rolled his eyes, he said, "Yeah, we had sex, all right?"

"I know what hooking up means," Katie groused.

Brady shrugged. "She was hot. I knew she was in love with some other guy, but she wasn't about to live like a nun while she waited for him to come around. And I don't want a commitment right now. Ya know what I mean?"

Katie could feel her face flush. "I believe I get the picture, *Mr.* Brady."

"Don't go getting all prim and proper with me," he said, with a smirk. "I know it was your boyfriend she was hoping to get her hooks into." He leaned forward. "So, tell me—did you kill her?"

"No," she said evenly. "Did *you*?"

"Nope. And I have an alibi if you or anyone else wants to check it out." He sat back, clasped his hands behind his head, and propped his feet up on the desk. "Do you? Have an alibi, I mean?"

Katie stood and glared at the man, not dignifying his question with an answer, and walked out of the office without a backward glance. She didn't even remember to say goodbye to Izzy. What an insufferable jerk Matt Brady was! Had he not paid his rent just a few days before, she'd be sorely tempted to throw him out on his ear. Oh, well, there was always next month.

A part of her felt like going back to Tealicious and eating the rest of that coffee cake, but she knew that would only do more harm than good. Instead, she went to her office, picked up the phone and switched it to Intercom.

"Rose Nash, please report to the manager's office. Thank you."

Less than a minute later, Rose appeared at her office door.

"Hey," she said brightly. "What's up?"

"Close the door, please. I really need to see a friendly face about now."

But before she did so, Rose collected cups of coffee for both of them and then closed the office door. She sat down in the chair by Katie's desk, and said, "Spill. Or not. We can merely sit here and drink if that would make you feel better?"

Katie smiled. "Did you spike my coffee?"

"No. Would you like me to?"

"No." She inclined her head. "Okay, maybe." Then Katie told Rose all about the morning's events.

"I never have liked that pompous so-and-so," Rose said of Matt Brady. "I bet he's the bird who killed Erikka and is trying to pin it on you."

"Well, if he did, I'm going to find evidence of that fact and throw it right back in his smirky face," Katie said.

"How?" Rose asked.

Katie opened her mouth to answer, but then frowned. She didn't have a clue.

CHAPTER 19

After Rose had gone back to her cash desk, Katie began scrolling through her email.

Junk. Delete. Junk. Delete. Junk.

And then there was an email from Sue of Sweet Sue's Confectionery. She opened it and read it. Sue was upset because Janey Ingram had led her to believe the merchants were responsible for providing refreshments for the Harvest Festival kick-off party.

Sue ranted, "I thought the party was *for* the merchants! If I'm supposed to provide refreshments for the entire Square, I'd have liked to have been consulted about it first. I'm not even sure I want to attend if my opinion isn't going to be asked for or respected!"

Heaving a sigh, Katie rolled her eyes heavenward and then penned a response: "Hi, Sue. I'm so sorry for the misunderstanding. The food for the Harvest Festival party is being catered. We're giving the merchants the opportunity to showcase their products—such as food samples, trinkets, demonstrations, etc.—but merchants are in no way required to participate. As you pointed out, the party is *for* the merchants' enjoyment."

After she sent the email, Katie grabbed a peppermint from her desk jar and ground it between her molars. She'd asked Janey to help out to save herself some time, not so she'd have to go along behind her and smooth ruffled feathers.

She called Janey's cell, got no answer, and left a voice mail asking for a return call at Janey's earliest convenience.

A ping alerted her to incoming mail. She scrolled to the top and saw that the message was from Sue.

"What a lovely idea!" Sue's enthusiasm oozed from the computer screen. "I *do* have a new turmeric truffle recipe I'd like to test out. I'll make up a batch and bring them for everyone to try. Have an awesome day! Toodles!"

Toodles?

Katie reached for another peppermint.

Rather than returning Katie's call, half an hour later Janey decided to "pop in."

"I was here to see Vance when I got your message, so I decided to drop by and say hello." Janey sat, took off her sunglasses, and crossed her long legs. "While I'm here, we can discuss what's going on with the party planning."

"That's why I called you," Katie explained. "I got an email from Sue Sweeney, who was upset because she thought we were requiring her to provide refreshments for the party."

Janey shook her head. "Oh, that's ridiculous. She can be so all-fired quick to jump to conclusions sometimes. But, as the wonderful Dolly Parton once said, 'I don't kiss nobody's butt.' And I'm not kissing up to Sue because *she* misunderstood what I said."

Taking her third peppermint of the day from the jar, Katie said, "I smoothed everything over with her. I simply wanted to make sure all the merchants realize the food is being catered and that we aren't expecting anything from them except for them to show up and have a good time."

"Fine. I'll have Izzy send out an email or something," Janey said with a wave of her hand.

"Actually, I'd prefer for you to take care of it." She wondered if she should be venturing into this territory, but given the day she was having, she might as well. "I don't think Izzy is up to doing much today."

"Why? What's wrong with her?" Janey leaned forward, placing her hand on her chest. "Is she sick?"

Katie blew out a breath. "I had to go by Matt Brady's office this morning, and I found Izzy in tears. It seems she and VJ have broken up."

Gaping at her, Janey asked, "Why? They're *perfect* for each other!"

"I think your high opinion of Izzy—and her relationship with VJ—might be part of the problem. Izzy told me they broke up because you like her too much."

Janey deflated back into the chair. "Oh, my gosh. I never meant to cause VJ to break poor little Izzy's heart. What am I gonna do?"

"Maybe you should talk with VJ and ask what happened." Katie shrugged. "It could be that there was something else about Izzy that he didn't like—or maybe he even found someone else—and used your feelings about her as an excuse to break up."

"My VJ would never cheat on a girl he was dating," Janey said in umbrage, drawing herself back up in the chair.

Yeah, that's what I thought about Andy. "I'm not saying he did. But he might've become interested in someone else, realized he didn't care for Izzy as much as he thought and broke up. All I'm saying is that you can't know what's going on between two people involved in a relationship and perhaps you should ask your son what's going on before you try to convince him to get back together with Izzy."

Janey frowned. "So you're saying there might be *more* to this than Izzy is saying?"

"Exactly," Katie said. "It could just be that the relationship has run its course. They're only kids after all."

"That's true," Janey said sadly and stood. "Well, I'll let you get back to it, and I'll go find VJ. I'm guessing this entire thing with Izzy is a silly misunderstanding—like Sue thinking she was being required to bring food for the party!"

With a nod, Katie said, "You're probably right." She actually doubted Janey was right. How often are breakups caused by "silly" misunderstandings? Because all misunderstandings come from a grain of truth, right?

She sighed. Who knows? Maybe it *was* a silly misunderstanding. She really needed to stop looking at every relationship through the lens of her breakup with Andy.

"I'll talk to you later," Janey promised and headed out the door.

Feeling a need for more caffeine was in order, Katie got up and went into the vendors' lounge for some coffee. She was glad to find the room empty because she didn't feel like chatting with anyone else at the moment.

Katie returned to her office and closed the door. Sitting back at her desk, she looked at the queue of unanswered emails and decided she didn't want to deal with them at the moment, either. She sipped her coffee and clicked on her favorite social media account. The little bell in the top right corner heralded twenty-four notifications, but she wasn't interested in those. She was interested in Matt Brady and whether or not he and Erikka were more involved than he'd led her to believe.

Starting with Erikka's page, she quickly realized she was simply covering the same ground she'd already worn a path through—the sonogram, the selfies, the photos with her sister and the rest of their family, the photos of her with her friends. Not a single photograph of her with Matt Brady.

But, then, if Matt was right in his assertion that he knew Erikka was in love with some other guy and was simply waiting for him to come around, would Erikka have had photographs of *anyone* she was dating on her page? That wouldn't make sense if she really was waiting for Andy to realize she was the one for him.

And what about the photos Matt had taken of Erikka? Was that when they'd started "hooking up?" How conniving *was* this woman if she was sleeping with a photographer hired—at least, Katie assumed he was hired—to take sexy photos of her for another man? The man she professed to *love*. It made Katie wonder just how many sets of those bedroom photos were floating around?

Maybe Matt's page would yield more information. His page was, naturally, filled with his work—landscapes, portraits, and action shots. He also had taken selfies with several beautiful women, many of whom were kissing his cheek or hanging on his shoulder. Erikka wasn't among them.

Katie wondered if, again, Erikka had asked Matt not to post anything indicative of their sexual relationship in an attempt not to drive away Andy. Had Andy known Erikka was sleeping with other men at the same time they were having an affair? The thought made Katie nauseous. She and Andy had always used protection—and she was particularly glad of that now—but the thought of even having *kissed* Andy given what she now knew made her sick.

Scrolling down, she found photographs of an adorable baby boy. In one photo, a woman was holding the baby. It was Erryn—Erikka's sister. Matt had tagged Erryn in the post, so Katie clicked the name to go to Erryn's page. It was apparent she wasn't going to find anything helpful on Matt's page.

Although she'd been through Erryn's page almost as many times as she'd been through Erikka's, Katie still thought there might be something yet to be found...some clue as to who might've wanted to harm Erikka. Surely, she'd been overlooking something.

Erryn hadn't posted since her sister died, so there was no new information. But maybe there was something here—not necessarily something Erryn was *hiding,* but something that would help lead Katie to the truth. But what?

There was the sonogram. Old news. There was a party photograph. Wait—someone there at the far right, almost out of the frame, looked familiar. His back was to the person taking the photograph, but—

And then, Erryn's page was gone. In its place was an error message.

What? No! There was something familiar about that guy! I need to enlarge that photo.

She tried again to access Erryn's page and again received the error message. Having a sneaking suspicion she'd just been blocked, Katie went back to Matt Brady's page. She scrolled down to the photos of Erryn's baby but could no longer see that Erryn had been tagged in the post.

Erryn *had* blocked her…and at the very moment she'd found something she could possibly use. Why? Katie knew it was impossible for Erryn to know that she'd been looking at her page then—wasn't it? She thought about what Ray said about surveillance and shivered.

When her phone rang, she started. Looking at the screen, she saw it was Seth.

"Seth, hi."

"Are you all right?" he asked. "You sound out of breath."

"I'm fine. I was…um…engrossed in my work, and your call startled me, that's all," she said.

"Okay. I'm calling to let you know that Jim Trammel can see us in his office on Monday morning at nine. I'm sorry he couldn't see us today, but he doesn't keep weekend hours. However," Seth continued, "should you need him this weekend, he'll be available to help."

"Why should I...?" She trailed off. "Oh. You mean, if I get arrested, I can call him, and he'll come to the police station?"

"Right." Seth's voice had a resignation to it that was hard for

Katie to hear. He thought her getting arrested was a very real possibility. "I don't believe that will happen, given the fact that the searches turned up nothing substantial, but call me if it does. I can get to you quicker than Trammel can, and I'll contact him en route."

Katie's breath caught in her throat. "Okay."

Just what did Seth think Schuler and Spence had on her? She voiced the question.

"Nothing, just a gut feeling."

"Can you take something for it?" she asked, not at all amused.

"Honey, I wish I could."

CHAPTER 20

As if things weren't going swimmingly enough already, Andy showed up at Katie's door. Giving him an exaggerated blink, she asked, "What are you doing here?"

He held up a bag. "I figured you probably hadn't taken time for lunch, so I brought you a calzone." She'd opened her mouth to protest, but he hurried on. "*And* I brought the information you asked me to get from my staff."

She nodded toward the vacant chair. "Fine."

Andy entered the office, closed the door, and took a seat. He placed the bag in front of her. "I included plenty of napkins."

"Thanks." She had to force the word between her tightly clamped lips. Seeing Andy was the last thing she needed that day. But, admittedly, she wanted to know what he'd learned from his staff about Erikka. And she *was* hungry. She opened the bag and took out the calzone. After all, it didn't deserve to be tossed in the garbage. *It* hadn't cheated on her. "So, what did you find out?"

Suddenly remembering Ray's warning about the listening devices, she quickly stood and said, "Wait! I can't eat this yet. I didn't power walk the Square this morning."

"Can't you do that after work?" Andy asked.

"I could. But I'd rather we do it now...together. It'll be good for both of us."

He gestured toward the calzone. "But your lunch will get cold."

"If it does, I'll pop it in the microwave when I get back," she said. "You know, you burn more calories if you exercise prior to eating than you do if you try to burn those calories after." She opened her desk drawer, placed her phone inside, and locked the desk. "See? I'm even leaving my phone here, so there will be no distractions. Want me to put yours in there, too?"

Looking at her as if she'd lost her mind, Andy said, "No. What if there's an emergency?"

"We'll be walking on the Square. Anyone who'd be looking for us in case of an emergency could simply look out and see us. But here." She grabbed a notepad. "I'll leave a note on the door."

"If it'll make you happy..." Andy handed over his phone, but his gaze remained puzzled.

Katie tried to hide her relief as she locked his phone in the desk drawer with hers. If the police were somehow listening in on her phone calls, they were likely listening in on Andy's as well. Leaving her office and foregoing carrying their phones, they were less likely to have their conversation overheard. She wondered again if she should tell Andy the real reason she'd been adamant about leaving the office and the phones, but she could hear Ray in her head: *Let Andy worry about Andy.*

As they stepped onto the tarmac, Katie looked all around before taking a step. She spotted a black van parked near Nona's quilt shop. Could it be a surveillance van?

"Why are you acting so weird?" Andy asked.

"Why *shouldn't* I be?" she fired back. "Or have you forgotten what happened yesterday?" She jerked her head toward the door. "Let's walk inside. It's a little chilly out here."

"Want me to grab you a jacket? I have an extra one in Angelo's."

"No. I'd rather walk inside—let the vendors see me. I like for them to feel I'm looking out for them." Okay, so that was a hypocritical comment. She was looking out for herself because that really could be a surveillance van parked in front of Nona's. And, knowing Nona, she was helping them out.

As they walked back in, Andy gently touched her shoulder. She flinched.

"Is that it?" he asked. "Are you afraid to be alone with me? You know I'd never hurt *you*, Sunshine."

Had he emphasized you, *or was that just my imagination?*

"I'm not afraid to be alone with you, Andy. My nerves are on edge—that's all." She reentered the building's lobby. "Come on. Let's walk and talk. What information did your staff have to offer?"

"Apparently, Erikka had a lot of friends who did favors for her," he said.

"Men friends?" Katie asked as they climbed the stairs to the second floor.

He shrugged. "That's the impression I got. But everybody liked Erikka. Even Schuler got her out of a speeding ticket once. And, hey, shouldn't that create some sort of conflict of interest and jeopardize the case—Schuler doing favors for the victim?"

"Back when he was in uniform, Schuler issued me a warning instead of a speeding ticket, too, but then I was only doing three miles over the limit. Now he's treating me as if I'm Lizzie Borden. I think you'll lose if you try to take that argument to court." She stopped walking and looked at him squarely. "Why are you so concerned about having the case thrown out on some sort of technicality? We need to be focused on alternative suspects."

"I know, but I don't want to ignore any weapons we might have in our arsenal," Andy said.

"Did your guys say anything else?" Katie asked as they rounded the southwest corner of the balcony that overlooked the main showroom.

"Only that it was funny how differently most of the men acted toward Erikka when they came in alone as opposed to when they came in with their wives." He gave her a half-smile. "But that didn't seem that suspicious to me."

Katie bit her tongue to keep from saying, *No, it wouldn't, would it?*

* * *

AFTER ANDY WENT BACK to work, Katie reheated the calzone in the vendors' lounge microwave. It smelled delicious, and it was tasty, but she didn't have much of an appetite. Picking at the crust, she wondered about those men who acted differently toward Erikka when their wives were present. If Erikka would cheat with Andy when at one point she'd professed to being Katie's friend, would she also cheat with a married man? If so, could the situation have turned deadly when the man's wife found out? It had been horrible enough for Katie to learn Andy had cheated on her, and they didn't share a home or children. She decided to ask Roger what he might know the next time she saw him. She hesitated to ask Andy to speak with any of his staff again. In fact, because of his infidelity, she wanted to put as much distance between the two of them as possible.

She'd taken the uneaten calzone to the vendors' lounge wastebasket and was returning to her office when she saw John Healy heading her way. "Hi, John."

"Hey, Katie. I've finished the last of the little jobs in your new apartment." He grinned. "That cat of yours is a real charmer."

"I have two, but you probably didn't see Della. She's a bit of a scaredy-cat. She runs and hides whenever we have visitors." She jerked her head toward the door. "Could we walk over and take a look at the apartment together? I'll bring my checkbook so I can pay your remaining balance, and you can tell me anything in particular you think I might need to know."

"Sounds great." He walked over and held open the door.

"Did you know Erikka Wiley?" Katie asked Healy as they made their way to Tealicious.

"The girl who was killed the other day?" he asked.

She nodded.

He shrugged. "I saw her at Angelo's a few times, and Roger speaks highly of her, but I didn't really know her."

"Did she ever come by the apartment to speak with Roger while you were working?" Katie asked.

"Not that I recall." He was squinting, but then his brows rose. "Oh. I imagine you're asking because of the police search."

"Yeah. I mean, I never knew of Erikka going there—or to Artisans Alley, either, for that matter—so I can't imagine why Detective Schuler insisted on searching those places." Of course, Katie knew it was because they were places where *she* had access, and she was considered a prime suspect, but she figured Healy had to know that, too. And, if he didn't, she didn't want to be the one to point that out to him.

He gave her shoulder a reassuring pat. "I don't know, either, but I'm sure everything will be all right. From what little I know of Erikka, the girl was a free spirit. She might've gone anywhere and done anything. I'm guessing the Sheriff's Office knows that, too, and that's why they're so overwhelmed."

"Maybe so," Katie hedged. "But they targeted *my* office and residences. You know, I'm learning things about Erikka that I never knew when she was alive."

"Ah, that's the way with all of us, isn't it?" He gave a half-hearted smile. "We have so many facets to our lives that few people actually know our real selves."

Our real selves? An image of Andy flashed into Katie's mind.

"By the way," Healy continued, "I was rechecking the smoke and carbon monoxide detectors, and I discovered that the smoke detector wasn't the one I installed."

Katie decided to play dumb. "What do you mean?"

"I hate to say it, but someone other than me or another of my crew changed it."

She knew exactly what he meant, and he was more than kind to point it out to her. Stomach turning, Katie forced a laugh. "I hope you didn't give away your secret chili recipe or anything."

"I didn't. And, in fact, I replaced the device," he said and winked. "I couldn't trust that a smoke detector I didn't install would adequately do the job, could I? My reputation as a contractor is on the line."

Katie swallowed down the lump of fear that had taken residence in her throat. "Thank you, John."

"Glad to do it," he said. "I just wanted you to know before we go into the apartment and you see the bogus smoke detector on your kitchen table."

"Do you think it's still working?" she asked.

"Well, I, for one, wouldn't light a cigarette around it. At least, not until you've examined it, taken out the batteries, and done whatever you think you need to do."

Katie paused at the bottom of the stairs. "You could get in trouble for taking it down, you know."

"For what? Replacing the smoke detector? Why? I'm just doing my job."

She smiled. Thanks to John, she could feel more comfortable in her home now.

But Schuler was sure to notice his device had been made useless when it ceased to work. Maybe she should leave it as it was. But was the bug left in her apartment even legal? She'd have to ask Ray—or maybe Seth. Either way, she needed to keep her mouth shut while in her new home.

Nobody should have to fear they were being monitored in their own home—especially by clandestine measures.

Nobody.

CHAPTER 21

Rather than returning to Artisans Alley following the meeting with her contractor, Katie walked over to Wood U. If anyone could give her advice about how to approach the disguised smoke detector—aka listening device that had been planted in her apartment—it would be Ray.

The former detective barely glanced up from his work when she walked through the door. "Be right with you," he said.

A lanky man was standing in front of the counter watching intently as Ray used a V tool to "line in" a pattern on a wooden plank.

"Use a medium gouge in a low angle grip," Ray instructed, handing the tool to his customer. "Here. Give it a try." He glanced in her direction and his expression brightened. "Be with you in a few minutes, Katie."

"That's all right," she said. "I just wanted to speak with you about the…um…the upcoming Harvest Festival."

Wandering around his shop, Katie realized she didn't often take the time to appreciate Ray's work. She ran her fingers along an intricately carved panel depicting a family of elephants. Hearing him encouraging his customer to improve his craft made her smile. As impatient and irascible as the man could be, Ray was thoughtful and considerate toward his students and customers.

When at last the student left, Katie turned to her friend with a broad smile.

"What?" he groused.

"I'm just admiring your exquisite work," she said. "You know, you're a talented artisan."

"Tell me something I don't know. Like why you're really here? Harvest Festival, my ass."

Katie frowned. "John Healy found the listening device in the apartment over Tealicious. It's hidden in a smoke detector." She shrugged. "Or designed to look like one anyway."

Her revelation made his bushy eyebrows rise. "Did you have him looking for bugs?"

"No. He noticed the smoke alarm wasn't the one he installed," she said. "He switched it out with his own and told me about it."

"But how did he know the smoke detector was a listening device?" Ray asked.

"He didn't say. Maybe he made an assumption—a correct one, I might add—since he'd been in the apartment when the police came to conduct their search."

Stepping out from behind the counter, Ray rubbed a hand over the lower half of his face. "Possibly. But he was awfully quick to point out this smoke detector listening device to you."

"I was employing him to do a job," Katie said. "Plus, I'd like to think he and I are friends. I'd point out a listening device to you if I found one in your apartment."

"Yeah, okay." He waved away her protests with a broad right hand. "Just be careful around the guy. You don't know him that well. And having Healy find that bug might've been a ploy the police are using for him to gain your trust and get you to confess."

"Are you this skeptical about everybody?"

"Yes, I am," he said.

She'd known him long enough to realize that was probably the truth. "Even if I was guilty, I wouldn't confess it to someone I'd only known a few months. Heck, I wouldn't tell anyone... except you."

He grinned. "Really? You'd tell me?"

"Okay, probably not. Unless it was an accident or self-defense and I didn't know what to do."

"Well, I'm flattered. Does that make me your ride-or-die bitch?"

Rolling her eyes, she said, "Whatever."

He laughed. "Now you're reminding me of my daughters."

"Of whom John Healy thinks I am one," she reminded him. "So...would you mind coming over to my apartment after work and disabling the listening device? I did an online search after John left, but I couldn't find any instructions. Oddly enough, there's not much about that sort of thing online. However, if you'd like to know how to disable a beeping or chirping smoke detector, I'm your gal."

"I'll take care of it for you after work. It's not that big a deal," he said.

"I ordered a device online that's supposed to help me find hidden listening devices, but it won't be delivered until Tuesday." She paused. "What about my cell phone? Do you think the Sheriff's Office is listening in on my calls too?"

"If your home and workplace are bugged, then the Sheriff's Office is absolutely intercepting your calls."

She emitted a growl of frustration. "I hate this! I didn't do anything wrong, and I'm so paranoid about everything I say and do. I'm terrified I'll do or say something that will...will..."

"Be used against you in a court of law?" Ray finished.

Katie nodded.

"I understand. I've been there. Remember?" He opened his arms. "Could you use a hug?"

Again, she nodded and stepped into his comforting embrace. Stepping back a moment later, she said, "Thanks. The hug was nice, but what I really need is a suspect."

"I'm working on it."

"Me, too." She sighed. "I even thought I might have a halfway promising lead until Erikka's sister blocked me on social media."

"What lead?"

Before Katie could answer, another customer entered Wood U. She gave him a wave. "Don't forget that Merchants Associations meeting this evening."

"What Merchants Associations meeting?" he called. "Today is Saturday."

She turned and glared at him. Like she was going to say, *See you later when you come to disable the listening device!*

"Oh, yeah...yeah, I remember," he said. "I'll be there."

* * *

ONCE BACK AT ARTISANS ALLEY, Katie sat at her desk and surveyed the tiny office. Everything looked the same, but she had to be missing something. There had to be a listening device somewhere in this room, too. The only thing she knew for certain, though, was that it was not disguised as a smoke detector. The closest one of those was located in the vendors' lounge; and while she wasn't sure what type of range these listening devices had, she guessed the Sheriff's Office would prefer to have one that was actually in her office where her conversations didn't have to compete with those of dozens of other people throughout the day.

Although she'd combed the office the day before, knowing there had been a device in her apartment gave her renewed purpose. She crawled beneath the desk and was looking up under it.

A shout of "Yoo-hoo! Katie, are you in here?" made her rise up and smash her head against the bottom of the desk.

"Ow! Yes! I'm here."

Moonbeam stuck her head around the desk to peep at her. "What are you doing under there? Are you hiding?"

Rubbing her head, Katie said, "No...just looking for the pen I dropped. It wouldn't be such a big deal, but...well...it's a really good pen."

"I sympathize. It's hard to find your perfect writing implement, and when you do, you sure as heck don't want anything happening to it." She stepped back. "Are you all right?"

"Yeah, I'm fine. I've been told I have a thick skull." She stood and ran her hands down the sides of her jeans. "What brings you by? Did you have questions about the Harvest Festival?"

"No. I came by because I'm concerned about you," Moonbeam said. "I did a tarot reading for you, and the cards revealed that you have a powerful enemy."

Yeah. Detective Schuler. Katie could have told her that.

"Do you really think so?" Katie asked.

"I'm sure of it. The person who killed Erikka Wiley is stalking you. You're in the murderer's sights. And this person is closer to you than you can imagine."

Reaching for a peppermint from the jar on her desk, Katie blew out a breath. "Could the cards be more specific?"

"I'm afraid not." Moonbeam's bracelets jangled as she spread her hands. "Believe me, I tried."

"I hope I don't sound disrespectful by asking, but is there any way you could simply conjure Erikka up and ask her what happened?"

Moonbeam smiled sadly. "I wish I could, darling, but I'm not a medium. Even if you found a medium who could interact with Erikka, she might not know or be willing to name her killer."

"Why would she not be willing to name her killer?" Katie

asked. "If I'd been murdered, I'd want someone to know it and give me some justice."

"Just like any living person might, she could have blocked the trauma and be unable to remember it." She held up her hands for emphasis. "Hopefully, she's in a place of peace now and doesn't want to think about her death."

Katie nodded, although she wasn't agreeing with Moonbeam. Of course, she hoped Erikka had found peace—but she'd love for the dead woman to be able to point the finger at her killer, help someone find the necessary evidence, and put the killer behind bars for the rest of his or her life.

Since issuing her warning, Moonbeam seemed to feel that she'd done her duty and decided to ask about a hundred questions about the upcoming Harvest Festival celebration. Were the vendors supportive of each other? Could she bring soap cubes and tea bags to share with the vendors to see if they might enjoy visiting her shop? Should she bring her tarot cards and offer to do free readings?

Katie told her she should probably leave the tarot cards at The Flower Girl the first time she met some of her fellow vendors. She could vividly imagine Nona having a conniption fit right there in the midst of the event.

Once Moonbeam had gone and Katie was alone with her thoughts, she remembered the photograph she'd glimpsed on Erryn's computer screen before being blocked. Was she grasping at straws, or *had* there been something familiar about the man in the background?

She sighed, took another peppermint and then leaned back in her chair, unwrapping the cellophane wrapper. What did she really know about Erikka's killer? Absolutely nothing. She couldn't account for anyone's whereabouts on that fateful night except her own. Where had Andy been? And what about Matt Brady? Was he telling the truth about not caring who else Erikka was involved with? Was Ray right about John Healy being used by the police to lull her into trusting him enough to confess? And why was Ray so quick to take Erikka's ring and hide it? Was there something else he was hiding?

Katie knew she was being paranoid, but right now, the only person she was certain she could trust was herself.

CHAPTER 22

Exhaustion pulled at every muscle in Katie's body as she finally climbed the stairs to her new apartment that evening. She decided to curl up on the love seat for a moment after feeding the cats. She didn't want a repeat of the previous night, but she knew she'd be awakened when Ray came to disable the listening device. And she could certainly use a quick nap before he arrived.

Unfortunately, she was thinking of Moonbeam's warning when she dozed off, and her nap was plagued by images of herself in various hunters' gunsights: Andy, Schuler, Erryn, Brady, Healy, Ray, and even Moonbeam herself. Katie's heart was thudding so loudly in her nightmare that it was all she could hear.

Thump! Thump! Thump!

"Katie! Hey! You home?"

Shaking off the fog and becoming fully awake, Katie realized it wasn't actually her heart she heard but Ray pounding on the door.

She stood, smoothed her hair, and opened the door to greet

him. "Sorry," she said, pulling the door wide, "I didn't hear you at first."

"What I can't understand is why you didn't get John Healy to put a doorbell in this place," he grumbled.

"I didn't expect to have many visitors."

Ray frowned. "Didn't *expect* any or didn't *want* any?"

Ignoring his question, she led him into her galley kitchen. "Here you go. Do you think you can take care of it?"

"Sure. Leaky faucets aren't a big deal...although you should've had Healy take care of that, too." The intense gaze he leveled at her let her know he was talking in code.

"I know," she said. "I just didn't want to bother him again."

"Bother him? It's his job." Ray took a multi-tool knife from the front pocket of his jeans and sat down at the table in front of the smoke detector listening device. "But I'll take care of this one."

Katie watched over his shoulder as Ray opened the device and inspected it before cutting a blue wire and a yellow wire.

"That should do it," he said.

"So, we're good?" Katie asked.

Ray turned to face her, put a finger to his lips, and shook his head. "I wanted to ask you about Sasha's birthday gift while I'm here." At Katie's frown, Ray nodded toward the now-disabled listening device. "I'm not sure it's the only one...you know, that I should give her."

"Oh, I see." He was telling her there might be another device. "Well, you should definitely look around some more and see what else you might find."

Returning the blade to the case and pulling out a screwdriver implement from the knife, Ray stooped down and removed a vent.

"I did that," Katie said. Catching herself, she said, "I looked high and low when I was searching for a gift for Rose."

"Some places are worth returning to—especially when they've had an opportunity to restock." He replaced the vent and stood.

Katie understood that he was referring to his suspicions about Healy that he'd expressed earlier in Wood U. Ray obviously thought Healy might've shown her one device but replaced it with another one—or more. But why would Healy do that? Why would he work with the police to get her to confess or try to catch her saying something incriminating? In the movies, the only people who cooperate in police investigations are those who have something to gain—the justice-seeking family of the victim or the criminal who wants a plea deal. Of course, all they had to do was threaten to have his permits pulled and he might sacrifice one client to save working with half a dozen more. And, Katie had paid him in full.

After looking around for a few minutes, Ray asked Katie for a drink of water.

"Sure." She reached into the cabinet above the sink and got him a glass.

He turned on the water full blast, but he didn't catch any in the glass.

Frowning, she asked, "What are you doing?"

"Drowning out the sound of our voices," he whispered.

"Why?" She glanced around the room. "Did you find something else?"

"No, but I won't feel a hundred percent comfortable talking about Erikka or the murder investigation in this apartment until your bug detector gets here."

"You were a cop for…forever. Don't *you* have a bug detector?"

Ray shook his head. "All of that kind of stuff belonged to the department. I could probably borrow one but not without raising eyebrows and alerting the department and, thus, Schuler—that we, namely you—are on to him watching everything you say or do."

"And that makes me look even more suspicious, even though all I'm trying to do is protect my privacy while helping to find out who killed Erikka Wiley. Besides, we just disabled the bug we *did* find."

Ray shut off the water.

"Thank you," she said. "I appreciate that, and so does my water bill."

"I don't know about that. Utility companies usually love it when you adopt a more-the-merrier mindset," he responded with a smirk. "And did you notice there's a great lake less than two miles away as deep as eight hundred feet in some parts?"

"Well, I don't want to use more than my fair share *or* run up my tab." She hesitated for a moment before diving headfirst into the question that had been on her mind. "What did you do with the—?" She mouthed the word "ring."

Eyes widening, Ray turned on the water again. "The less you know about that, the better."

"Why did you take it? Why didn't you instruct me to immediately turn it over to the police? After all, even if someone planted the thing, it's ostensibly the reason the Sheriff's Office obtained a search warrant and searched my residences and the office at Artisans Alley." Katie warmed to her argument. "After all, you *were* a detective. Why would you volunteer to conceal evidence in a murder investigation?"

He got so agitated, he forgot to control the volume of his voice. "Because I don't trust Schuler, that's why! When I came under suspicion for the murder of Ken Fenton, Schuler wouldn't give me the benefit of doubt—and the man *knew* me. He'd worked with me for years. And he tried to convict me on evidence manufactured by other people. Do you honestly think I could stand by and let that happen to you?"

Katie placed a hand on his arm, hoping to both calm him down and reassure him. "I appreciate your concern, but I feel compelled to turn the object over to the police. It could hold traces of the killer's DNA or something."

"That *object* was found in your apartment and likely *is* contaminated with *your* DNA," Ray reminded. "Besides, how are you going to tell Schuler or one of his deputies that you found it *after* their extensive searches turned up nothing?"

"I won't let on that I found it here," she said. "I'll say I found it on the street or inside Artisans Alley somewhere other than my office—like, near the cash desks. That would work, wouldn't it?"

"No. Turning that thing in now with some lame explanation about just happening to run across it—the very thing they turned your apartments upside down looking for—is going to make you look even more suspicious to them than you already do."

"Fine." She turned and leaned against the sink, wondering if dousing her head beneath the cold running water would help clear her thoughts…or if dunking Ray would clear his. "Why don't you give it back to me until I decide what to do with it?"

"I can't," he said. "It was only a few hours ago that you told me you trusted me. Have you changed your mind?"

"Of course not. But you're acting like *you* don't trust *me*."

"I don't trust you not to possibly condemn yourself by turning damning evidence over to police," he said.

"How would that be condemning myself?" she asked.

He lowered his voice to a whisper. "You know that ring was taken from the finger of a dead woman, presumably after she died and presumably by the killer." He gently cupped her chin and turned her face up to look at him. "I don't know if the killer planned to use the ring to misdirect police or if he intended to hang on to it as a keepsake. The fact of the matter is that it ended up in *your* apartment. Let that sink in."

Katie turned the water off. "I can't do this."

"Then let's go downstairs and have a cup of tea," he suggested.

"I—" She started to say no, but she decided to hear him out. "One quick cup."

"That's all I want."

They used the interior stairs to go down into the now-closed

Tealicious. At the bottom of the stairs, Katie asked, "Do you really want tea, or was that merely a ruse to get out of the apartment?"

"I'd drink some tea."

She put a kettle on before turning to Ray and folding her arms over her chest. "You told me you didn't suspect Andy, and yet upstairs you mentioned that the killer might've held onto the ring as a keepsake."

"I still don't suspect Andy," he said. "He wouldn't have kept the ring even if he had killed her."

"Why do you say that?"

"He didn't need a trophy, and he wouldn't have used the ring to implicate you in Erikka's murder." He shrugged. "Had Andy killed the woman, his motive would have been because he felt she stood in the way of your relationship. He wouldn't have wanted you to be convicted of the crime."

"Fair enough. Who do you think *did* kill her?"

The tea kettle whistled, and Katie started at the sound.

"Have a seat," Ray said. "I'll pour the water over the tea bags."

"I don't need to sit down. I need answers. What did you do with the ring?"

"I threw it in the lake."

She gaped at him. "*Why*? Ray, do you honestly think I killed Erikka?"

"No, of course not." He avoided her eyes, carefully pouring the boiling water into the mugs and dunking the teabags up and down.

"Then why would you throw her ring in the lake?"

His eyes narrowed. "Dammit, I'm just looking out for you, Katie."

Despite the warmth of the tea shop, she felt a sudden chill. *He does. He thinks I killed Erikka Wiley,* she thought with horror. That implied indictment hurt almost as much as Andy's betrayal.

CHAPTER 23

Katie felt as if a weight were pressing on her chest when she awakened on Sunday morning. The fact that a cat sat on her sternum wasn't the root cause of the feeling. Rather, it was days of stress and exhaustion without a break. She desperately needed a break—even if it was for only a couple of hours.

Before she even fed the cats, Katie reached over to the nightstand for her phone and called Rose. As her second in command, Vance would've been her first choice; but Katie knew he and his family would be at church.

Sounding as chipper as if she'd been up for ages—which in Rose's case was likely—Rose answered, "Good morning, Katie. Isn't it gorgeous out today?"

"I…um…I haven't looked out my window yet," Katie said. "I'll take your word for it. I'm calling to let you know I'll be late coming into Artisans Alley today. If anyone needs me, tell them I'll be there soon."

"Is anything wrong?"

Katie nearly laughed at the unintentional absurdity of Rose's question. *Is anything in my life going right?* "I'm simply taking a little time this morning to adjust to the new apartment and to spend some time with Mason and Della."

"Oh, how nice. Yes, you should absolutely do that," Rose said cheerfully. "You can count on me to hold down the fort."

"I know. Thank you."

After speaking with Rose, Katie took a few more minutes to align her body and mind to the fact that she was awake and that she couldn't lie in bed the entire day. So, as tempting as that thought was, she pushed back the covers, stretched, and got up. After making up her bed and hiding it in its wall niche, Katie leisurely fed the cats, made herself some scrambled eggs, and took her breakfast into the living area where she could curl up on the love seat while she ate.

Clicking the TV remote's on button, she saw that an episode of the classic show *I Dream of Jeannie* was playing. She wished she had her own personal genie who could magically blink away all her problems. She imagined herself striding into an antique shop and manically rubbing every lamp in the place, and then she wondered what she'd wish for first.

I'd wish for Aunt Lizzie to still be here. And Chad. And that Chad and I were running the English Ivy Inn bed and breakfast.

But that thought brought her up short. Had she and Chad purchased the mansion, Nick and Don wouldn't be in her life, either. Nor would Artisans Alley or Tealicious. Or Ray. Of course, meeting Erikka, and being suspected of her murder, and Andy wouldn't be in her life either.

There would have been other heartaches though. No life was free from those. Now that her appetite had deserted her, Katie turned off the TV, divided the remainder of her eggs between the two cats' bowls, and sat behind her new desk. She opened her laptop, checked her social media accounts, and ensured that she was still blocked from seeing anything pertaining to Errika's sister. The fleeting glance of the photograph she'd seen still bugged her. VJ was a computer whiz—talented in all things tech.

She wondered if he could somehow find the photograph and enlarge it for her?

Checking the clock, she decided he was likely still at church with his parents. She'd call him when she got into her office at Artisans Alley. Meanwhile, it was time for a bath in that new soaker bathtub.

As she strolled into Artisans Alley at a little after eleven, Katie felt more relaxed than she had in days. Sadly, that sensation was short-lived.

She found Rose in the vendors' lounge refilling her coffee cup. Her cheerful demeanor had evaporated as well. "We've got to do something about that mean old Nona Fiske," Rose said in lieu of a greeting. "She's telling her customers and everyone on the Square that Moonbeam Carruthers is a hippie and a witch and that people should stay out of her voodoo shop."

Having been the recipient of Nona's malicious gossip, Katie knew Rose was right—something had to be done before the old meddler did any real damage. "I doubt Nona has ever even visited Moonbeam's shop. If she had, she'd know how charming it is."

"I agree. I love her lavender-scented soaps," Rose said. "And the hand lotions are nice, too."

Katie thought about it for a moment, considering what approach to take. "Given Sue's misinformation about the food for the Harvest Festival vendors' party, and Nona's rumors, it might be a good idea for me to call a special meeting of the Merchants Association."

The Victoria Square Merchants Association had been in place long before Katie became its president. The organization had been formed to provide the merchants a place to express concerns, share promotional ideas, and—most recently—become business partners.

Rose returned to the Alley's main cash desk, and Katie headed for her office. She'd planned to call VJ first thing, but now she realized a call to his mother should be her priority.

Katie scrolled through the contacts on her cell phone and tapped Janey's name. She answered on the third ring.

"Hey, Katie. What's up?"

"Hi, Janey. I'm going to call a special meeting of the Merchants Association, and I'd like for you to be there."

"Oh? What's going on?"

"It seems that Nona Fiske is spreading gossip about our newest merchant, Moonbeam Carruthers."

"Well, that's just uncalled for," Janey huffed. "I've met her and Moonbeam is as sweet as can be."

"I agree. But I can't very well call the meeting so the merchants can see that Moonbeam is great and that Nona is merely being a busybody."

Laughing, Janey said, "If you called a meeting every time Nona stuck her nose into someone else's business, the Merchants Association would have to get together on a daily basis."

"Isn't that the truth?" Katie said and laughed. "That's why the *official* purpose of the meeting will be to provide an update on the Harvest Festival. That's why I'd like you to be there—to give a progress report on the vendors' party. Can you to it?"

"I'm honored you've asked me, and I'll be happy to do whatever you need me to do," Janey said. "When will the meeting take place?"

"I'll try to schedule it for tomorrow evening at Del's. Does that work for you?"

Janey said it did, and Katie asked her if VJ was around.

"He's not here at the moment, but I can call his cell and have him get in touch with you," Janey said.

"Thanks. I'd appreciate that. I'm having a…a computer issue… I hope he can help with." She didn't want to tell the boy's mother that she hoped he could print out a picture from Erikka's sister's social media account. She wasn't sure how Janey would feel about that.

"I'll let him know." Janey paused. "By the way, I think I've taken care of that whole situation with Izzy."

Something in Janey's voice made Katie apprehensive. "What did you do? I mean, did you talk with VJ?"

"I did." The woman sounded downright triumphant. "And I told him I absolutely couldn't stand that snooty little Izzy."

"What? I thought you *liked* Izzy," Katie said. "You told me you thought she was a good influence on him."

"I still do, hon. Izzy's an amazing young woman. I'm using the old reverse psychology on VJ."

"Oh...okay." Katie thought that was a terrible idea, but of course, she didn't tell Janey that.

"Do I need to bring anything to Del's?" Janey asked.

"Just yourself. If you want to do a handout or anything, let me know and we can work it up before the meeting."

"Sure thing. I'll let you know."

"Okay. See you tomorrow."

Katie hit the end-call icon and set her phone on the desk. Now all she had to figure out was how she was going to approach the Nona problem. Perhaps she should have made sure Moonbeam could attend the meeting before she made arrangements at Del's. And that was another expense the Association would have to eat. They needed to figure out a place to meet that wouldn't cost them an arm and a leg, not that Del overcharged them for special meetings. But he was in business to make money, after all. When they had their monthly dinner meetings, everyone paid for their own meals.

First things first. Katie needed to call Moonbeam to ensure she could actually attend the meeting.

* * *

After speaking with Moonbeam, Katie contacted Del's Diner and was happy to find no one had booked their party room for the following evening. She sent an email to the Merchants Association members scheduling the special meeting for the following evening. She was working on the agenda when VJ stopped by her office. Like his father, the boy was tall and lanky and Katie could see the resemblance between them grow more and more each day.

"Hi, there," she said, turning away from her computer to give him her full attention.

"Hey. My Mom said you were having computer issues." He frowned at her laptop. "Is this the one?"

"Um…" She didn't know how to dive right in and tell him what she wanted him to do. It felt awkward without a little upfront small talk. "You sure got here fast. It wasn't that long ago that I spoke with your mom."

"Yeah, I was at Brady's studio when she called."

"Do you help Matt out often?" she asked.

"Sometimes. Today I was there talking to Izzy." His gaze dipped to the floor. "I guess I hurt her feelings. I kinda don't know how to make it up to her," he said sheepishly.

"It's none of my business," Katie said, "but I found Izzy in tears after the two of you broke up. She said you were upset because your mom likes her too much."

VJ met Katie's eyes. "That's the thing—Mom has changed her mind about Izzy. She doesn't like her anymore."

"When I was in college, it was considered a good thing for your parents to like the person you were dating," Katie said.

"Yeah, but you don't want them to like the person *too* much, or then it's just weird—especially if things don't work out and your parents pressure you to get back together. That happened to a friend of mine," he confided somberly.

"I see." Katie took a peppermint from the jar, offered one to VJ, and he accepted. "I can understand why that would be a problem. But you should date someone because you like her, regardless of how others feel. Do you like Izzy?"

VJ's expression brightened. "Izzy's awesome. She likes me even though she's a whole six months older than me. I just didn't want to end up in a bad situation like my friend, Adam." VJ unwrapped the peppermint and tossed the cellophane wrapper into her wastebasket. "But, then, you know all about that—am I right?"

Katie frowned. *Great. Even the kids around here know I'm screwed.*

When Katie didn't answer, VJ took a seat in the chair beside her desk and nodded toward the laptop. "So, what's going on with your computer?"

Taking a deep breath, she said, "It's not so much my computer but a photo I'm trying to get off social media. Since you obviously know something of the predicament I'm in, I don't mind telling you that I'm looking for leads as to who might've killed Erikka Wiley. All I know is that it wasn't me." She added that last part not only for VJ's benefit but for the benefit of anyone who might be listening in.

VJ nodded thoughtfully. "That's understandable. I'd feel the same way."

She wrote Erryn's name and the date of the post on a sticky note and handed it to VJ. "If you could print and enlarge the photo posted on that account on the date I've given you, I'd be in your debt."

VJ shrugged. "That should be easy. Mind if I use your computer?" he asked.

"Not at all." Katie pushed the keyboard in his direction.

After logging in to his own online account, VJ frowned. "You have to be a friend to see the majority of her posts. Only friends and approved followers can see all of them."

"Rats." *There goes* that *lead.* "I appreciate your trying, VJ."

"No problem." He held up the sticky note. "May I keep this? I might think of another way of getting access to the account."

"Thanks, VJ."

As the young man left her office, Katie wondered if Andy followed Erryn on social media. Of course, since Erryn had blocked Katie, the only way she could know was if she called Andy and asked him. Was she that desperate?

Maybe.

And then it occurred to Katie that she might be blocked from Erryn's page, but as VJ had showed her, the world at large could at least see she *had* a profile.

Logging out, she went to the sign-up page and used Artisans Alley's generic email address and set up a new account. In seconds, she typed Erryn's name into the search bar. Sure enough, her profile page flashed onto Katie's screen. As VJ said, she could only see a couple of Erryn's posts, the latest being some ten months before, and the other two from several years past. Katie decided to check out Erryn's friends' pages. When she typed Andy's name in, it came up in less than a second.

So, Andy had friended Erikka's sister—or had it been she who'd befriended him?

Again Katie considered calling Andy.

Again, she decided not to. He had cheated on her not once, but twice, and maybe more. She had loved him and he'd betrayed her.

Katie swallowed, worried that after being betrayed first by her husband and now by Andy, that she might never trust—or love—a man ever again.

CHAPTER 24

The workday had come to an end, and Katie had shut down her computer, locked her desk, and was on her way out the door when her phone rang. She glanced at the text on her screen and saw it was Jordan Tanner. She tapped the call-accept button.

"Hi, Katie." Jordan sounded breathless and annoyed.

She inwardly groaned. "Hi, Jordan." *What now? Has there been another miscommunication about the Harvest Festival party?* She was beginning to regret spearheading the entire event.

"I know you've got help at the Alley, which is why I'm calling you. It's Ann," Jordan continued. "She fell here in the bakery and it looks like she broke her wrist."

"Oh, no!" Katie cried, berating herself for thinking he was calling with something as trivial as a Harvest Festival party complaint.

"I hate to ask, but would you mind coming over and waiting for a customer who's picking up a birthday cake just before closing so I can take Ann to the ER?"

"Of course," she said. "I'm on my way there now."

To save time, Katie retrieved her car which she'd parked

behind the vendors' lounge and drove across the Square, parking it near the bakery's entrance. Ann sat at a table near the front of the shop with an ice bag on her right wrist, her face was contorted with pain. She tried—but failed—to smile as Katie entered.

"Oh, Ann, I'm so sorry," Katie said.

"She slipped in some coffee that a customer spilled," Jordan said angrily. "Not only did the person not clean up the mess, but they also didn't tell either of us so we could take care of it. For goodness sake, if a customer had fallen, we'd be facing a lawsuit right now!"

Ann and Katie shared a glance.

"Honey, why don't we ask Katie if she minds taking me to the emergency room?" Ann asked. "That way, you can be here when Mrs. Logan comes in for the cake...you know, in case she has questions or something." She gave Katie a desperate look.

"Uh, sure," Katie said. "That's a great idea. I'll take Ann on to the ER, and you can join us as soon as your customer is taken care of."

"Are you sure it won't be too much trouble?" Jordan asked.

"Hundred percent." With that, Katie put a comforting arm around Ann's shoulders, then helped her to her feet and led her to her car.

"Don't forget your purse," Jordan said, and went to grab it from the backroom.

Meanwhile, Katie buckled Ann's seat belt for her. "I appreciate your driving me. Poor Jordan is my rock, but he tends to fall apart during an emergency, and he handles it by ranting and raving. I'm glad I won't have to listen to that all the way to the hospital."

"He's probably using his anger to cover his concern," Katie said, with a smile. "I know he's worried sick."

Ann nodded. "He'll be all right once he gets to the hospital and sees that I'm going to live."

Katie closed the door and got in the driver's side just as Jordan returned with Ann's purse.

"I'll be there as soon as I can, honey," he said through Katie's open window.

Ann gave him a nod, and Katie fired up the engine. In no time at all, they were on their way to the hospital in nearby Greece.

Upon their arrival at the hospital, Katie steered toward the circular drive in front of the ER's drop-off zone. "I'll stop the car and get a wheelchair for you," Katie said.

"Nonsense. It's my wrist, not my legs." Ann nodded toward the seat belt. "If you could just undo this thing...."

"Okay."

The ER's lot wasn't full and Katie found a space near the front and parked. She yanked the keys from the ignition. "Stay put until I come around and get you." Katie unfastened her seat belt, got out of the car, and rushed around to the passenger side. She opened the door and gingerly helped Ann from the car. They walked through the double sets of doors and into the waiting area where they were greeted by a security guard.

"I think my friend has broken her wrist," Katie explained.

The guard handed her two Day-Glo green visitor stickers. "Check-in is straight ahead," he said and nodded in the appropriate direction.

"Thank you."

Katie steered Ann to a chair in the waiting area, and Ann fumbled in her purse to come up with her driver's license and insurance card, pressing them into Katie's hand. "Thanks."

Approaching the reception desk, Katie's stomach did a swan dive. Erikka's sister, Erryn, sat behind the counter in front of a computer. Would she behave professionally or blow a fuse as she had at the antique store?

"Excuse me, I need to—"

Erryn looked up from her keyboard, her expression changing from passive to angry in a heartbeat. "What are you doing here?"

she interrupted. "You can't harass me at my job. Get out of here before I call the guard over."

"I brought my friend here," Katie said evenly. "She has a broken wrist and needs to be seen immediately."

Erryn narrowed her eyes at Katie before scanning the waiting room and seeing Ann sitting on one of the blue plastic chairs still holding the ice bag around her wrist. Erryn let out a breath. "Fine. Name, ID, and insurance information," she barked.

"Ann Tanner. Believe me—I had no idea you worked here."

"Really? You didn't see it on *social media*?" Erryn hissed. "Andy told me you saw my sonogram and recognized it as the one Erikka used to prank him. That's why I immediately blocked you. My life is *none* of your business."

Through gritted teeth, Katie said, "I only looked at your page to see if your sister might have had a stalker or something—I want to find out who killed her."

Erryn lifted her chin defiantly. "Then look in a mirror."

"Do you honestly believe that?" Katie asked.

"All I know is that my sister told me you'd do anything to hang onto Andy, even though you knew it was *her* he was in love with."

"Then Erikka was either delusional, or Andy was lying to us both," Katie said. "But right now, I only care about my friend getting to see a doctor as soon as possible. Delay her treatment, and I'll report you."

"I'd never do that to a patient to spite *you* or anyone else," Erryn said, snatching the cards from Katie's hand and going back to work. It took her just a minute or two to input the information before handing the cards back. "Have a seat. You'll be called as soon as someone is available to see your friend."

"Thank you," Katie said sweetly and returned to Ann's side, taking a seat. "It shouldn't be long."

"It seemed a little tense up there," Ann said, her eyes wide. "Anything wrong?"

"No. I was merely making sure they don't dawdle getting you in to see a doctor."

Ann managed a half-smile. "And I thought Jordan was a pit bull."

Within minutes, Ann was called back to see one of the ER physicians. As Katie remained in the waiting room, she thought about everything Erryn had said. How weird was it that Erryn had known about—and allowed—Erikka to use her sonogram to announce a fake pregnancy? Of course, Erryn called it a *prank*, but Katie didn't believe it. She was convinced Erikka intended to use the news to persuade Andy to leave Katie for her.

It made her blood boil to know that Andy told Erryn she recognized the sonogram from Erryn's social media page. Why on earth would he do that? Why would he even be in touch with Erikka's sister? Andy's relationship with Erikka had obviously been more involved than he'd initially let on, but *had* he told the woman he loved her? Had he been lying to both of them, stringing them both along?

Still, other than the night Katie had stayed with Ray's daughters, she and Andy hadn't spent many nights apart. Had he spent the ones without her with Erikka? Erikka had to have been the aggressor in the pursuit of a long-term relationship with Andy, but did he meekly accept her pursuit? Yes, he admitted sleeping with her; but according to Brady, Erikka wasn't sitting at home pining for Andy, either. Katie took that to mean that Andy hadn't made Erikka any promises. The woman had simply plotted and waited.

As much as she hated to do it, Katie was going to have to talk to Andy again. If nothing else, he owed it to her to go on Erryn's social media page to download and enlarge that photograph to help identify the mystery man.

And to think, the entire situation really *was* all Katie's fault. She thought she was doing a kind thing by introducing Erikka to Andy after his assistant manager had quit. The woman had been broke and needed a job, and Katie had come to the rescue. As repayment, Erikka had deliberately come between Katie and Andy. And now her death might land Katie in jail!

A pale and concerned Jordan arrived at the ER waiting room. Katie rushed to him.

"Where is she?" he asked, his expression tense.

"In one of the treatment rooms. I'm sure they'll take you right to her. She led him back to the reception desk. They waited, and one of the nurses came to take him to Ann.

"Will you give me an update?"

"Sure," he said. "Just give me a few minutes."

Katie watched as Jordan accompanied the nurse, noticing that Erryn kept flashing her a nasty glare every so often.

Ten minutes later, Jordan returned with a report. "They took an x-ray, and it's broken all right." He let out a heavy breath. "She might need surgery. I don't know how we're going to keep the bakery going without her. She could be out of work for up to two months. We've got Halloween and Thanksgiving coming up, and they're always a busy time of year for us."

"How's Ann taking it?"

Jordan shrugged. "Like a trooper. They've splinted her wrist and the nurse is looking up the name and address of the orthopedist so we can make a follow-up appointment. He'll decide her course of treatment."

"Is there anything I can do to help?" Katie asked.

Jordan shook his head. "We'll have to hire someone."

"I could ask one of my girls at Tealicious if she needs some extra hours. That might tide you over for a few days until you can find someone."

"Thanks, Katie. I'd appreciate that."

"When do you think they'll release Ann?"

"Any time now. They already phoned in a prescription at the pharmacy down the road. The one in McKinlay Mill is already closed. I think I'll pick up a container of chocolate cookies-

and-cream ice cream. It's her favorite," he said, his voice dipping.

Katie patted his arm. "You're a good guy, Jordan."

"And I've got the best wife and partner in the world," he said, his voice breaking. He sniffed and seemed to shake himself. "I'd better get back to Ann. Thanks for bringing her here. You're a good friend, Katie."

She said nothing and watched as he returned to the big automatic door that led to the treatment rooms.

Yeah, Katie was everybody's friend. But when it came to lovers, they always seemed to take advantage of her good nature. Was there an invisible KICK ME sign on her back?

Maybe.

Feeling more than a little depressed, Katie turned and headed for the exit.

* * *

AFTER LEAVING Ann in Jordan's care, Katie headed back to McKinlay Mill. As she drove, she reflected on the care and concern Jordan showed toward his wife. She knew the couple had been married for over thirty years and had opened their bakery and café nearly ten years before. It had been a struggle at first, but now that business had improved for all the merchants on Victoria Square, they could probably handle the strain of hiring additional help while Ann recuperated.

Katie thought about Jordan's expression as he told her about Ann's favorite ice cream and wondered if she'd ever have someone care for her the way those two cared for each other. Andy had cared about her at one time…hadn't he? Now she was no longer sure. These days, she was uncertain about every aspect of their relationship. Had everything they'd shared been a sham?

As she passed Andy's house, she noticed his truck was in the driveway. He should have been at the pizzeria. Had he left one of the boys in charge? Was he too grief-stricken, still mourning the loss of his beloved Erikka?

Hesitating for only a moment, Katie pulled into his driveway. The house had originally belonged to Andy's parents. He'd taken it over when they'd become snowbirds, splitting their time between their summer cottage on Lake Ontario and a condo in Florida. He hadn't done a lot of updating to the place, although from time to time he spoke of doing some renovations. He kept saying he was waiting for him and Katie to make it "official." And, yet, he'd never asked her to marry him. He'd never even asked her to move in with him. Looking back, she could see he'd always held some part of himself back. Admittedly, so had she. Maybe they'd both known all along that things simply weren't right between them.

As she sat in the car contemplating the house and feeling herself deflating, Andy suddenly appeared at her driver's side door.

"Are you all right, Sunshine?"

Katie stepped out to her car. Having no good answer to his question, she simply said, "We need to talk."

"Of course." He held out a hand to escort her to the house, but when she didn't take it, he let it drop to his side.

Once inside, Katie bypassed the living room's couch and took the armchair to further underscore the fact that she hadn't come to rekindle their relationship. In case he didn't take the hint, she began with, "I'm not here to make up. After all that's happened, we'll never get back together."

Andy started to speak, but she held up her hand.

"Please let me finish."

He nodded.

"I have to let go of my hurt and anger toward you and concentrate on taking care of myself. That starts with finding out who killed Erikka, and I need your help to do that."

"You know I'll do anything to prove to you that I didn't hurt her." He sat on the edge of the couch closest to her. "Hell, I even offered to confess to throw Schuler off your trail," he reminded her.

"Yeah, and we decided that more lies were not going to solve this murder," she answered tartly. "But, hopefully, the truth will. I know you're friends with Erikka's sister, Erryn, on social media."

He shifted his gaze. "Yeah. I might've inadvertently misled Erikka into thinking that she and I might have had a future together if things ever went south between you and me."

Katie glared at him and waited. He had more to tell her, and she'd found the silent treatment was the best way to get Andy to talk. She just had to wait him out.

It didn't take long.

Andy slapped his knees, got up, and started pacing. "Okay, I wanted a backup, all right? You kept getting closer and closer to Ray Davenport, and then you hired that GQ model of a chef to run Tealicious. Things were strained between us and—"

"It doesn't matter anymore," Katie said evenly. "None of it does. Maybe one day we can move past your betrayal enough to consider each other friends, but right now I see no point in rehashing what was done or what should have been done or—"

Andy dropped to his knees in front of her chair, his eyes beseeching. "Katie, please, I still love you. What can I do to prove it?"

She hadn't gone there to debate. She'd come for one purpose. "Please go onto Erryn's Facebook page and download a photo for me. There's someone in one of her posts who looks familiar, and I want a better look."

"Sure thing." He got up, retrieved his laptop, and set it on the coffee table. Sitting back down on the couch, he revved up the computer and opened his social media account. "What the—?"

Moving behind the sofa to look over Andy's shoulder, Katie saw that her visit had been in vain. Now Andy, too, had been blocked from Erryn's page.

CHAPTER 25

"Well, that was unexpected," Andy muttered, staring at his news feed.

"Why's that?" Katie asked.

"Because I thought we were—"

"*Real* friends?"

Andy didn't answer.

"Just how well do you know Erikka's family?" she pressed.

Again, Andy seemed to retreat into himself. "I've met them a few times—at the shop."

Katie glared at him. Sure. They drove all the way to Victoria Square when there were scores of pizzerias between Fairport, Greece, and McKinlay Mill. Katie stood. "I'd better be going."

"Wait," Andy said, and reached for her arm. She shrugged him off and headed for the door.

When she got to her car, Katie saw Andy watching her from behind the screen door.

She got in, started the car, and pulled out of the driveway without a backward glance.

So, he wanted a backup in Erikka in case things didn't work out with her. He was allowed to have a friendship—and apparently a very close one—with Erikka, but she couldn't be friends with Ray, a man old enough to be mistaken for her father, and the chef she employed at Tealicious? Talk about a double standard. Katie had remained faithful when Andy….

But then she remembered the kiss she'd shared with Ray and a cloud of self-doubt descended upon her.

Katie gave herself a mental shake. She had other things to think about. Like the meeting with the criminal defense attorney the next morning. She'd done some research and his billable hours could put her in the poor house.

Yes, she had a lot of other, more important things to think about besides Andy Rust.

* * *

KATIE SPENT the rest of the evening finishing her unpacking, but since she'd pared down her possessions before the move, it didn't take all that long. She avoided the computer and even turned off her phone. She didn't want to be in contact with the world at large. If someone needed her, they could knock on her door.

She pulled down her Murphy bed, turned on the TV, found a chick-flick, and promptly fell asleep. Waking hours later, she found two hungry cats staring at her while the tube droned on and on. She fed the felines and went to bed, but after napping found it hard to fall asleep, and when she finally dozed off, she dreamed of handcuffs being snapped around her wrists.

It was light when Katie rolled over in bed, took a deep breath, and looked up at the ceiling. She was glad Artisans Alley was closed on Monday, so she didn't have to explain her absence that morning. She was both apprehensive and relieved about her appointment with J.P. Trammel, the criminal attorney. Della headbutted her chin—as if Katie needed to be reminded that the most important thing in the world was feeding the cats.

The next hour passed in a blur of routine—feeding the

cats, taking a shower, trying and failing to eat a piece of toast vetoed by her nerves, dressing in a conservative navy suit, and hurrying down the steps to exit the teashop's back door.

Brad caught her eye and gave her a wink and a thumbs-up—he knew where she was going. She tried to smile but was afraid the expression was more of a grimace.

Seth was waiting in the parking lot. She opened the door and sank into his Mercedes' buttery leather seat.

"Are you all right?" he asked.

She puffed out her cheeks as she considered her answer.

"Should I take that as a no?" he persisted.

"No...maybe...I don't know." She gave him a rundown of the previous evening's events: Ann's fall, Erryn at the hospital telling Katie that Andy was in love with Erikka, and then stopping by Andy's house.

He groaned. "You went to Andy's house? Why would you do that?"

"For access to that stupid photograph," Katie said. "But, guess what? Erryn decided to block him, too."

"What makes you think this one particular photograph is the Holy Grail?"

She sighed. "I don't really know. Maybe it isn't. But the glimpse I got of that photo—fleeting though it was—made me think that something about the man in the far-right corner with his back to the photographer was familiar...and, yet, out of place."

"The man isn't even facing the camera?" Seth asked.

"No, but I could still see a sliver of his profile. I'm telling you—it set off alarm bells."

Seth braked for the village's only traffic light. "Could it be Andy? That would explain your visceral reaction to a photo you merely glimpsed."

"No, it definitely wasn't him. If it had been Andy, then why wouldn't he have told me so when I asked about the picture?" she asked.

"Maybe to avoid throwing another log on the fire." The light changed, and the car eased forward.

Katie shook her head. "No. He didn't use that as an excuse to avoid showing me the photo. Erryn blocked him."

"Why are you so convinced the man you spotted at the edge of a photograph—someone not even central to the image—is so important? Don't you think you're grasping at straws?"

"Yes. But right now, straws are all I have."

He glanced over. "That's not true. You've got me—and we're going to get you out of this mess."

She sure hoped so.

J. P. Trammel's sleek office in downtown Rochester was filled with a lot of chrome-and-black furniture. An administrative assistant wearing a gray suit and light-blue tie escorted Katie and Seth to a conference room. She sank into one of the cushy leather chairs at the glass-topped table. The window beyond looked out on the Genesee River not far from the High Falls.

"If you need anything, I'm Patrick. Mr. Trammel will be with you momentarily. Would either of you like coffee, tea, or water?"

"I'd like a water please," Katie said.

Seth shook his head.

Patrick returned with a bottle of Perrier and a crystal glass filled with ice, set them in front of Katie, and left the room.

Katie twisted the cap off the bottle. "I can't help but wonder how much this will cost me. Am I going to have to mortgage my...everything?"

Before Seth could offer reassurance, a handsome man in his mid-forties burst into the conference room clutching an expensive-looking leather binder.

"Seth! Good to see you!"

Seth stood, and the men shook hands.

"Good seeing you, Jim. Although, naturally, I wish it were under more pleasant circumstances," Seth said.

"Me, too, buddy." He stretched out a hand to Katie. "J. P. Trammel."

"Katie Bonner."

They shook.

"Nice to meet you. Thank you for making time for me."

"Not a problem." He sat at the conference table across from the two of them. "I called the DA's office a few minutes ago and learned that there is currently no evidence against you whatsoever, Ms. Bonner."

Her relief was expelled in a puff of air as she sank back in her seat. "Thank you." She wasn't sure if she was addressing Trammel or the almighty.

Trammel smiled. "Right now, everything Detective Schuler is trying to use against you is pure conjecture. Granted, there wasn't a lot of evidence at the crime scene—no fingerprints, no DNA, no business card from Artisans Alley lying beneath the body..."

His attempt at a joke landed flat.

"Sorry," he said.

Pouring the water into the glass, Katie asked, "What were the police looking for when they searched my residences and office?"

"As you both know, the search warrant was cagey, and the DA's office isn't about to share that information with me unless and until you're charged with a crime." Trammel spread his hands. "However, it's promising that no evidence was found."

Katie recapped the water, took a drink from the glass, and then looked at Seth, feeling guilty.

"What?" He knew her too well. "What aren't you telling me?"

The thought of her conversation with Ray flooded her mind. He wouldn't want her to tell Seth and Trammel about the ring. He'd warn her that it was crazy. The ring was gone, he'd say, it's pointless to bring it up. Why sabotage her credibility with Trammel? Why make Seth think she'd kept such a huge secret from him?

On the other hand, Seth was her friend. She loved and trusted him like a brother. And if she wound up being charged for Erikka's murder, Trammel was going to be her attorney. Shouldn't they know everything she knew?

"Katie?" Seth prodded.

"I—I found something." The words tumbled quickly from her lips. "Before the search. I was doing a walk-through of the apartment over Tealicious, and I spotted something glistening on the windowsill. It was a ring—Erikka's ring."

Seth's expression darkened. "Why didn't you tell me about this before now?" he asked through gritted teeth.

"What did you do with it?" Trammel spoke at the same time as Seth, so she decided to answer his question first. It seemed to be the easier of the two…for now, anyway.

"Well, Ray Davenport was doing the walk-through with me—you know, he's experienced in carpentry and…whatever—so when he offered to come along, I said okay." She shrugged. "I didn't let on to anyone—well, Ray or John Healy—that I'd found the ring, and I slipped it into the pocket of my jeans."

"Where is it now?" Seth asked. "Do you have it?"

She took another drink of water—a sip, really, because her hands were shaking so badly, she was afraid she'd drop the crystal glass if she didn't put it back down. "No. When we—Ray and I—got outside, he asked what I'd put in my pocket."

"So you *told* him?" Seth asked. "How do you know he's not the one who put it there?"

"Why would Ray try to frame me for Erikka's murder?" she asked.

Trammel regained control of the conversation. "Did you tell Ray what you'd found?"

"Yes. I showed it to him. And he—" She began fidgeting with a button on her jacket's cuff. "He said I should give it to him for... for safekeeping."

Seth shook his head, disappointment furrowing his brow. "And I suppose you did?"

"Well, sure. I mean, the man is a former homicide detective," Katie said. "I thought he was trying to help me."

"Why didn't you call me?" Seth demanded. "Why am I only finding out about this now?"

"I don't know." Katie lowered her head. "I'm sorry."

"That's all right." Trammel's voice was as warm and soothing as hot cocoa. "Where is the ring now?"

Katie refused to raise her eyes to either man. No way was she going to look at either of them when she admitted the truth that would infuriate Seth and call her credibility into question with Trammel. "It's...gone."

"What do you mean it's gone?" Seth asked.

"After the search, I asked Ray to give it back to me," she said. "I wanted to turn it over to the deputies. Ray told me it would look bad for me to have held onto the ring and that I couldn't take it to them now." She took a deep breath. "When I insisted he give the ring back, he told me he'd thrown it in the lake."

"Did he—a veteran homicide detective—explain to you *why* he threw away an item that was potential evidence in a murder investigation?" Trammel asked.

"He said he was looking out for me." Katie's voice was barely above a whisper, but she felt sure both men had heard her. Especially when Seth spoke again.

"Looking out for *you* or looking out for someone else?"

Trammel's good mood had also evaporated. "Walk us through finding that ring again from the beginning and tell us why you didn't immediately turn it into the deputies—or seek the advice of your attorney."

After taking a drink of the cold, bracing water, Katie started at the beginning. "I walked from Artisans Alley to the apartment at Tealicious to do the walk-through."

"And Ray Davenport was with you." Trammel opened the binder, took out a pen and set it on the yellow legal pad.

"Yes, sir."

"Was it your idea or his that he accompany you on this walk-through?" Trammel wrote as he spoke.

"It was Ray's," she said. "But I was glad—he knows much more about carpentry and electricity, and—"

"That's fine," Trammel interrupted. "Tell us about your finding the ring and Mr. Davenport's actions thereafter."

"Sure." She explained that she spotted the ring on a window sill, eased it into her pocket as unobtrusively as possible, talked some more with the contractor, and then she and Ray left the building. "When we got out onto the tarmac, Ray asked me what I'd put in my pocket. I told him I didn't want to discuss it there, so we returned to my office at Artisans Alley."

"And it was there in your office that you showed the ring to Mr. Davenport," Trammel said.

"Yes. I took it from my pocket and placed it on the desk between us. He said he guessed the ring wasn't mine," she said. "I told him I thought it belonged to Erikka. He asked when she had been in that apartment, and I said I didn't know if she ever had."

"Is that when Mr. Davenport took possession of the ring?" Trammel still didn't look up from his notepad. Katie could well imagine him to be an intimidating presence in a courtroom.

"Yes. He said he believed the ring had been planted and that it would be best if he held onto it." She wracked her brain for more information from their conversation. "I asked him how we'd find out where the ring had come from and why it was in my new apartment, and he said that if it was important, someone would ask about it." She shrugged. "No one ever asked about that ring specifically, but I'm guessing that's what Schuler was looking for with the search warrant."

"And now the ring has been tossed into the lake." A thread of anger shot through Seth's words.

"I'm sorry I didn't come to you with the ring," Katie told him.

"So am I," he grated.

"This makes me look really bad, doesn't it?" she asked.

Trammel finally looked up from his legal pad. "Actually, Ms. Bonner, this makes Ray Davenport look really bad."

CHAPTER 26

Despite the sunny day, there was no need for any air conditioning in Seth's car as they pulled into the city's mid-morning traffic. The chill emanating from Seth was more than enough to dispel the day's heat.

"How do you think our meeting with Mr. Trammel went?" Katie asked.

"Fine." His clipped tone and lack of eye contact reinforced his mood.

"I get it." Katie placed a hand on his forearm, but he jerked it away. His reaction stung. "I'm sorry. I realize now I should've told you about the ring before going into the meeting. I was nervous, and I didn't—"

"You should've told me about the ring the instant you found it! In fact, you should never have touched the thing. You should've called me and waited until I got there. Then I'd have called the police." He shook his head. "Don't you realize you could be guilty of concealing evidence and perverting the course of justice?"

"I didn't think—"

"No, you didn't," he interrupted. "You're a grown woman, Katie. When are you going to start thinking for yourself?"

"I *do* think for myself," she protested.

"Really? Were you thinking for yourself when you let Ray Davenport have that ring?" he asked. "Or were you simply relieved to have a protector—a knight to save your distressed damsel?"

"Take that back!" she snapped and wished *she* could take *her* words back. They made her sound like a child trying to stand up to a playground bully. She took a breath to calm herself. "I trusted Ray because he was an excellent homicide detective."

"You trusted Ray because you know the besotted old fool would do anything for you, including cover up a murder."

Katie gasped. "You can't possibly believe I killed Erikka."

Seth's voice softened slightly, but his words were harsher. "No, I don't doubt you're innocent. You're merely a pathetic little girl who wants someone to save her. I thought you were a hell of a lot stronger than that."

"I don't need *anyone* to save me—I can save myself," Katie asserted.

"Ha!"

Katie refused to accept his lack of faith. She turned to look out the passenger-side window to fume.

Seth's silence angered her more than it should have. For the rest of the drive, they both simmered in their own feelings—a foot apart and yet miles away from each other. Katie could only guess at what Seth was thinking, but she couldn't get past his calling her a pathetic damsel who was looking for a savior.

Is that what she'd been? The thought horrified her, but looking back, she had to admit she'd been relieved to turn the ring over to Ray—she hadn't wanted to be caught with the dead woman's property when Schuler was so blatantly trying to find evidence that it was Katie who killed her. Besides, Ray *was* an experienced homicide detective. Who better to trust with evidence? How was she to know he'd destroy it? And what reason had he given? *He was protecting her.*

Katie prided herself on being a strong woman. Yet, she'd put on blinders when it came to the men in her life. Well...no more!

Seth took the Lake Ontario State Parkway exit for McKinlay Mill and headed south, driving straight through the village to Victoria Square and pulling up in front of Tealicious. Katie looked across the seat at him, but Seth stared straight ahead.

Katie got out of the car and bent down to talk to Seth, but he spoke first.

"Look for my bill in the mail," he said tersely.

"Seth!" Katie began, but he reached over to shut the door. The Mercedes tire's spun in the loose gravel as he took off. He hadn't even told her goodbye or said to call him if she needed him.

Katie swallowed. Okay, if that was the way he felt, it was fine with her. She was through being seen as needy. On the other hand, Seth *was* her attorney *and* her pseudo big brother. Was their relationship irreparably damaged?

Guilt and shame vied for prominence within her and despite her new vow for independence, Katie didn't want to be alone. Looking around the Square, she decided to head to Sassy Sally's. Nick and Seth had been friends for years. Maybe he could advise her on how to get back in her attorney's good graces.

Don was at the reception desk consulting their reservations computer when Katie entered the B and B's lobby. Greeting her with a smile, he said, "Good morning. How nice you look."

"Thanks." The smile she offered was nowhere near as bright and cheerful as his. "I had a meeting this morning. Is Nick around?"

"Nope. He's out, and all our boarders are, too. I'm blissfully alone."

"Oh, okay. I'll go and let you enjoy your peace and quiet." She turned, but Don called her back.

"No, wait. I'm sorry. Nick should be here any minute, and I've had all morning to enjoy my solitude. Come into the kitchen, and let's have a chat."

"Are you sure?" she asked.

"Positive." He moved from behind the counter and placed a hand on her shoulder. "You'll have to forgive me. Sometimes it gets so hectic here with the constant hustle and bustle—people coming and going all the time, chatting in the common areas. Nick thrives on it, but I love it when I get a little break from the chaos."

"I can imagine," Katie said. "You know, I never stopped to consider how little privacy the two of you have living and working here at Sassy Sally's."

"Don't feel too sorry for us. We do love it." He led her into the kitchen. "Coffee?"

"Please." She sat on a stool at the island.

Don placed a mug of coffee, a spoon, and two sugar packets in front of her before preparing his own mug and sitting across from her. "You appear to have something on your mind."

Katie glumly stirred the sugar into her coffee. "Seth and I had an argument. I think it's the first time he's ever been angry with me." She told him about the meeting with J. P. Trammel. "I'd found—something—" She didn't want to tell anyone else about the ring. "—that might've had some bearing on the investigation, but I didn't mention it to Seth before the meeting with Trammel. And then…um…I couldn't produce it for the meeting because I… I lost it." She also didn't want to tell Don she gave what might have been an important piece of evidence in the case to Ray, who'd tossed it in the lake.

"So, Seth is reprimanding you for being irresponsible?" Don asked neutrally.

"Yeah. And he's right. I didn't handle the situation as well as I should have."

"Ah, well, who among us isn't guilty of that?" He smiled encouragingly. "Sometimes daily. I imagine Seth is simply frustrated. He cares about you so much, and he doesn't want you to be in trouble."

"I don't want Katie to be in trouble either," Nick said, coming into the kitchen with a couple of bags of groceries in time to hear the end of Don's sentence. "But it seems to me she always is." He bent down to give her a peck on the cheek before kissing his husband hello. "Somebody fill me in."

Katie watched as Nick filled a mug with coffee. She could see exactly what Don meant about the man thriving on chaos. Nick was a little dynamo whose batteries never seemed to run down. He flourished in the midst of turmoil. Even the air in the kitchen seemed to have charged since he entered the room.

"Seth is upset with me," she said.

"That's right. You were meeting with Trammel this morning," he said and began to unpack the bags. "Didn't it go well?"

She repeated the version of events she'd given Don.

Nick's expression was grim. He let out a breath. "I can understand where both of you are coming from. I'm sorry for both of you."

Though she appreciated his sympathy, it didn't help her predicament.

"Any news on how the investigation is progressing?" Don asked.

"None." Katie sighed. "I feel as though if I don't find the killer, Schuler will come up with a way to implicate me in the murder."

"From what Seth has told me, that's exactly what he's trying to do."

I know," Katie said.

Nick finished with the bags, poured himself a cup of coffee, and borrowed Katie's spoon to stir in sugar and creamer.

Katie took a sip of her coffee, which was no longer as warm as she liked it. "This might sound silly, but I glimpsed a photo on Erikka's sister's social media page that I feel holds a clue. But Erryn blocked me before I could get a closer look."

Nick squeezed Don's arm. "Listen to our very own Velma from the Scooby-Doo gang uncovering clues."

"Does that make me Fred?" Don asked.

"Of course. I guess that makes me Daphne." He laughed. "Anyhoo, you're in luck. Erryn had her baby shower here—it was Erikka's idea—and she and I are friends on social media. I'll get the laptop and— "

"'Fraid not," Don interjected. "The internet is down."

"What? Squirrels again?"

Don nodded. "I've already called and have been reassured that service should be restored by later this afternoon."

Nick rolled his eyes. He grabbed a sticky note and a pen and handed them to Katie. "Do you recall the date the photo was posted?"

"I do." She jotted it down and described it in as much detail as she could remember.

"As soon as we have internet service, I'll download it and print it out for you," Nick said.

"Thank you. Could you enlarge it so I can get a closer look at the man in the upper right corner?" she asked. "He's barely in the photo at all, but he's the one ringing alarm bells."

"Sure." Nick grinned. "This is exciting." He spoke in falsetto as he said, "Come on, gang—let's split up!"

For the first time that day, Katie laughed.

KATIE ALWAYS FELT a little at loose ends on a Monday. With Artisans Alley closed, she had far too much time on her hands. And now that she wasn't having lunch dates with Andy at Del's, she felt a little socially deprived.

She'd cleaned up her lunch dishes and was thinking of grabbing a quick nap when her phone rang. It was Rose.

"Hi. Katie. I hope I'm not calling at a bad time."

"Not at all," she said, although it wasn't like Rose to call out of the blue on her day off. "Is everything okay?"

"Yes. Well, probably." Rose drew in her breath before asking, "Could you meet me at Moonbeam's shop? She's going to tell my future."

"She's going to *what*?"

"She's getting ready to do a tarot reading for me, and I wanted you to come and be with me—that is, if you aren't busy or anything. That way, I won't be alone if she says I'm about to kick the bucket or something."

"If you're afraid of what she'll tell you, maybe you shouldn't have her do the reading," Katie suggested.

"I know, but I'm going to do it anyway. I feel like I need it. Will you come, or should I call Edie Silver?"

Katie knew Edie babysat her grandson on Mondays. "No, I'll be there." It wasn't often that Rose asked Katie for a favor. Sitting through a tarot reading wasn't too much to ask. Besides, someday soon, Katie might be asking Rose to bake her a cake with a file in it.

Ten minutes later, Rose was waiting outside The Flower Child looking like a little girl who'd been promised a treat. Her blonde curls glistened in the sunlight, and she held a hand up to shade her eyes as she watched for Katie. Her smile broadened as Katie approached.

She gave Katie a hug. "I'm so excited! I've never done anything like this before."

"Never?" Katie asked.

"No...and it's kinda scary." She steered Katie toward the door.

"It'll be fine." Katie desperately hoped it would be. Moonbeam wouldn't give Rose bad news, would she? Of course, she *had* told Katie that Erikka's killer was stalking her, so...

They entered The Flower Child to find Moonbeam sitting at a small desk in a corner of the shop. "Good afternoon, ladies. It's so good to see you both. I wasn't expecting you, Katie."

"Rose wanted a little moral support."

Moonbeam gave Katie a conspiratorial wink. "What a good friend you are!" She turned her attention to Rose. "You want someone here to share your good news with."

"Or bad," Rose said. "*Que sera, sera.*"

"Come, sit. Rose, we can begin whenever you're ready."

"I'm ready."

They moved to the back of the shop where a small table sat ready, covered with a colorful shawl. A deck of cards swathed in blue silk fabric awaited them. Rose sat on one of the chairs across from Moonbeam and clasped her hands in front of her. "Thank you for permitting me to call Katie and have her be here with me."

Moonbeam unwrapped the cards and shuffled the colorful deck before handing them to Rose. "Think of what you'd like to know and then cut the cards please."

"All right." Rose clasped the deck tightly and closed her eyes as though she were about to blow out the candles on her birthday cake and make a wish. Within seconds, she opened her eyes, cut the cards, and handed them back to Moonbeam. "Hit me."

Moonbeam laughed. "It's tarot, not blackjack."

Rose shrugged.

With an amused shake of her head, Moonbeam laid ten cards on the table using what she called the Celtic cross spread. The first two cards on the table were the emperor and empress. The second two were the two of cups and the ten of cups. The next cards she took from the stack held in her left hand were the ace of cups, the ten of pentacles, the four of wands, the Knight of the Hierophant, and the Lovers.

Moonbeam steepled her fingers, her brows rising in what Katie interpreted as thoughtful. "Ah, this tells me there's a strong probability for love in your future, *if* you're open to it."

Rose's face practically glowed with excitement. "I'm definitely open to it. How do I meet him? What do I need to do?"

Moonbeam gave a gentle laugh. “Nothing. The two of you are *destined* to meet. Now all you have to do is relax and let it happen.”

“Do the cards say what he looks like?” Rose leaned in and peered at the cards as if the image of her mystery man might magically appear.

Katie suppressed a grin. “I think you’re a little confused as to how these things work. Actually, I wish they did provide photographs of people you need to see.” She shared a look with Moonbeam, as she recalled the woman’s warning days before.

“Me, too,” Moonbeam said. “We have to be patient.” She directed her next words to Katie. “And watchful.”

“Oh, you bet I will,” Rose said.

So will I, Katie thought.

CHAPTER 27

It was inching toward five forty-five when Katie touched up her hair and makeup before heading to Del's, although she wasn't sure why. After all, there was no one she wanted to impress. And she knew not everyone was likely to attend that evening's meeting since she'd called it on such short notice. But at least Janey would be there to smooth over any ruffled feathers caused by her prior miscommunications, and Moonbeam would be around to dispel any negativity toward her brought about by Nona Fiske's nasty gossip.

Katie idly wondered if Andy would join them—he hadn't responded to the email she'd sent the merchants. Telling herself it didn't matter, she squared her shoulders and walked the two blocks to the diner.

As they hadn't booked far enough in advance, Del wouldn't be catering the meeting, but a number of the Association's members still had dropped in to have their evening meal. At a corner booth, Rose was regaling Sue and Gilda with the tale of her tarot reading. Katie waved at the group before heading over to Jordan Tanner.

"Hey, Jordan. How's Ann?"

"Hi, Katie. Thanks for asking. She says she's not in much pain," he said. "I'm bringing a take-out dinner home to her. Our daughter, Lila, is with her now to keep her company."

"If you're unable to stay for the meeting, I'll be summarizing the key points and emailing them tomorrow," Katie said.

"I plan on staying for a little while." Jordan waved to Conrad Stratton, who'd just walked in. "Ann would kill me if I didn't bring her some news to go with dinner. Not being at the bakery today nearly drove her bonkers."

"Poor Ann." Katie's thoughts drifted to what Don had told her about needing to get away from the chaos sometimes and wondered if Ann was like Nick in that she needed the stimulation. "I'll try to go see her tomorrow."

"Thanks. I know she'd enjoy that."

Katie left Jordan and joined Rose, Sue, and Gilda. She ordered a ham sandwich on rye from the waitress taking their orders as she slid into the booth.

"So, Katie," Sue said. "Did Moonbeam tell your fortune, too?"

"Nope," she said. "Today was all about Rose."

Her sandwich came in record time and Katie ate in silence, as Rose extolled Moonbeam's virtues. It looked as though one objective for this meeting was well on its way to being met. Of course, Rose wouldn't stay for the meeting—she was only at Del's for dinner—but Katie knew she was there to do her part in tearing down Nona's nasty rumors.

Katie noticed Vance sitting in a nearby booth. While he wasn't a member of the Merchants Association, he must have come with Janey to provide moral support. Katie knew Janey was nervous about talking to the group about the Harvest Festival vendors' party. Katie didn't know why Janey had the jitters about speaking to the group as a whole when she'd spoken to each one individually, but hopefully, all miscommunications would be laid to rest.

Upon finishing her meal, Katie rallied her troops to head for the diner's party room and the meeting. She stepped up to the head of the long table. From her vantage point, she could see a smiling Moonbeam. Nona, cheapskate that she was, hadn't dined at the restaurant but had arrived a few minutes ahead of the scheduled meeting and gone straight to the party room. She sat at the bottom of the table, scowling. Ray hadn't eaten at the diner but was seated a chair to her left. The other merchants ambled in and took their seats. As she was about to call the meeting to order, Andy walked in. He took the chair across from Ray, glaring at him.

"I apologize for calling you all to this last-minute meeting," Katie began, "but Janey Ingram and I wanted to clear up some misunderstandings that have occurred while planning the Harvest Festival—she'll address those items shortly. But first I want to welcome our newest member, Moonbeam Carruthers." She nodded toward Moonbeam, who stood and acknowledged the group. "I hope those of you who haven't done so will check out Moonbeam's charming shop, The Flower Child."

Ignoring Nona's scoffing, Katie continued. "Before I turn the program over to Janey, is there anything anyone would like to discuss?"

Katie purposefully avoided looking in Nona's direction, since she was frantically waving her hateful little hand, but the diminutive demon cleared her throat and stood. "I have an issue I believe needs to be addressed."

Here we go, Katie thought. But she was surprised by the next words out of Nona's mouth.

"I feel we should discuss the fact that *you're* being accused of murder, Katie Bonner," Nona said. "Don't you believe it's time you step down as president of the Merchants Association and let someone who *isn't* facing a murder trial take your place?"

As Katie's jaw dropped, Ray stood. "I don't know where you're getting your intel," he said, "but Katie *hasn't* been accused of anything."

Not to mention the fact that Katie had been trying to unload the responsibility of running the Association ever since she'd been drafted.

"My friend Mae heard the victim's sister accuse Katie to her face of killing Erikka Wiley." Nona lifted her sharp nose in the air to punctuate her statement. "And she said it's only a matter of time before the police make an arrest. We *all* know they've already searched Katie's office."

"Whether that's true or not, Katie has not been charged with any crime." Ray glared at Nona. "You need to apologize to her right now."

"Oh, sit down and hush, Ray. Just because you're in love with her doesn't mean everyone else is." She pointed a finger at Andy. "*He* certainly wasn't, now was he?"

Katie ran a hand over her face as the meeting erupted into pandemonium. How would she ever restore order?

From the left side of the table, Jordan muttered, "Ann's gonna hate that she missed this."

"Now just a second." Andy stood and stalked toward Nona. "You know nothing about me and my life."

Nona folded her arms across her chest. "I know one of your girlfriends is dead, and the other one is suspected of killing her."

Nona facing off against Andy looked like a chihuahua refusing to back down from a pit bull. Since she had no gavel, Katie slapped her hand on the table in an attempt to get everyone's attention and regain control of the meeting. It didn't work.

"Katie is my *only* girlfriend, and she didn't hurt anyone." Andy's expression was dark, and Katie decided now wasn't the time to remind him that she was *no longer* his girlfriend.

Ray stood. "Oh, really?" His mouth quirked up in some mixture of a smirk and a snarl. "You still think you can make Katie happy after you've shattered her trust?"

Great, Katie thought. *Why not toss an old bloodhound in between the chihuahua and the pit bull to make matters worse?*

"I can make her happier than you can, *old* man," Andy growled and circled around the table. "You're pathetic. You don't realize how ridiculous you look chasing after her!"

"Katie and I are friends—that's it," Ray said. "I care about her, and I take her feelings into consideration. That's more than you can—"

Ray didn't get the opportunity to finish that thought because Andy's fist connected with his jaw. Several women screamed; Katie was pretty sure one of them was her and even more certain that Nona was not.

Ray fired back with a punch to Andy's face, and the fight turned into a full-blown *Beating in the Meeting*—as opposed to the *Thrilla in Manilla.* All they needed was the late, great Howard Cosell to commentate.

Katie absolutely had to get this meeting back under control—or else give up on it altogether—before Del called the police and banned the group from ever gathering at his diner again. Fortunately, Vance and Jordan were already pulling the two pugilists apart.

"Please!" Katie called. "Everybody *please* calm down!"

No one calmed down.

A shrill whistle pierced the air. Miraculously, everyone stilled and looked around for the source. Like Katie, they probably feared Del had already summoned the authorities. But, to her relief, she saw that it was Moonbeam who'd blown the whistle. Smiling at Katie, she dropped it into her purse now that it had served its purpose.

"Thank you, Moonbeam," Katie said. "Since this meeting has become such a fiasco, I think it would be best if we adjourn. I'll send everyone an email tomorrow covering what Janey and I intended to address here. I'll also write Del a formal apology." She fixed her glare on Nona. "Some of *you* might want to do likewise after your unconscionable behavior."

Nona merely threw her head back, sniffed, and left the room.

As Katie gathered her materials into her tote, she heard Vance tell Janey, "See? I told you there was no need to be nervous about speaking in front of these people."

"You sure were right," Janey replied. "Do you think these Merchants Association meetings are always this exciting?"

* * *

KATIE KICKED off her flats as soon as she walked through the door of her new apartment. Waiting for Mason to wind around her ankles and stepping over Della, who was rolling from side to side directly in front of her, Katie took the shoes to the closet. She changed into shorts and a T-shirt before returning to the living room to turn her attention to her cats.

Snuggling Mason up under her chin, she asked, "What do you think are the odds that the three of us could simply pack up and start our lives over somewhere new?"

The cat offered up a *purpt* that Katie took as his agreement. He was in his third abode within days—what was another move?

"I *know* it's ridiculous, and I don't really want to leave. At least, I don't believe I do. It's just that tonight—heck, my entire life lately—has been such a complete wreck."

She'd never considered it before, but who would look after Mason and Della if she weren't around? She couldn't bear the idea of her beloved cats being turned over to the county humane society—which was a kill shelter—and she pulled Della over to include her in the embrace. Though not as affectionate as Mason, Della seemed to sense Katie's need for reassurance and submitted to the cuddles.

As she was telling herself not to be ridiculous and that she was definitely *not* going to prison, there was a rap on her door. Katie put the cats down and decided that if either Andy or Ray was dumb enough to show his face here tonight, she wasn't going to let him in.

"Who is it?" she demanded.

"Nick." He paused. "Who are you expecting?"

"No one." She opened the door. "Thank goodness, it's you."

Stepping inside and arching one brow, he said, "I brought the gift of salted caramel," he said, holding up a bag that held a container of premium ice cream. "Sorry Don and I couldn't make it to the meeting. We had a future bride come by to look our place over."

"I was afraid it might be Andy or Ray knocking on my door." She filled him in on the debacle that was the Merchants Association meeting as they filled their bowls and sat down on the love seat to eat it. Two curious cats milled around, no doubt hoping to lick the bowls clean.

"I'm sorry I missed it," Nick said. "Sounds delightful."

Katie frowned. "Trust me. It wasn't."

Nick grinned. "I imagine Nona Fiske would beg to differ. It'll be interesting to see your suitors' faces tomorrow. I'm thinking cinnamon buns for breakfast and a trinket from Wood U would be a bright start to my day."

"Very funny." Katie gouged a big hunk of caramel from her ice cream and ate it. "For your information, I have no suitors."

Nick raised an index finger. "And again—Nona would disagree."

"Well, Nona is wrong," Katie grumbled, flopping back against the back of the love seat.

Nick spooned up some ice cream. "Is she? Tell me how you feel about Messrs. Rust and Davenport."

Katie rested her head against the top of the love seat and stared up at the freshly painted ceiling. "Up until very recently, I loved Andy. I was happy with him and thought we had a future together."

"And now?" Nick prompted.

"Now I realize I was living a lie. Andy wasn't the man I thought he was." She raised her head to look at Nick. "He actually told me he was stringing Erikka along in order to have a backup since Ray and Brad are apparently such a big part of my life. He even referred to Brad as a GQ model of a chef."

"Was he justified in being afraid you might stray? Maybe not physically but in your heart?"

"Of course not!" Katie cried.

Nick raised a hand in defense. "I'm just playing devil's advocate."

Katie glowered at him. "Sure, Brad is gorgeous, and we work well together, but we're just friends."

"And what about Ray?"

Rolling her eyes, Katie asked, "What about him?"

"You have a soft spot for Papa Bear." Holding up a hand to further fend off her protests, he asked, "Had it been one of the boxing bachelors on your doorstep instead of me, which one would you have preferred it to be?"

"Ray," she answered grudgingly. "But only because I'd like to make sure he's all right. And I'm not angry with him. We don't have the turmoil Andy and I have between us right now."

"Uh-huh. You don't care whether or not Andy is okay?" he asked. "I imagine Ray can still pack a wallop."

"Of course I hope Andy is okay." She rubbed her forehead. "I don't mean to be rude, but I'd rather not discuss Ray *or* Andy right now."

Nick merely shrugged.

"Have you spoken with Seth?" Katie asked quietly.

Nick lowered his gaze. "Yeah. You really should've told him about the ring."

"I know. Believe me, I know. Do you think he'll ever forgive me?"

"He will." He scratched his head. "In time. You need to leave him alone for a day or two."

"I don't want to leave him alone. I want us to fix this." She took Nick's hand. "Please tell me how to make this up to him."

"Katie, you can't. You found something that could be potential evidence, you didn't trust him with that information—"

"I do trust him!" she interrupted.

"But you didn't trust him with that," Nick said. "You trusted Ray. Ray, who's in love with you. Ray, a former homicide detective who thought damning evidence might've been placed in your apartment and got rid of it."

She sighed. "We don't even know for sure it was Erikka's ring."

"I'm not getting in the middle of your argument with Seth but take it from someone who knows him better than most people, give him a couple of days to cool off before reaching out to him. Otherwise, you'll only end up making it worse."

"But you do feel that ultimately things will be all right between us?" She desperately wanted Nick to give her hope that Seth would forgive her.

He nodded, but Katie still didn't feel terribly hopeful. Not reaching out to Seth would be a challenge.

"What about the photograph?" she asked. "Were you able to pull it from Erryn's social media page and print it out?"

"Yes. Did you doubt me?" he asked.

"Doubt *you*? Never. Doubt the Internet? Yes."

He marched over to the kitchen counter and retrieved a kraft envelope from the bag the ice cream had come in. He returned to the love seat and handed it to Katie.

Katie pulled out the papers, spread them onto the coffee table and studied them. "Are you kidding me?" she whispered.

"What is it?" Nick asked.

She tapped the man in the sliver of the frame. "That's Schuler."

Leaning closer to the image, he asked, "Are you sure?"

Katie's eyes narrowed. "Absolutely positive."

CHAPTER 28

When she sat up in bed the next morning, Katie's head was throbbing. Spending the night tossing and turning while wondering what to do with the knowledge that Schuler was in the photograph's background on Erryn's page had not been conducive to restorative rest. While she hadn't come to any definitive conclusion, and although she was adamant about not turning to any of the men in her life, Katie did wonder if asking Seth's advice might get her back in his good graces.

On her way to the kitchen to wash down a couple of pain relievers and feed the cats, she decided not to heed Nick's warning about giving Seth a few days before getting in touch with him. Seth, however, must not have wanted to speak with her because he didn't answer her call.

She sent him a text saying: *Nick brought over a photograph from Erryn's social media account last night. He'd printed out an original and one with the section I wanted to examine enlarged. We agree the man in the photo is Detective Schuler. Please let me know if I should contact Mr. Trammel with this information.*

There—he could do with that whatever he chose. If she didn't hear from him by the end of the day, she'd contact Trammel anyway and ask for his exorbitantly priced advice.

After dressing and tidying her tiny apartment, Katie went down the interior stairs to Tealicious.

"Good morning," Brad said, with a smile. "I have fresh-from-the-oven caramel apple scones. Want one?"

"Oh, my goodness, yes." She closed her eyes and inhaled the wonderfully sweet aroma. "May I?"

"You bet." Picking up a pair of tongs, he placed one on a small plate for her and even garnished it with a Granny Smith apple slice.

"Wow. You're spoiling me." Katie poured herself a cup of Earl Grey tea from the pot he'd already made.

"I figure you could use a bit of spoiling. You've been through a lot in such a short time. Are you okay?"

Sinking onto a stool by the counter, she said, "I'm holding my own. Could I use a tropical vacation? You bet. But I'm taking everything else day-to-day."

"Good." He smiled slightly. "I heard you had quite the productive meeting of the Merchants Association last night."

"It's unreal how fast good news travels." She bit into the scone and moaned in delight. "Oh, Brad, this is delicious."

"Thank you. It's my own recipe."

"You could sell it and make a mint," she said, but then sobered. "So, what did you hear about the meeting?"

"Eh, not much. You know...the usual. Problems were addressed, notes were taken, motions were made, quorums were met, punches were thrown..."

"You were obviously misinformed." Katie enjoyed another bite of her scone. "There were no notes taken or quorums met. I suppose one problem was addressed, but many more arose. And the only motions made were the punches thrown."

He grinned. "At least, it wasn't boring."

"It certainly was not. I expect membership to increase exponentially. Business will boom here on the Square just so entrepreneurs may join our elite group." Taking a sip of her tea, she added, "That is unless Del's Diner sues us for disturbing the peace of his other customers. I don't *think* any property was destroyed, but I can't be a hundred percent sure of it. I'm going to email him as soon as I get to Artisans Alley and offer to reimburse him for any damage."

"I heard what caused the fight—Nona's accusations," Brad said. "I want to assure you she's alone in her belief that you could've harmed Erikka."

"She didn't say she thought I could've done it." Katie sighed. "She said I was being *accused* of it—and I am. But I simply can't understand why the police are fixated on me rather than—"

"Rather than Andy?" Brad asked.

Inclining her head, she said, "Him or anyone else who is taller and stronger than I am. I believe Erikka was overpowered from behind. I like to think I'm a tough woman, but I'm not stout enough to sneak up on and strangle a woman five inches taller than me with her own scarf."

"I suppose the killer did have the element of surprise," Brad mused. "But why was Erikka alone in that deserted warehouse, anyway? Had she gone there to meet someone?"

Katie stood so quickly she nearly dropped the plate she'd been holding. "You're right! Surely the police have obtained her phone records. I should get my attorney on that immediately." She gave him a quick hug. "Thank you."

"Serving up great advice and even better food," Brad said with a smile. "That's what I'm here for."

* * *

KATIE USED Artisans Alley's back entrance hoping to avoid any and everyone. Joking about the meeting with Nick and Brad was one thing. Having other vendors or merchants smirking or whispering as she walked by was another.

First things first, Katie decided as she walked into her office and closed the door: damage control.

She booted up her computer and found an email address for Del's Diner on the restaurant's website.

Dear Del:

Sighing, she wondered how to begin.

I apologize for the commotion wrought at your diner last evening by the Victoria Square Merchants Association. As president of the group, I take responsibility for any damages or losses you might've suffered. Please send me an itemized list, and I will reimburse you.

Hopefully, she wouldn't live to regret that last sentence.

I'm sure you realize this was an anomaly and hope that you'll continue to allow us to meet at your establishment. Del's Diner is a favorite among the people of McKinlay Mill, and we'd hate to lose your support.

There. That should do it. Surely, she didn't need to remind Del that it was he who was being supported by the Merchants Association—both during meetings and on a regular basis by the individuals who made up the group. She and Andy had met for lunch there at least twice a week for a year before...well, before.

Dismissing the pain that thought caused her, she signed and sent the email. Now, on to the next one.

As she was taking the folder Janey had given her from her tote, Rose knocked at the door before poking her head inside.

"Hey, there. Are you okay?" the older woman asked. "Vance said there was quite a kerfuffle at the Merchants Association meeting last night."

Katie groaned.

"Now, now. I'm not here to gossip," Rose assured her. "I only wanted to tell you that no one—except maybe Nona—thinks you killed Erikka. Nona just likes to keep things stirred up."

"Thank you."

Rose held out her arms, and Katie stood and gave her a brief hug.

Rose gave her one last pat on the back. "I'll be off now. But call me if you need me."

Katie thanked her again. As she sat back down at her desk, the phone rang. Caller ID told her who it was.

"Hello, Seth," Katie said timidly.

"Good morning." His terse tone told her he still hadn't forgiven her for the ring incident. "Would you please email me the photograph and the enlargement you mentioned in your text? Once I've taken a look at it, I'll see what I can do."

"At the very least, it should be enough to get Schuler thrown off the case, right?" she asked.

"I doubt it. Merely because two people are in close proximity doesn't mean they know each other well or at all." He paused. "Still, if the photo combined with Erryn's testimony about the event can prove Schuler had a connection to Erikka, then we might be able to call his objectivity into question. But don't get your hopes up."

"I won't."

"Should you be served by Del's later today, send that over to me as well," Seth said. "I'll bill you on a retainer."

"Ha-ha," she said flatly. She was happy he was extending an olive branch by giving her a glimpse of the Seth she'd always known. "Has everyone in McKinlay Mill been regaled with the misadventures of the Victoria Square Merchants Association meeting over their morning coffee?"

"Don't underestimate your reach." He had a side conversation with an imaginary third party. "Hey, turn on the TV, please. I want to see if Katie made the national news. No, no, no, not for murder—for turning Del's Diner into the Pelican's Nest."

They both laughed, albeit a bit forced.

"I'll take that over the other any day," Katie said.

"I know," he said softly.

A wave of shame passed over her. "I really am sorry, Seth. I'm scared, and when I'm scared, I can make very bad decisions."

"I know. If you're ever scared witless again, please, *please* trust me to help you out."

"I will. I promise. Are we okay?" Katie asked, almost afraid to hear his reply.

"Yeah, we're good," he said grudgingly.

Katie heaved a sigh of relief. "I'm glad. I can't imagine my life without you in it."

"Me, too," he said. "But I'm still going to bill you," he said.

"Do I get the friends and family rate?"

"Of course," he said.

"Thank you. And thanks for being such a good friend. Right now, I really need one."

As soon as they ended the call, Katie used her printer to scan to photograph the images Nick had given her. The photographs probably weren't as good as Nick's copies, but Seth would be able to see what he was working with and call her if he needed to see the originals. She emailed them to him with yet another heartfelt thank you. They might not be back where they were yet, but she felt the two of them were on much firmer ground than they were the day before.

Turning her attention back to the Merchants Association email, she began by apologizing for allowing yesterday evening's meeting to spiral out of control.

From now on, anyone who cannot behave in a civilized manner—whether by making derogatory remarks toward others or by acting inappropriately—

She thought that sentiment should let Nona, Ray, and Andy know where they stood.

—will be asked to leave immediately. Any conflict with any member of the group will be addressed on an individual basis outside of a Merchants Association meeting. Anyone who cannot abide by these rules will be asked to resign her or his membership.

How she'd love to tell Nona, "Bye, Felicia!"

And now to address the issues meant to be discussed at our scheduled meeting. There was a misunderstanding about food being provided for the vendors' party kicking off the start of this year's Harvest Festival.

She reached for the folder so she could peruse Janey's notes before setting forth the details of the party. Del's was catering the food, and their agreement was on the top of the stack of papers inside the folder. Looking at the bottom line, Katie told herself there was no way Del's would give the Merchants Association grief over what had happened there last night.

Flipping through the rest of the pages, she came upon something that stopped her cold: one of Erikka's racy pictures. What was it doing in Janey's folder?

Did it belong to Vance or VJ?

CHAPTER 29

Katie flipped the photo over to see if there was anything written on the back. The only notation was Matt Brady's copyright. Why was this photo among Janey's things? Had she found it among her husband's or her son's belongings and was waiting for the proper time to have a confrontation?

After debating for a few minutes, Katie called Janey Ingram.

"Hello!" Janey sang, sounding quite chipper. Katie would've considered hanging up had she not known her number had shown up on Janey's caller I.D.

"Hi, Janey. I'm really sorry to bother you with this, but I found a photo in the file you brought me with the Harvest Festival party information."

"What kind of photo?" Her voice had gone from chipper to wary in two seconds flat.

"It's...it's a lingerie picture of Erikka Wiley."

"Oh, no," Janey wailed. "I'm so sorry you found that! I don't know how it got into that folder! I found it in VJ's room and was going to ask him about it. I'd put it on my desk, and I must've picked it up with my other papers by mistake."

"I'll put it in an envelope and keep it here for you, if you'd like," I said.

"Thanks. I'll be glad to collect it—or have Vance pick it up." She sighed. "We're terribly disappointed in VJ, but I'm trying to give him the benefit of doubt. I mean, I understand his wanting to see the photo—she is, or rather was, a beautiful woman—but I want to know where he got it." Janey hesitated. "I don't think he'd simply walk off with Matt Brady's property, even something as insignificant as one photograph."

"Do you think Erikka could have given it to him?" The question was innocent enough, Katie thought, but Janey's response was explosive.

"Certainly not! He didn't *know* that woman. There was no reason whatsoever for her to give him a picture of herself in lacy, barely-there lingerie."

"I didn't mean to imply anything," Katie told her. "It just seems Erikka had a lot of those photos to spread around."

Janey calmed. "Oh, well...I suppose she was pretty proud of herself, huh? She must have adhered to the old adage *if you've got it, flaunt it.*"

"I guess so."

"Knowing VJ, he might've even picked that photo up by accident—you know, like I accidentally put it in your folder," Janey said. "I'll bet you that's exactly what happened. If you don't mind, just throw the thing away. I'm not even going to ask VJ about it now. No sense embarrassing him over doing the same thing I did, right?"

"Right," Katie murmured in agreement, even though she didn't agree. She wanted to know why VJ had the photo. Why didn't his mother? Was Janey afraid of the answer she might get?

Janey laughed. "I'm sure you'll delight in ripping that picture into a million teeny tiny pieces. I would! So you just do that, and put it in the trash, okay?"

"Yeah," she said, "I'll take care of it,"

After ending the call, Katie opened her desk drawer and put the photo inside face down. She didn't want to look at Erikka every time she opened her drawer, but she did want to know why VJ had the picture. But was she willing to confront the young man herself? She didn't want Janey and Vance upset with her, but she didn't want a lead to go unexplored either. Maybe VJ could tell her something about Erikka that could help find her killer.

Why had Janey been so defensive? Had she merely not wanted Katie to get the wrong impression of her son? Or was she afraid VJ was hiding something?

Katie went back to composing the email to the Merchants Association. It seemed to her that the stupid thing was taking forever to get finalized and sent. At this rate, the Harvest Festival vendors' party would be in full swing, and she'd still be sitting at her desk typing the email.

As she composed the message, her mind kept going back to Erikka being found on the entryway of the empty warehouse. Why had she been there? Was she waiting for someone? Surely, the killer had lured her there and had lain in wait to murder her.

Even though Katie was certain the police had conducted a thorough search, she wanted to see the crime scene for herself. Maybe being there again would trigger a memory of something she saw that morning that she'd been too traumatized to remember before. And maybe it would jog Nick's memory as well.

She texted and asked him if he'd like to meet her at the warehouse at noon.

He replied, *Jinkies, Velma, I'd love to. P.S. The boxing bachelors don't look as bad as I'd hoped—bruising minimal. Nothing for Nona F. to gloat over. But Don liked the hand-carved elephant I bought him... despite knowing why I went by Wood U.*

Katie shook her head. There was no one else in the world—or, at least, *her* world—like Nick.

As she finally finished the missive to the Merchants Association and hit send, she got an email from Seth. He'd spoken with Captain Spence about the photo and had then emailed it to him. Spence was going to investigate. Katie replied, thanking him for his help.

A rat-a-tat knock resounded in the office before Rose opened the door and said, "Quick—come with me. I believe I've found him."

"Found who?"

"*Him,*" Rose insisted. "Come on."

Katie got up, locked the office door, and went with Rose. When they got to the lobby, the older woman jerked her head toward a bench where an admittedly handsome older gentleman sat reading a book.

Rose faced Katie so she'd have her back to the man when she said, "Can I pick 'em or what? Good looking *and* smart."

Katie winced when the man was joined by his wife, for whom he'd obviously been waiting.

"What?" Rose whirled around to see the couple leaving together.

"I'm sorry," Katie said. "It looks like *she* could pick 'em too."

Rose shrugged. "That's all right. I wasn't crazy about that shirt he had on anyway." She lifted her chin. "So, that one wasn't *him.* My guy is still out there—Moonbeam told me so."

"She also told you that the two of you will find each other," Katie reminded her gently. "You won't have to go looking for him."

"Oh, pooh," Rose said. "I didn't go anywhere—he came right to me. But, like I said, he wasn't the one." She looked around the lobby as if to zero in on *the one.*

Katie gave her friend a one-armed hug. "It'll happen when the time is right."

* * *

About eleven forty-five, Katie left her office and crossed the back lot, heading for the warehouse. Seeing Nick coming from the other direction as she neared the building, she quickened her pace and met him halfway.

"This is exciting," he said, as they power walked to the door.

"Or incredibly stupid," she said. "Do you think we're making a mistake by going inside?"

"No! Hurry up before someone sees us."

Katie was relieved that the crime scene tape had been removed, and even more surprised the building hadn't been secured. As head of the Victoria Square Merchants Association, she should probably contact the owner—who'd rejected an invitation to join the association. Their loss. Still, she wouldn't have tried to enter the building if the crime tape was still there, although she wasn't certain Nick felt the same way. "Did you tell anyone where you were going?"

"Of course not," he said. "Don already thinks I'm too nosy for going to check out Andy's and Ray's post-fight faces. Why? Did you tell someone?"

"No. After we leave here, I'm planning to go to Tealicious and get a few sandwiches to take to Ann Tanner's house," she said. "Want to join me?"

"All right, but let's do our investigating first."

Inside the warehouse, everything looked much as it had the morning she and Nick had found Erikka's body, with thick dust and cobwebs everywhere except the spot on the floor where Erikka had been lying. And since the crime scene techs had worn booties over their shoes, the floor around where the body had lain was covered in indistinguishable footprints.

"What are we looking for?" Nick whispered.

"I don't know," Katie said. "I thought maybe we'd remember something we'd seen that morning. Why are we whispering?"

He shrugged. "It seems sacred or something in here."

"I think you're confusing morbid for sacred." Something in the corner of the room caught her eye. "Look at that."

Following her gaze, he squinted. "I don't see anything."

"Exactly. There's a perfect square in that corner that's clean—no dust. Why do you think that is?"

"Maybe the crime scene techs put a blanket down, and they transferred Erikka to the blanket to remove her from the warehouse," he suggested.

"Or maybe someone put a blanket here because they'd been setting up a rendezvous."

"You're reaching," Nick told her.

"Am I?" she asked. "Think about it. Why had Erikka come here? She was bound to have been meeting someone. And if this was a regular trysting spot…"

Nick shook his head. "Why not get a hotel room?"

"I think that's pretty obvious." Katie eased closer to the spot. It was perfectly square. "I really believe this was a meeting place between Erikka and one of her lovers."

"Do you think it could have been Andy?" he asked.

"Anything's possible." She didn't want to think so, but she realized that yes, it *was* possible.

CHAPTER 30

As they were walking from the warehouse toward Tealicious, Katie pulled out her phone to call Brad to asked him to box up a selection of tea sandwiches. "Nick and I are taking lunch to Ann Tanner."

"You're a sweetheart," Brad said. "I'll have them ready for you when you get here. I'll throw in some cookies, too."

"Thanks." Katie put her phone away.

"He's a great guy," Nick said after Katie had ended the call. "You could do worse, you know."

Her voice was pleasant but firm. "I adore Brad—as a friend—but I'm swearing off men for a while—maybe forever."

Nick laughed. "In that case, there's a nice young woman I know who just broke up with her—"

"Hush," she interrupted with a laugh.

He gave her an impish grin. "Good to see you laughing today. I think you're on the mend already."

"Maybe my heart is, but my mind is still terrified I'll end up in the hoosegow."

"Now, *there's* an old-fashioned word for you." He arched a

brow. "Have you been doing crossword puzzles with Don behind my back?"

Katie arched an eyebrow. "Maybe."

Once they'd retrieved the boxes of sandwiches and cookies, they piled into Katie's car and drove over to Ann's house. If she wasn't delighted to see the two of them, she put up a great front.

Giving one-armed hugs to Katie and then Nick, Ann said, "Look at what the cat dragged in! And just in time—I'm starving! Come on in to the kitchen."

Nick and Katie followed Ann into her charming, spacious kitchen where she invited them to sit at the breakfast table.

"What would you like to drink?" Ann asked. "I can't pour, but I have canned drinks and bottles of water."

Both opted for water, and Ann got herself a bottle as well, then grabbed some sandwich plates from the cupboard and distributed them before joining them at the table.

As they dug into the sandwiches, Ann asked, "Have you heard anything new in Erikka Wiley's murder investigation?" Then before Katie could answer, she said, "You know, someone told Jordan that Erikka wasn't even really pregnant. Imagine going around telling people you're expecting a child when you aren't." She tsked and shook her head. "The day before she died, she came into the bakery and bought some mini cupcakes—we call them babycakes, you know. She said her baby wanted a baby cake and patted her tummy. Jordan asked when she was due, and she said April."

"Were there a lot of people in the bakery at the time?" Katie asked.

"Oh, sure. It was full. We're always extra busy when we make baklava, and we only make it once a week," Ann said. "And that was baklava day."

"I always snag some for Sassy Sally's." Nick winked at Ann. "Sometimes I'm selfish and don't share it with our patrons though. It's hard to find guests I like more than I like Tanner's baklava."

Smiling, Katie asked, "You wouldn't happen to remember if Matt Brady was there, would you, Ann?"

"Yes, he was." Ann bit into a tea sandwich, looking thoughtful. "And so were Ray, Nona, Vance, Detective Schuler, Gilda...the whole Square loves our baklava."

Katie shot a look in Nick's direction, but he made no comment, and Ann turned the conversation back to her bakery and how she felt at loose ends sitting at home while her husband ran the business.

They stayed chatting for another half hour before Katie announced that she needed to get back to work.

"Stop by with those wonderful sandwiches anytime," Ann said and waved to them from the front door.

They got in Katie's car and headed back to Sassy Sally's.

"Penny for your thoughts," Nick said, sounding serious.

Katie scowled, her hands tightening on the wheel. "I'm not sure they're worth that much, but here goes. Do you think one of the men in the bakery when Erikka announced her pregnancy could've been her killer?" she asked.

"What?"

"I'm serious. I mean, think about it—there was Erikka bragging about the baby she was going to have in April. If someone in there thought he was about to be a father, he might've gotten nervous."

"Are you thinking of Matt Brady?"

Nodding, Katie said, "He admitted the two of them were hooking up."

"Yeah, but Erikka had also posted the sonogram on social media, and she'd told Andy even before that," Nick pointed out.

"True, and Matt knew Erikka was in love with Andy. He'd have to have known she intended to pass the baby off as Andy's whether the child belonged to him or not."

"You're assuming—probably based on Andy's reaction-that the real father would not have wanted the baby. Maybe he—Matt or whomever—*did* want the baby, if it belonged to him."

"Andy wanted the baby, too," she said quietly. "At first he told me that he didn't. That it wouldn't mean anything to him, but I think he truly did. After Erikka died, he seemed pretty upset to think he'd lost his son, but also relieved when he learned she'd lied about being pregnant."

Nick inclined his head. "Believing you're going to have a child is life-changing, but don't limit your suspect list to just the men in the bakery when Erikka made her announcement. Like you, the suspect could've seen the sonogram on social media. And, don't forget, Nona was there. Telephone, tell-a-Nona!"

"True," she said with a laugh, "but I still want to talk with Matt Brady again." And she thought she had the perfect excuse to do so.

* * *

KATIE PARKED BEHIND Tealicious and walked to Matt Brady's studio. Izzy wasn't there, and Katie was relieved to find Matt in the studio changing his main backdrop from summer flowers to a fall setting.

"To what do I owe the pleasure?" he asked sarcastically. "Now that you know Erikka and I were hooking up, do you want to find out for yourself if I'm a better lover than Andy? Or how you measure up to her?"

Clenching her fists, Katie used every single ounce of restraint she possessed not to punch Matt in his smug, leering face. "I'm not interested in you in the slightest. I'm here because VJ Ingram's mom is concerned because she found one of those sexy photos of Erikka in his room. I don't think for a second that VJ would steal. I believe he either picked it up accidentally or you gave it to him."

"Of course, I gave it to him," Matt said. "Erikka was one hot babe and he's a young man." Brady waggled his brows suggestively. "The kid's been good to help me out around here for nothing, so I was doing him a solid."

"Do you know whether Erikka and VJ had any sort of relationship?" she asked.

Matt snorted. "He wishes."

Katie turned to leave but paused to look over her shoulder. "Did you and Erikka ever use the abandoned warehouse as a meeting place."

"No." He gestured to the sofa. "We *met* right there on that sofa...and sometimes on a faux fur rug I have in the back. Which would you prefer? With the sofa, there's a chance we could be interrupted, but Erikka liked thinking someone might see us. She found it exciting. What about you, Katie? How adventurous are you?"

She merely glared at him and walked out of the studio to the sound of his mocking laughter.

Feeling as if she could use a scalding shower, Katie hurried to the comfort of her office at Artisans Alley. But there was no peace to be found there either.

Detective Schuler was standing in the vendors' lounge drinking a cup of coffee. Had he chipped in for it or just helped himself? "Katie Bonner, I've been waiting for you."

Quickly suppressing her annoyance at finding him there, Katie said, "I'm sorry—did we have an appointment?"

"No." He slammed his paper coffee cup into the nearest trash receptacle, and Katie could smell the sweet aroma as the remainder of its contents sloshed out into the bin. It made her stomach flip.

"How may I help you, Detective?" she asked, pleased that her voice didn't betray her inner turmoil.

"Let's talk in your office where we won't be disturbed."

Katie lifted her chin. "Do I need to have my attorney present for this meeting? If so, I'd prefer to conduct it at *your* office. As you well know, mine is rather small and cramped."

He didn't react to her pointed reminder of him and his men searching her office. "That's entirely up to you. We can have an informal chat, just the two of us, or we can conduct a more formal interview. I'll warn you, though—a formal interview could lead to official charges."

While she had nothing to hide, she didn't want to antagonize this man further…at least, not until she could learn what he had up his sleeve today. Jerking her head toward her office, she indicated he should follow her. As she traversed the short distance, she thought she should take measures to protect herself. She took her key from her purse and unlocked the door.

My phone... I've got to find a way to record this conversation on my phone.

Detective Schuler stepped inside as soon as she opened the door. With his hands on his hips, he waited for her to get inside and seated, then he loomed over her, watching her closely. She was afraid she'd be unable to set her phone to record without tipping him off.

Placing her purse under the desk, she dropped her keys beside it. "Darn it." Making it appear she was fumbling for the keys, she tapped the buttons necessary to make the phone begin recording. She straightened and gave Schuler a tight smile. "Sorry."

With a smirk, he asked, "What's the matter? Are you nervous?"

"Just clumsy." She hoped the phone's speakers could adequately detect their voices, and she tamped down the desire to speak louder than usual. "What do you need to talk with me about?"

Schuler moved farther into her personal space, towering above her, no doubt trying to intimidate her even more. "I had a meeting with Captain Spence this morning. He was concerned about a photograph you apparently produced."

"What photograph is that?" she asked.

"You know very well the one I'm talking about," he said. "It shows me at a crowded—*very* crowded—party."

"And?" She shrugged. "You're here to ask me to see if I can get you a copy, too?"

A muscle worked along Schuler's jaw, and Katie could tell he was grinding his teeth. When he spoke again, his voice was steely. "I am here, Ms. Bonner, to inform you that jeopardizing my job in any way would be an egregious mistake."

Stiffening her spine, Katie asked, "Is that a threat, Detective Schuler?"

"It's a promise," he said.

"So, are you saying Captain Spence removed you from the case?" *That would be damaging in itself if Schuler came here to threaten me about a case to which he's no longer assigned.*

"I have most certainly *not* been taken off the investigation, but I find it very interesting you want me to be." He leaned closer. "Why is that?"

"Whether you're on the case or not is of no consequence to me," Katie said. "I merely thought that if you were well acquainted with the victim, it would be a conflict of interest for you to be investigating. I know you wouldn't want anything to hamper the veracity of your evidence."

"Nothing will, Ms. Bonner. I can personally assure you of that." With that rebuke, he turned and stormed out of her office.

Waiting until she heard the side door open and close, Katie checked her phone. While their conversation had been adequately recorded, Schuler had been too clever to say anything really damning. Even his threat against her was sufficiently vague to have been "misconstrued" or "taken out of context." But she hadn't recorded the conversation to attempt to have it hold up in a court of law—she'd done it to protect herself and to prove to herself, if to no one else, that Schuler was hiding something.

Using her phone, she emailed Seth a copy of the recording. In the subject line, she wrote: *Apparently, I poked a bear...*

Seth called soon after. "Sorry, Katie, you don't have much to go on with this recording. How'd you get it anyway?"

She explained how she'd seemingly fumbled with putting her keys in her purse and used that opportunity to set the phone to record.

"You need to be careful," he said. "Spence didn't think Schuler's being at the same party as Erikka Wiley was a big deal. Schuler explained to him that it was a fundraiser for a charity to which his wife's parents contribute generously and his wife is on the board."

"But why was Erikka there?" Katie wondered aloud. "Doesn't that *prove* that Erikka was—or could have been friends with both Schuler and his wife?"

"Not necessarily," he said. "There were apparently a lot of people at the event, and many of them were arguably strangers to each other."

"You are *not* being helpful," Katie said.

"Sorry, darlin', but I assume you wanted my legal opinion."

"Yes," she grudgingly replied.

"Good. Keep your head down."

"More legal advice?" she asked.

"Only the best."

"Yes, *big* brother."

"Goodbye, *little* sister."

Katie tapped the end-call icon.

So, the Sheriff's Office didn't find it at all suspicious that Schuler and Erikka had been seen at a prominent social function, but that made Katie even more suspicious. Erikka didn't have enough money to contribute to a fundraiser. Either she'd gone on the arm of someone who *did* have deeper pockets than she, or else she'd gotten in some other way.

Katie sat back in her chair and crossed her arms across her chest. She needed to learn the identity of the women who were in the photo with Erikka. Unfortunately, the best way to do that was to ask Erryn.

Did Katie dare approach the woman?

CHAPTER 31

Wracking her brain for half an hour before she circled back to her original conclusion, Katie decided to call Erryn. Since she didn't have her personal information, she tried reaching her at the hospital only to be told that Erryn was off work. Despite her resolution not to rely on her male friends, she called Nick.

"Hey, Velma," he answered, obviously seeing Katie's number on his caller I.D. "Are we going out looking for clues again?"

"Not exactly. I was hoping you might be able to help me figure out where Erikka's sister Erryn might go on her day off." She explained why she needed to speak with Erryn and how she'd had no luck calling the woman at work.

"Um…not to sound mean, but she'd have probably just hung up on you anyway," he said. "I think she's made it abundantly clear she doesn't want to talk with you, love."

"True, but if I could make her understand that we're on the same team—that I want to find out who murdered her sister as badly as she does—then surely, she'd help me. Right?"

"I don't know." He paused. "Let me reach out to her and see if I can arrange a meeting here at Sassy Sally's."

Katie breathed a sigh of relief. "Thank you." If anyone could talk the woman into meeting with her, it would be Nick. The man could charm a snake right out of its skin.

"I'm not promising anything," he warned.

"I know, but I appreciate the fact that you're willing to try. You're the best."

"Well, that is true. Talk to you soon."

Katie smiled and shook her head as she put down her phone. Back to work!

A knock on her office door interrupted the check of her email for responses to the Merchants Association update she'd sent out earlier. Since her meeting with Schuler, she was double wary of visitors.

"Who's there?" she asked.

"It's me—VJ. May I come in?"

Putting her PC to sleep, she called, "Of course."

VJ came into her office, shut the door, and stood with his hands stuffed into the front pockets of his jeans. "I…I know I have no right to ask you this, but could you not…you know…say anything to Izzy about…about what you found?"

"You mean the photo?" she asked.

He nodded. "Mom told me you found it in the folder she gave you. She was awfully embarrassed and upset about that." He shrugged. "Anyhow, Izzy and I just made up, and we're doing all right, you know? I don't wanna blow it with something that I didn't even want."

"You didn't want it?" Katie asked.

VJ took his hands from his pockets and slumped against the file cabinet, looking boneless as only a teenage boy could look. "No. I mean, I only took it because Matt pushed it on me. I didn't want to come across like a jerk." The side of his mouth quirked up. "Izzy would say it's all right to be rude sometimes, but I didn't want to get on Matt's bad side. Plus, Izzy didn't like Erikka anyway."

"Why not?" Katie asked.

"A guy Izzy used to date got his head turned—to use her words—by Erikka. He and Erikka didn't date or anything, but Izzy says it was disgusting how Erikka would manipulate the guy."

Who would Erikka be manipulating? It could certainly be any of the boys from Angelo's. "Did she tell you the guy's name?"

"Nah." He straightened. "I'd better get back. So, are we good? You won't tell Izzy about the picture, right?"

She smiled. "Picture? I don't know anything about any picture."

VJ grinned. "Thanks, Ms. Bonner. You're the best."

* * *

KATIE SPENT the next half hour slogging through the emails from the few members of the Merchants Association who'd bothered to respond. It appeared no one had questions—not about the Harvest Festival vendors' party anyway. There had been some about the meeting itself, but she chose not to answer those, simply advising the merchants to contact Janey Ingram with any further concerns about the party.

The phone rang. Katie recognized the number and immediately picked up.

"Am I the master or what?" Nick asked.

"You tell me."

"I've arranged for you and Erryn to have a meeting at Sassy Sally's this afternoon at four o'clock. Don is going to watch Erryn's baby, and I'm going to mediate…or referee, whichever is necessary."

"Thank you!" Looking at her phone, she saw that it was close to four already.

"Don't thank me yet."

"I'll be right over," she said.

As Katie stepped out of Artisans Alley's front entrance, she saw Roger's sister Regan exiting Angelo's. The young woman had updated her spiky blue hair with some lavender highlights.

"Hey, Regan! How've you been?" Katie asked.

"Pretty good." She jerked her head toward the pizzeria. "I took Roger some cookies from Tealicious and I got a calzone out of the deal," she said indicating the small to-go box. "Rog got addicted to sweets while he was working on your apartment."

Katie grinned. "Brad makes some delicious goodies. That's why I try to get in a power walk every morning. Now that I'm living above the tea shop and smelling all those delights every day, I might have to start walking every evening, too."

Regan laughed. "I sure would. And Roger might have to join you."

Inspiration struck, and Katie asked, "Hey, did Roger ever date a girl named Izzy? She works for Matt Brady."

Regan's expression went from sunny to suddenly wary. "Yeah. Why?"

"Oh, I met her recently, and someone later told me she used to date one of the guys at Angelo's." She reasoned that wasn't really a lie. For Erikka to be manipulating a young man, the odds were good that he worked at Angelo's. "And since Roger is the cutest guy there..."

Regan laughed. "That's true. But don't tell *him* that—he's already too full of himself. He and Izzy weren't together for very long, but she seemed cool. I liked her."

"I like her too. It's a shame they didn't work out," Katie said. "By the way, how is he holding up since Erikka's death? I mean, since Andy and I aren't together anymore, I haven't felt comfortable checking in on the staff."

"They're all taking it hard," Regan said. "Roger included. Erikka went out of her way to be kind to them, and her death was a shock—especially since...well, you know."

Since she was murdered. Yes, she did know. Too well. "If there's anything I can do, please let me know."

"Just have Brad keep making those chocolate chip cookies."

"I will," Katie promised.

As she walked away, Katie wondered if Roger—or any of the young men who worked at Angelo's—might have misconstrued Erikka's kindness for love and then killed her when learning she didn't feel the same way. Plus, that kindness could have very easily been mistaken for something more if Erikka was using it as a way to manipulate them...although for what reason? Just a tease...or something more?

When Katie stepped onto the porch at Sassy Sally's, she saw that Nick had prepared a tray with lemonade and homemade butter cookies. The tray sat on a white wicker bistro table, and Nick and Erryn were already seated there.

Erryn stiffened as soon as she saw Katie. "This was a mistake."

Nick placed a hand on her arm. "Please hear Katie out—that's all I ask."

Shooting a brief glare in Katie's direction, Erryn said, "You have two minutes."

Rather than taking the empty chair, Katie remained standing at the bottom of the steps. "I have reason to believe Erikka was meeting someone at the warehouse—not just the night she was killed, but on a regular basis. I think that person scheduled a rendezvous with her, Erikka got there ahead of time, and he crept up behind her and strangled her."

"Forty-five seconds," Erryn grated.

"Erikka was strong," Katie said. "She had to have been murdered by someone she knew—someone who could overpower her. She'd have never put herself in a dangerous position if she feared for her life. Look at me." She waited until Erryn lifted her eyes. "Erikka was taller than I am. You must know from the evidence that the person who murdered Erikka was at least two inches taller than she."

Erryn closed her eyes but couldn't stem the sudden tears that flowed. "I know the killer was most likely a man. But Detective Schuler had been so adamant that *you* were involved."

"I swear to you I'm not, and it's because of Schuler's bias against me that I'm so desperate to find out who *did* kill your sister."

"What do you want to know from me?" Erryn grudgingly asked.

"There was a photo on your social media page of Erikka at some sort of charity event. Detective Schuler was there, and I later learned his wife is on the organization's board." Katie waited for Erryn's nod before proceeding. "Are the Schulers friends of your family?"

Erryn shook her head. "No, I've never even met Mrs. Schuler. I don't think I'd ever spoken with Detective Schuler until...until this happened." She took out her phone, pulled up her social media page, and scrolled to the photograph in question. Pointing to the blonde woman to Erikka's right, she said, "This is Laurel Westin. She invited Erikka to the party. She thought Erikka was too hung up on Andy and wanted to introduce her to some other guys."

"What was the event?" Katie asked.

"Some stupid fancy-schmancy society for saving butterflies, of all things. They're bugs. Who cares?"

Katie cared. Not only were they beautiful, but they were beneficial to the environment. They help pollinate plants, eat harmful insects, and are sustenance for other species.

"Where did you get the picture?"

"Laurel. She'd known Erikka since grade school."

"Could it have been one of the men from that party that Erikka was meeting at the warehouse?" Katie asked.

"I don't know." Erryn frowned and let out a weary breath. "I'm sorry to say that my sister enjoyed living life just a little dangerously. Although she was clearly in love with Andy, she wasn't going to miss out on any fun while she was waiting for him to come around." She looked down at her slim hands, and Katie knew this had been a hard revelation for her to make.

"What about Luke Stafford? Is there any chance she could've been meeting him?"

Erryn shook her head. "I don't think so. Erikka knew how I felt about that jerk."

"Then she wouldn't have mentioned it to you," Katie pointed out.

"I guess you're right," Erryn admitted, her gaze dipping to her untouched glass of lemonade.

Katie's questions seemed to be wearing her down. Dare she ask for a favor?

"Do you know how I can get in touch with Laurel Westin?"

Erryn shrugged. "Sorry. I know her—but it's not like we're friends." She stood. "I'd better check on the baby. I haven't heard a peep out of him."

Nick smiled. "He and Don are probably asleep on the sofa."

Erryn wiped her eyes. "Let's see if you're right." She opened the front door and went inside the house. Katie watched her go.

"Thanks again for arranging this meeting, Nick," she said quietly. "While I realize Erryn and I will never be friends, I don't think she believes me guilty of killing her sister. That's a huge improvement."

"I'm glad I could help." Nick blew Katie a kiss. "Now I'm going inside, too. I don't want Don getting *all* the baby time for himself."

CHAPTER 32

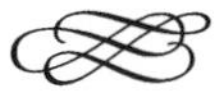

It had been a while since Katie had spent a lot of time on her own. Sure, Andy worked long hours, but he'd often pop up the stairs to have dinner with her and help wash the dishes. And he seemed to spend more nights in her bed than his own. While Katie had more friends than after her break-up with Chad, she didn't have anyone to hang out with in the evening or weekends.

It would take some time to get used to the new normal.

That evening, Katie decided to concentrate her investigative efforts on finding out where the picture of Erikka and Detective Schuler had been taken and turned to the Internet for answers. While there were several area organizations dedicated to butterflies, including the Dancing Wings Butterfly Garden at the Strong Museum of Play, it seemed the only recent fundraiser was held by the Rochester Area Butterfly Conservation Project, hosted by its benefactor Bethany Schuler.

The next morning, after her power walk around the Square and a quick shower, Katie called Vance just before she headed out of McKinlay Mill to tell him she had an errand to run.

The office resided in an impressive brick building off Linden

Avenue with a lovely garden on the right. Beautiful asters and mums of rust and gold and lavender were neatly arrayed in beds and planters alongside white marble benches and wooden arbors. Katie wondered if the garden had been created as a habitat for the butterflies the organization sought but had now been dressed for the fall season.

She walked into the building, found the location of the Conservation Project, and strode purposefully down the hall to her left. When she opened the heavy wooden door, she was surprised by the office's opulence. Although it was a charitable organization, the mina-khani daisies indicated the floor covering was either Varamin or an excellent fake. The walls were decorated with impressionistic paintings, not photographs, of the delicate butterflies the charity was sworn to protect.

"May I help you?"

Katie turned to see an elegant young woman sitting behind a large, curved desk. "Yes, hi." She smiled. "I'm Katie Bonner, and I'd like to speak with Bethany Schuler if she's available."

"Do you have an appointment?" The woman frowned.

"I don't," Katie said. "But we have a mutual friend, and I promise not to take up much of Mrs. Schuler's time if she'll agree to see me."

"One moment." The woman rose from behind the desk and went to an office down the hall. She returned momentarily and said, "Mrs. Schuler has ten minutes she can spare before her next appointment. Right this way."

"Thank you." Katie followed the receptionist back to Mrs. Schuler's office where she immediately noticed the expensive Jonathan Charles furniture and the attractive Decasso desk set. She'd known from reading about Bethany Schuler's parents that the detective's wife came from money, but she hadn't realized it was *this* much money.

Bethany Schuler stood and extended a hand across her desk. "Bethany Schuler. What can I do for you?"

"Katie Bonner," she said and shook Mrs. Schuler's hand, noticing that the woman wore a large diamond and emerald ring encircling one finger and a dainty gold butterfly ring—exactly like the one Erikka had worn—on another. "I appreciate your taking the time to see me. I came to speak with you about Erikka Wiley. She attended one of your organization's recent events."

Mrs. Schuler indicated the chair in front of her desk and both women sat.

"Ms. Bonner, a lot of people attend our events. You'll need to be more specific."

Taking the photo from her purse, Katie said, "Maybe this will jog your memory."

Mrs. Schuler glanced at the photo. "I know the blonde—she's Laurel Westin. She, and I imagine your friend, typically come to the RABC events on the prowl for a husband. Many of our patrons are wealthy."

"So, you didn't know Erikka Wiley personally?"

"Wiley?" Mrs. Schuler tapped her right index finger on her chin. "The name does sound familiar. She was the woman who was recently murdered in McKinlay Mill, right?"

"Yes. Your husband is investigating the case."

Mrs. Schuler showed no emotion but she nodded. "Right. Such a tragedy, but no, I didn't know her."

"Is it possible Erikka met one of your organization's patrons at the party and started seeing him romantically?" Katie asked.

"I highly doubt it," Mrs. Schuler said, a sneer marring her seamless face. Was she a fan of Botox or had she lived a life devoid of smiles? "I'm privy to the gossip inside this organization, and I haven't heard any rumors about this *woman*," she said with disdain, "dating any of our eligible bachelors." She looked down her nose at Katie. "Besides, none of the men at my gala would've murdered anyone. We're all about preserving life here, not taking it."

"I'm glad to hear that," Katie said, keeping her expression bland.

"Is there anything else I can help you with?" Mrs. Schuler asked, her tone not at all helpful.

Oh, yes. Like why had her husband decided to target Katie as a murderer with nothing in the way of evidence?

Etiquette demanded Katie bite her tongue—at least on that account. "How is it that Erikka even received an invitation to your fundraiser?"

Bethany Schuler narrowed her eyes. "Our tickets are sold to the public at large. We can't control those who attend." Did she loathe the rabble who might show up? But Katie also knew that such fundraisers gave away tickets to corporate sponsors so that they could pack the event with warm bodies so that it would appear to be better attended.

"Will you be making a donation to our cause today?" Mrs. Schuler asked pointedly.

"I'd like to study some of your literature before I make such a commitment," Katie said affably.

"Of course." Mrs. Schuler pulled a brochure from her top desk drawer and handed it to Katie, then forced a smile and nodded toward the door. "It was very nice to make your acquaintance. I'm sure you can find your way out."

Katie stood. "Again, thank you for seeing me."

Instead of acknowledging Katie, Mrs. Schuler picked up her phone and asked the receptionist about her next appointment.

As Katie strode through the receptionist's office, a box of shiny bling caught her attention: Golden butterfly rings. She waited until the receptionist set down the receiver before speaking.

"Excuse me," she said.

The receptionist looked up. The name plaque on her desk said RITA.

"What are these rings for?"

"We give them to our contributors at events."

"May I have one?" Katie asked.

"If you give us a check," Rita said blandly. She seemed to have taken on the same attitude as her boss.

Katie eyed the half-empty box of rings and smiled. "I'll think about it."

"You do that."

Katie left the office and headed for her car. So, Erikka's ring wasn't all that unique after all.

Could there be hundreds of them being worn by hundreds of women in the area?

* * *

ONCE BACK AT ARTISANS ALLEY, Katie logged into her favorite social media account and searched for Laurel Westin. It wasn't terribly hard to find the attractive blonde, and Katie sent her a friend request and a message asking if they could meet for lunch later that day. To sweeten the pot, Katie provided a link to the Tealicious web page. If Laurel Westin was on the prowl for a husband, gorgeous—famous—Chef Brad might induce her to accept Katie's invitation.

A hesitant tap on Katie's door caught her attention and she called, "Who is it?" trying to swallow down a fit of nerves. She expected push-back from Schuler once he learned she'd spoken with his wife, but he wouldn't be timid about knocking. He might not even knock at all. But she feared it could be someone with even more bad news.

"It's Roger."

Katie let out a sigh of relief and told the young man to come on in.

Roger entered and closed the door back behind him. "Are you busy?"

"Not too busy for you. What's on your mind?"

The young man looked embarrassed. "I'm afraid I'm in trouble."

Katie directed him into the chair beside her desk. "Do I need to get you some water or something? Or do you just need to get whatever it is off your chest?"

"I just need to say it," he said, his cheeks going scarlet. "A day or two after...after Erikka was found—I can't remember exactly which day—I found that little butterfly ring she used to wear." He gulped. "It was on the sidewalk in front of Tealicious. I saw it lying there with the sun glinting off it, and I just... I put it in my pocket. I didn't know what else to do."

Aware that their conversation was possibly being overheard by Sheriff's deputies, Katie said, "You couldn't know that was Erikka's ring. It's a popular design. Why, just this morning I saw the exact same ring being worn by Detective Schuler's wife."

"Well, picking up the ring isn't what got me into trouble," he said.

"Then, what is?" Of course, she already knew. But she wasn't about to tell him—or the officers who were probably listening—that.

"I took the ring inside Tealicious with me and, at some point, while I was working, I took it out of my pocket and put it on the windowsill. I told Mr. Healy about it, and he said I should tell the cops."

"And did you?" Katie asked.

He nodded. "I called and told Detective Schuler I'd found the ring. He asked if I could come by later that day and sign an affidavit saying I'd found it. I said I would and asked if I should bring the ring with me. He said no, to leave it where it was for now."

"And did you sign the affidavit?"

"Yes, and the next day, the police came here and searched," he said. "But the ring was gone. I don't know what happened to it. Mr. Healy said he didn't take it, and none of the other workers would own up to taking it either. And now, they're telling me I'm in trouble if I don't tell them where the ring is. They said I could be charged with filing a false report."

Katie frowned. "Who's telling you? You know what? It doesn't matter. You *didn't* file a false report. You did the right thing when you reported finding a ring you believed *might've* belonged to Erikka."

Roger's eyes were wide and scared. "But they're saying I lied."

"John Healy will testify that you didn't," she said. "Besides, that ring wouldn't do police any good even if it did belong to Erikka."

"Why's that?"

"Those rings—Erikka's and the ring exactly like it that Mrs. Schuler was wearing today—" She'd said that extra loudly for the benefit of Schuler himself should he be listening. "—were given away by the hundreds recently at a charity event. They're delicate, with a thin band. It would have had so many fingerprints on it that the police wouldn't have been able to get any clean trace evidence from it."

Roger's mouth dropped open. "Wow, Katie, you must watch a ton of crime shows to know so much about the law."

She winked. "Nah. But I *am* an avid reader. And I don't think you have anything to worry about from the police. Still, if they should try to badger you, refuse to talk with them without an attorney present."

"If I could afford one."

"I know several who might help.

He frowned. "Okay. Thanks."

"You're welcome," she said.

Okay, she didn't really know *several* attorneys, but she wanted Schuler to *think* she did. If he was listening in on her conversation with Roger, she hoped he got an earful. It crossed her mind that he might've even put Roger up to coming here and talking with her, hoping she'd confess to the young man that she'd taken the ring. But she wasn't foolish enough for that. And she didn't say anything to Roger that wasn't legally sound.

"I guess I'd better get back to work," Roger said.

"Don't worry," Katie told him. "Things have a way of working out."

She just hoped what she said would turn out to be true.

* * *

LESS THAN AN HOUR LATER, Katie got a response from Erikka's friend, Laurel Westin. She said she'd love to have lunch with Katie and that she'd meet her at Tealicious at a quarter past twelve.

At twelve-fifteen, Katie exited Artisans Alley through its back door and hurried across the parking lot to Tealicious. Laurel Westin was already there, leaning across the counter as if she were trying to see something…or someone.

"Hi, Ms. Westin? I'm Katie Bonner."

"Hi, Katie. Please call me Laurel." She gave Katie a distracted smile and then looked again not in the display case but toward the kitchen.

"Would you like to meet Chef Andrews?" Katie asked. "We're lucky to have him here at Tealicious."

"I'd *love* to meet him," Laurel gushed, her eyes going wide.

"Wait right here." With a bright smile, Katie left her new acquaintance to enter the kitchen to speak with Brad.

Upon seeing her, his eyes narrowed, as though he could see she wanted a favor. "What?"

"There's someone in the dining room who'd like to meet you," she said.

Blowing out a breath, he asked, "This isn't a fix-up, is it?"

"Of course not! I simply want you to come out and smile at a young woman," Katie said. "Just turn down the charm to seventy-five percent or so—I don't want her fainting on me."

Brad scowled. "Ha-ha."

"I'm serious." She drew back and placed a hand on her chest. "You don't realize the power of your influence."

"Uh-huh. And am I using that power for good or evil?" he asked.

Katie shrugged. "Eh, it's a gray area. I'll explain later." Taking his arm, she walked with him out into the dining room. "Chef Andrews, I'd like you to meet Laurel Westin."

Brad gave a slight bow. "I'm delighted. How do you do, Laurel?"

"How do *you* do?" Laurel asked rather huskily. "I'm so glad to meet you. I absolutely *adore* cooking."

He smiled. "So do I. And now I'd better get back to it."

"Wait," Laurel said. "Could you give me some tips sometime?"

Brad shot Katie a murderous look before turning back to his admirer. "Of course. Contact me through our web page with your questions."

"I sure will. Thank you!" Laurel sighed and beamed at Brad's retreating back and then seemed to melt. "Isn't he *marvelous*?" she breathed.

"Yes, he is." Katie smiled, wondering if she should've given her words more emphasis. Laurel seemed to emphasize about every other one. "Why don't we have a seat and order?"

Once they'd settled in at a table with their tea and sandwiches, Laurel said, "I was surprised to get your invitation. I mean, it was a *nice* surprise, but—" She shrugged. "Well, why did you want to have lunch with me?"

"I know you were friends with Erikka Wiley, and I'm so sorry for your loss," Katie said sincerely.

"Oh, well, thank you. That's so nice." But then her smile faded. "Wait, you're *Katie. The* Katie who was dating Erikka's boyfriend."

"Actually, Erikka was dating *my* boyfriend." Katie sipped her tea to steady her nerves. "Although, I don't think you could call what they were doing *dating*." *Oh, my goodness,* Katie thought. Now Laurel had given *her* the emphasis sickness.

"Well, that's true enough." Laurel picked up a sandwich and took a small bite out of it. "In fact, I told her that over and over. I said, 'Erikka, he's not going to leave that other woman for you. If he was, he wouldn't be sneaking around.' I mean, it's not as if the two of you were married and he had assets to lose or a custody battle to fight or something."

"That's true," Katie said with a nod. "I understand that you took Erikka to the butterfly gala to introduce her to some other guys?"

Laurel rolled her eyes. "Yeah. That turned out to be a dud, though, even though we got these awesome rings." She held up her hand to display one of the dainty butterfly rings with which Katie had become overly familiar. "Anyway, everybody wound up drinking too much—as per usual at these things—and the only guy Erikka flirted with all night was the Schuler woman's husband. I don't even know why—he's not that cute or anything. You think maybe it's because he's a detective? You know, some girls are badge bunnies."

Katie blinked in disbelief. "You're telling me that Erikka flirted with Detective Schuler at the gala?" she asked. "Did he flirt back?"

Laurel giggled. "Oh, absolutely! It was so bad that the Schuler woman told me to never bring Erikka back to one of their functions. Isn't that a hoot?"

Katie let out a shaky breath. "Is it ever."

CHAPTER 33

Katie felt a tad guilty for judging Laurel to be a vapid bimbo, but apart from the information she'd imparted about the butterfly gala and Erikka's behavior there, she seemed to have the mental capacity of a sex-starved hamster.

Katie hadn't been back at Artisans Alley for very long before Rhonda Simpson, one of her vendors, burst into her office. Strands of Rhonda's long blonde hair had escaped their French braid, and her face was flushed.

"Katie, you need to come quick!"

Hopping out of her chair and hurrying behind Rhonda, Katie asked, "What's wrong?"

"Some woman is about to kill Rose," Rhonda called breathlessly, not slowing down.

Rhonda dashed out of her office, and Katie struggled to catch up until she arrived at the cash desks where it looked as if some woman Katie had never seen before was indeed considering murder, her venomous gaze fixed on Rose's face. Vance was attempting to pull the woman away from Rose, but she had a good fifteen pounds on him and appeared to be a lot stronger than him.

"Hey, what's the problem here?" Katie shouted.

Everyone turned and looked at Katie guiltily—except the would-be Rose killer who encompassed the group in her glower.

With the scuffle and the noise abated, at least, for the time being, Katie asked, "Would someone please tell me what's going on?"

"This *old* floozy made a pass at my husband!" Would-be Rose Killer said.

Katie looked at her friend, hoping she was going to dispute the woman's account. "Rose?"

Rose nodded toward the woman's husband, a handsome man in his mid- to late-seventies. "Well… he winked at me."

The man looked as if he wished the floor would open up and swallow him.

"He does that all the time!" his wife yelled. "He's flirtatious. And I've warned him it was going to get him unwanted attention."

"All I did was wink back and slide my phone number across the desk to him," Rose explained. "I didn't realize this hateful shrew was his wife. I thought maybe she was his sister or something."

"You know better now, don't you?" the man's wife demanded.

"I do. And I'm terribly sorry for the misunderstanding," Rose apologized.

"I too am sorry for the misunderstanding," Katie said sincerely. "Let me give you a twenty-percent discount on your purchases."

The woman glared at Katie. "No, thanks. We don't *want* these things anymore, and we'll *never* step foot in this nasty little establishment again."

"I'm sorry you feel that way." Katie watched them go and then turned to Rose, finding it difficult to keep her voice level. "A word in my office, please?"

Rose nodded. "I'm sorry."

Katie ignored Rose's attempts at conversation until they were in her office with the door closed. "What happened out there?"

"The man winked at me, and I—"

But then Katie lost it. "And because of some ridiculous fortune Moonbeam Carruthers told you, you cost us a customer and potentially every other customer who witnessed the altercation. Rose, please stop thinking about your mystery man and start considering your fellow vendors." She paused to take in a breath.

Dropping her head, Rose said, "I didn't mean to..." Her voice broke, and she began to sob.

Katie let out a breath, feeling terribly sorry. "I apologize for losing my temper, Rose. I'm under a lot of stress."

"You don't know how lonely it can be," Rose said and continued to weep.

Oh, how wrong she was. Katie's husband, Chad, had betrayed her trust by investing in Artisans Alley and she'd endured a terrible year of isolation with no family and few friends to soften it. It had been the worst year of Katie's life. Rose had been alone for almost a decade, which was definitely worse, but to say Katie didn't understand the depth of her feelings was simply untrue.

Handing Rose the box of tissues from atop her desk, Katie said, "You're going to find that guy who's destined to be with you, Rose. Moonbeam said so, and I...I believe her. But please just let nature take its course rather than trying to help it along."

Rose nodded.

Sighing again, Katie took a peppermint from the jar on her desk, unwrapped it, and smashed it between two molars with a satisfying crunch. She looked at Rose's drooped shoulders and lowered head and wished she could take back her harsh words. But, the truth of the matter was that Rose needed to rein herself in. She *had* cost her fellow vendors by making the woman customer change her mind about shopping at Artisans Alley, and she'd represented the arcade in an unfavorable light.

"Why don't you take the rest of the day off?" Katie suggested gently.

"I'm surprised you aren't telling me to leave and never come back," Rose said.

"I'd never do that. You're more important to the Alley than a million customers," she said and patted Rose's hand. "But I know that altercation was stressful. Are you all right?"

"I'm fine…but I do believe I'll take you up on your offer and take off for the rest of the day."

"I agree. But I hope you'll be back tomorrow. You're one of Artisans Alley's most important assets. We need you. *I* need you."

"Thank you, Katie," Rose said, still sniffling.

Katie gave her friend a heartfelt hug. "Now go home and treat yourself to something special."

"When you get to my age, there isn't much to celebrate," Rose remarked.

Katie hugged her friend once more and Rose left the office, Katie gave a sigh, sat down, leaned back in her chair, closed her eyes, and wondered if things could possibly get any worse. But, of course, they could. One should never underestimate the power of a crappy day.

* * *

AFTER CLOSING Artisans Alley and walking back to Tealicious, Katie heard footsteps on the pavement behind her. Twilight had descended and while it wasn't that late—it wasn't unusual for other people to be walking or jogging around the Square. But there was something about those particular footsteps that unnerved her. She whirled and came face-to-scowl with Detective Schuler.

"How dare you," he growled, his face scrunched into a leer.

Determined to stand her ground, Katie drew herself up and lifted her chin. "How dare I what, Detective?"

"Don't you *ever* go near my wife again."

She shrugged. "I visited her charitable organization. I'm interested in butterflies. Is that now a crime?"

He squinted at her. "You didn't go there because of your interest in butterflies. You went there to question my wife about Erikka Wiley."

Katie squared her shoulders. "Fair enough. I did. Did you know Erikka was using the abandoned warehouse as a meeting place with one of her many lovers? And that she *might* have been meeting someone she met at your wife's gala?"

"I know you're a ridiculous woman who thinks she knows far more than she actually does." He leaned down so she could smell his stale breath as he hissed into her face. "I know that if you know what's good for you, you'll leave the investigating to the professionals and that you'll leave my wife and me alone."

"Why are you so defensive about your wife?" Katie asked.

Schuler clenched his fists. "My wife is none of your concern, and you'd be wise to give her a wide berth."

Katie recalled reading about Bethany Schuler's family's political influence. "Is it because you want to run for office at some time in the future? I read that Bethany's family was influential in Western New York politics."

"Shut up!"

"Is that the plan?" she continued, realizing she was walking a dangerous path but not willing to get off it just yet. "You and Bethany see yourselves as the next governor and first lady?"

Schuler's lip curled and he raised one of his clenched fists. Katie recoiled, certain he was about to strike her.

"You'd better get out of my sight," he warned.

"Or what?" she challenged. "You are trespassing in front of my store. Leave now, or I'll call the Sheriff's Office and have you removed. And then I'll ask them to transfer my call to Internal Affairs."

Schuler glared at her.

She turned and, despite her bluster, she was half afraid that he'd grab her and pull her back but was too stubborn to let Schuler see her fear. As calmly as she could, she walked to the stairs leading up to her apartment over Tealicious. It was only when she reached the steps and saw him stalking off in the other direction that she felt she could let her guard down.

With fumbling fingers, she unlocked the door, walked into the apartment, and immediately locked the door again, throwing the deadbolt. Mason and Della ran to her and with trembling hands, she gathered them up and hugged them.

Opening her fridge, Katie took out the already opened bottle of wine and poured herself a glass. She spied the landline phone she hadn't abandoned. To further calm her nerves, she called Rose. She needed to check on the poor woman anyway, and it would be good to hear a familiar voice.

"Hi, Rose. H-how are you?" she asked.

"How are *you*?" Rose asked. "You're the one who sounds like she's on the verge of tears. Are you calling to fire me?"

"Oh, I'd never do that." Katie took a deep breath. "I j-just...I just..." Her heart was pounding, and she took another deep breath. "I just had another run-in with Detective Schuler."

"Oh, my gosh! Did he arrest you?" Rose cried. "Do you need bail money? I can be there in—"

"No, Rose." Katie gave a soft laugh, thankful for Rose's unconditional friendship. "I appreciate the offer, but our meeting was no way near as civilized as his simply arresting me."

"What did he do?" Rose asked, her tone anxious.

Katie told Rose about Schuler's approaching her on the sidewalk outside Tealicious. "When he raised his fist, Rose, I really thought he'd hit me."

"If nothing else, you should immediately report him," Rose decreed.

Katie no longer trusted the Sheriff's Office. "Maybe," she sort of agreed. "I'll call Seth Landers and let him know."

"Why don't I come sit with you for a while?" Rose offered. "You shouldn't be alone right now."

"Thank you, but I'm all right. My doors are locked, and I'm not planning on going anywhere until tomorrow morning. I simply needed to hear a friendly voice," she said. "What about you? Are you all right? I know you were awfully shaken up when you left Artisans Alley today."

"I'm fine." Rose gave a rueful chuckle. "There's no fool like an old fool, is there?"

"You're certainly not a fool. You're wonderful. I'll see you tomorrow."

They said their goodbyes, and Katie placed her phone on the table. By now, her heart had slowed to a reasonable rate, so she fed the cats before preparing some dinner for herself. As she cut an apple to put in a quinoa salad, she remembered Rose's encounter with the jealous wife. Yes, the husband had flirted with Rose, and Rose had simply responded in kind. Okay, maybe she had taken it a step farther in trying to give the man her phone number. But the wife was furious, even though she admittedly knew flirting was common behavior for her husband.

Putting strips of grilled chicken in a saucepan, Katie thought about Laurel Westin telling her how much Erikka and Detective Schuler had flirted with each other that night. Granted, according to Laurel, they'd *all* been drinking. And it was possible neither Erikka nor the detective had meant anything by the flirting. But had Bethany Schuler taken it that way? Or had she been like the jealous wife at Artisans Alley that day? After all, she'd told Laurel to never bring Erikka back to another event. How angry had Bethany actually been? Did the woman have a reputation for blowing her top?

While eating dinner, Katie booted up her laptop and searched online for any information on Bethany Schuler. Several articles told of parties and other events, but there were also tales of a woman with a volatile temper. One chronicled a tirade in an airport over a lost bag, while another reported her being removed from a restaurant for verbally assaulting the wait staff, as well as throwing a tantrum in a nail salon and demanding, "Do you know who I am? Do you know who *my* parents are?" After the nail salon debacle, Bethany reportedly went on a spa retreat to "rest and rejuvenate because she was under so much stress over the plight of the local butterfly population." The charity was formed right after that, and Bethany hadn't received any more bad press. At least, not yet.

Katie pondered what she'd learned that day. Laurel said Bethany had been angry—angry enough to ban Erikka from all future events. But, judging by the most recent articles mentioning Bethany, she'd finally mastered control of her outbursts…at least, in front of the media. Self-control was an excellent quality for a woman who had political aspirations for herself or her husband. Lovely women with wild oats to sow were widely known to be detrimental to political careers. What might Bethany Schuler do if she thought Erikka Wiley was trying to seduce her husband?

CHAPTER 34

Determined not to let Detective Schuler push her around, Thursday morning Katie made the drive into Rochester to revisit the butterfly organization before heading to Artisans Alley. After reading about Bethany Schuler's antics online the evening before, she'd decided to go and apologize for upsetting the woman. Okay, her primary reason was to try to get more information about Detective Schuler's flirtation with Erikka at the gala, but she did plan to apologize.

The receptionist recognized her when she came into the office.

"Hello, Rita!" Katie said brightly. "How are you this beautiful morning?"

"Fine. Mrs. Schuler is—"

Before the receptionist could finish her sentence, Bethany Schuler came out of her office and handed a file to the young woman. Upon seeing Katie, her expression soured, but then she forced a smile. "Ms. Bonner, was it? Have you come to make that donation?"

"Actually, I have a few more questions, if you wouldn't mind taking the time to speak with me." Katie held up her hands. "I promise I'll be quick."

Mrs. Schuler nodded at the receptionist. "Rita is quite knowledgeable about our operations. I'm sure she can answer any questions you might have. I'm swamped today."

"She knows why you banned Erikka Wiley from future events then?" Katie asked.

Eyes narrowing to slits, Mrs. Schuler said, "That's none of your business. Rita can answer your *relevant* questions about our organization."

"I'd like to know if it's true that you told Laurel Westin not to ever bring Erikka to another of the charity's events," Katie persisted.

With a shriek, Mrs. Schuler snatched the stapler off Rita's desk and hurled it across the room. "Get out of this office and never come back. If you do, I'll have you arrested for harassment!"

"But I'm not—"

"Out!" Mrs. Schuler screamed, making poor Rita cower against the wall.

Katie didn't press her luck and left the office in haste. It appeared Bethany Schuler hadn't quite mastered controlling those violent outbursts after all.

* * *

IT WAS close to opening when Katie returned to Artisans Alley. She found Rose waiting for her in the vendors' lounge her expression quizzical. "Good morning. Is everything all right?"

Katie managed a smile. "Yes. I had a quick errand to run before I got here." Remembering Bethany Schuler's fury caused her smile to fade, but she quickly put it back in place for Rose's benefit. "How about you?"

"I'm fine, but Susan Williams said she could feel that spot in the floor upstairs between her booth and Chad's Pad give a little when she walked across it this morning," Rose said. "I reminded Vance about it, and he said he'd get on it as soon as he can."

Katie nodded. "He really should have fixed it by now."

"Maybe he doesn't know what to do," Rose suggested.

"That's a good point. Maybe I should ask my contractor to take a look at it. I'll speak to Vance about it."

While it was still on her mind, Katie took out her phone and texted Vance to ask him if the floor was something he could fix himself. She looked up from the phone and grinned at Rose. "Let's hope that's one less dragon to slay today."

"Slaying a dragon will be the least of our worries if Susan Williams falls through that floor," Rose said. "I don't know which she'd do first—kill you or sue you."

"Don't remind me. I have enough problems to worry about at this moment, remember?"

Rose patted Katie's shoulder. "Sorry. But, like you said, you've done all you can about the floor for now. And Susan knows about it, so she should avoid it. Oh, hey, do you want me to go ask Moonbeam if Susan is going to fall through the floor?"

Although she knew Rose was serious and meant well, Katie burst out laughing. "Please don't. Let it be a surprise." She liked Moonbeam as much as her friend did, but Rose was starting to rely too heavily on the woman's prognostications.

"My main concern is a customer who might trip or fall because of it. I need to get a sign up or block it some other way. Maybe a piece of plywood with duct tape holding it down as a stopgap.

"Good idea," Rose agreed. "I better get back to work," she said and headed back to her cash desk.

After settling in at her desk, Katie pulled up her agenda for the day to decide what she should do next, idly wondering how soon Vance would get back to her about the floor. Hopefully, he could fix it.

Before she could determine which task to tackle next, there came a brief knock before Andy strolled into her office with a picnic basket.

"Hey, there, Sunshine."

"Andy, I—"

He raised a hand. "Let me explain. Please."

She sighed as she looked at his handsome face, still marred with a purple bruise along his jawline.

"We owe it to ourselves to say all the things we need to say," he said. "We might never get the chance again. So, what do you say? Will you take a walk with me down by the lake and have an early picnic lunch?"

He was right. They might never have another chance to get closure. She'd never had it with Chad. In fact, the two of them were trying to reconcile when he'd crashed his car into a tree and died. Katie couldn't turn her back on establishing closure with Andy.

"Okay." She pushed back from the desk, stood, grabbed her purse, and followed him out of the office, locking the door on the way out. "I should tell Rose I'm leaving."

"I told her," he said.

She gave him a look of mock indignation. "Awfully sure of yourself, weren't you?"

"Let's say optimistic." He winked. "Don't forget, I know you well, Sunshine. I came determined to make you an offer you can't refuse."

Sadly, good food *was* her Achilles heel.

September was a fickle month. One never knew what to expect: balmy breezes or chilly rain. Andy couldn't have picked a more beautiful day for this impromptu picnic—Katie had to give him that. The sun was shining with a light wind and a hint of honeysuckle scenting the air. Although she wished it were under happier circumstances, Katie was happy to be outside strolling toward the lake. She could tell Andy how much he'd meant to her during their two-year relationship, but she was also determined to tell him goodbye.

Katie looked out at the sparkling water as she and Andy headed toward the picnic area. Surprisingly, quite a few boats still dotted the slips, and a catamaran and a couple of sailboats cut through the white caps out on Lake Ontario.

"This is gorgeous," she said. "I don't take time to appreciate this view as often as I should."

"Neither do I." He sat the picnic basket on a bench. "We often take things for granted that we certainly shouldn't."

She wasn't about to fall into that opening. The only thing she was referencing taking for granted was the beautiful view.

Andy opened the picnic basket and removed a blue cloth that he spread over the table. Then he took out a bottle of Chardonnay, a corkscrew, and two glasses.

"It's a little early in the day for wine, isn't it?" she asked.

"Since we both have to go back to work, we'll only have one glass each. I promise." He opened the wine and poured, then he gingerly retrieved a chicken pasta salad, a fruit platter, two plates, some silverware, and placed them on the table, along with a couple of paper napkins.

"Wow. I'm impressed," Katie said, taking a seat.

Grinning, he asked, "Did you forget I can make more than pizza, calzones, and cinnamon buns?"

"No," she said. "I didn't forget."

They ate their lunch, admiring the scenery, and making somewhat awkward, innocuous conversation. Katie had a feeling that once their meal was finished, Andy would reveal the real purpose behind this impromptu picnic, and she also thought she knew in what direction his line of thinking might go.

So be it. She already had an answer.

Once Andy had packed everything back into the basket, he turned to her and spread his arms. "Come here."

Katie hesitated.

"Please. Just let me hold you."

She got up from the table and stepped into his embrace. It felt good to wrap her arms around his waist one last time and press her cheek to the hardness of his chest. Memories flooded her, and she inhaled his spicy scent. Tears pricked her eyes.

"Oh, Katie, I've missed you." He tried to tilt her face up to him, but she resisted.

"I can't," she whispered.

"I love you. And you still love me. I know you do. You don't just turn your feelings off."

"I do love you. But you deceived me, Andy." She stepped back. "You know my marriage to Chad ended because of his betrayal. I told you when we first started dating that I'd never be with a man I couldn't trust."

"I messed up, Sunshine. I realize that. But, believe me, I'll never do it again."

"I never thought you'd do it the first time," she muttered.

He squeezed his eyes shut, tears leaking from beneath his lashes. "Marry me," he whispered huskily.

Right on cue.

"Let's start a family. I'll do anything you want to make this right."

Stepping forward, Katie took his hands. "You made choices that I just can't forgive."

"Can't or won't?" Andy asked.

"Won't," Katie declared. "I'm sorry, but nothing you do will ever make it right again."

"How can you be so hard-hearted?" Andy implored.

Because I never want to go through this again. If you'd cheat on me once, you'll do it again with someone else.

Katie swallowed. "I'd like to think we could still be friends. And we still have Erikka's murder hanging over both of us." *But mostly* me. "Our businesses are right next door to each other—and I intend to patronize Angelo's for pizza and cinnamon buns."

"But I won't be a part of your life?"

Katie squeezed his hands before letting go. "No. I wish you all the best. I really do. But we have no future together."

Andy's head dipped and he swallowed.

"You'll find somebody else." After all, Laurel Westin was available.

Katie mentally winced. *Meow.*

"It's time for both of us to move on."

Andy shook his head, still staring at the ground.

"Will you drive me back to the Alley?"

Long moments passed before Andy nodded. He picked up the picnic basket and led the way back to his truck.

CHAPTER 35

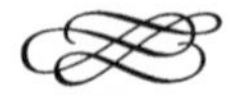

Even though she hadn't cried, Katie's face still looked blotchy. Upon returning to Artisans Alley, she took out her compact to powder her nose and then reapplied her mascara and lipstick.

Someone knocked on the door. "Come on in!" Katie called.

Rose stepped inside and closed the door behind her. "Are you all right? I saw you leaving with Andy."

Smiling slightly, Katie said, "I'm fine. Our relationship is now officially over."

"And you're okay with that?"

"I am." She truly was.

Rose handed Katie a note.

"What's this?"

"I don't know," Rose said. "Detective Schuler was nosing around the main showroom while you were out."

Katie had assumed as much, but since he'd searched the place before, she knew it wasn't out of the realm of possibility that he'd returned to scour over her office again. She had no idea if that was legal under the search warrant, but at this point, she wouldn't put anything past Schuler.

"What did he want?" she asked.

"He didn't say. But when he was around the cash desks, he picked that up—" She nodded toward the note. "—and said, 'Looks like you dropped something.' I told him, no I didn't, but I took it since it has your name on it."

Opening the desk drawer, Katie took out her letter opener and sliced open the envelope. She removed the note inside and immediately glanced at the signature at the bottom. "It's from Erryn, Erikka Wiley's sister."

"Really? What does it say?" Rose asked.

She scanned the words. "It says she has new information about Erikka's death, and she wants to talk with me this evening. She's coming by here."

"Do you trust her?"

Katie shrugged. "I'm not sure. But I'll listen to whatever she has to say."

"I'll stay with you, just in case—"

"You will not." She smiled. "I appreciate your thoughtfulness, but I'll be fine, Rose." "But it's weird that Detective Schuler is the one who found the note. Don't you agree?"

"I do. And he could be using Erryn to see if I know more than I'm telling him. But since I don't, it's an exercise in futility." She stood and gave Rose a quick hug. "After the day I've had, a chat with Erikka's sister will be anticlimactic."

Rose nodded. "You're probably right."

After the older woman left, Katie scanned the note again. Was it legitimate? Did Erryn have new information about her sister's murder? If so, why wouldn't she take it directly to Detective Schuler? Unless, of course, she'd come to distrust Schuler as much as Katie did.

She tried to call Erryn at work, but was told she had the day off. She left a message for Nick, asking for Erryn's home number, but he didn't get back to her until late in the afternoon. When she finally did get to call Erryn, she only got voice mail.

The day dragged on.

Evening was upon her when Katie checked her watch again. Artisans Alley had closed nearly half an hour before. She'd give Erryn five more minutes, and then she was leaving. Thinking maybe Erryn didn't know where Katie's office was, she wandered out into the arcade's main showroom.

While there, she decided to go upstairs to see for herself how bad the floor situation was. Vance had placed CAUTION signs in the middle of the floor and had told her he believed he could shore it up, but since he hadn't already done it, Katie thought she might rather have John Healy do the job. She wondered how to do that without hurting Vance's feelings—or his pride.

She gingerly stepped over to Chad's Pad and unlocked the door. Getting closure with Andy had brought up feelings about Chad, his death and how things had been left unresolved between the two of them. She walked into the room where his paintings were displayed. It was Katie's way of honoring her late husband. She ran a hand over one of the intricate frames holding a beautiful landscape. He'd been a talented artist—that was certain.

Hearing a noise from downstairs, she came to the top of the stairs and called, "I'll be right down!" When she didn't receive a response, she crouched down to get a better look into the lobby. She didn't see anyone.

A door opened and closed again.

"Darn it!" Katie raced down the steps. Had that been Erryn? Hadn't she heard Katie call to her? But why would she leave so quickly after driving all the way here? After arranging the meeting in the first place? Maybe she'd only forgotten something.

When Katie got to the lobby, Schuler stood up from behind one of the cash desks. He greeted her with a malevolent smile. "Rushing off somewhere?"

"Just locking up," she said, trying to act as if everything was fine. She didn't truly believe he'd be fooled, but she could try. "We should have closed before now, but I was waiting for someone."

"And where is this someone?" he asked.

"She didn't show."

"Oh, but she did." He took a snub nose revolver from his jacket pocket. "She was enraged that you killed her sister, and she came here to make you pay."

"No one will ever believe that."

"Sure, they will. I know of at least one member of your staff who is aware you were meeting Erikka's sister here after work," he said. "I know because I gave her the note."

"Rose doesn't know what was in the note," Katie lied. "The envelope was sealed."

He shrugged. "So what? It's in your office. I'll make sure it isn't hard to find."

Katie felt that stalling Schuler was her best defense. Maybe someone would come by and see that she was in trouble. "Did you fall for Erikka's ruse about being pregnant?"

"I'm not engaging in your idle chatter." He pulled her toward the hall. "Let's walk on back to your office, shall we?"

"You did, didn't you?" Katie persisted. "You thought she was going to have your baby and that—worse—she was going to tell your wife. Oh, ho, ho, you'd have been out on your ear had that happened, wouldn't you? No socialite wife, no political future, no inherited fortune."

Schuler backhanded her across the face with the hand that held the gun. She'd have fallen if he hadn't still been holding her by the arm. Her face stung, and she tasted blood.

Schuler half-dragged Katie down the aisle and through the vendors' lounge to her office. "Have a seat at your desk. Do it, and I'll kill you quickly. Don't, and I'll make you suffer." He pushed her toward the desk.

"Did you make Erikka suffer?"

"No. I made it quick and painless," he said. "After all, I thought she was carrying our baby."

Katie shuddered.

That made him laugh. "Are you frightened of me? You should be."

"I feel sorry for you," Katie said.

"Don't you worry about me," he said. "I'm going to be fine."

Katie grabbed her jar of peppermints, turned, and smashed him in the face with it. As he shrieked in pain, she shoved him to the side and ran for the side door, but Schuler was already scrambling after her.

Schuler grabbed a handful of Katie's hair and yanked her head back. "I'm gonna love killing you."

"Stop!"

At the sound of the commanding voice from the doorway, both Katie and Schuler stilled.

"Drop your weapon and raise your hands up over your head!"

Katie sagged in relief when she saw Captain Spence standing outside the vendors' lounge with a team of officers behind him.

"Thank goodness you got here in time!" a bloodied, wild-eyed Schuler shouted. "This woman is insane! She just confessed to killing Erikka Wiley and—"

"Save it," Spence said. "And put that gun on the floor. Now!"

Schuler turned a murderous glare in Katie's direction but did as he was told.

She moved aside and rubbed the back of her still-tingling scalp where Schuler had yanked her hair, watching and listening as Captain Spence read Schuler his rights and slipped the cuffs around his wrists.

Movement through the back door's window caught her attention, and she saw Rose standing in the back parking lot, wringing her hands. Katie opened the door and hurried outside to join her.

"Rose! What are you doing here?" Katie asked, leading her friend into the building.

"It was that note," she said, the agitation in her voice conveying her concern. "You know it didn't set well with me, and

I was afraid it might be a trap. I tried to call you, and when I didn't get through, I called nine-one-one."

"We had a patrol car on its way here, and when we heard what you told Ms. Bonner in her office, we moved," Captain Spence said. He turned back to Schuler. "You were right—it *was* smart to bug the place."

CHAPTER 36

Rose insisted on staying with Katie until late Thursday night. And though she'd never raised a child, her maternal instincts took over and she mothered Katie all evening —cooking dinner, making Katie hold a bag of frozen peas against her bruised cheek, and ensuring Katie had tea or wine whenever she wanted it.

She arrived back at Katie's apartment early the next morning with a basket full of warm, home-made apple-nut muffins and they shared breakfast before they crossed the parking lot to go to work at Artisans Alley.

"If Nona sees me, she'll be thrilled," Katie muttered, indicating the blue and purple splotches that marred her face. "I look like I've gone a couple of rounds with a boxer, just like Andy and Ray."

"Maybe more so, but I'll bet Detective Schuler looks worse. Surely he had to have quite a few stitches to repair the damage you inflicted. You were very brave to use your peppermint jar as a weapon!" Rose laughed. "I don't think our former detective knew just who he was dealing with."

When they walked into Artisans Alley's lobby, they found an

older man standing there with a bouquet of white tea roses and baby's breath. Katie assumed the man was a delivery person and that the roses were a possible peace offering from Andy. But she was wrong.

"Are you Rose Nash?" the man asked, his blue eyes twinkling.

"Yes."

"I'm Sergeant Walter Tillman of the Greece Police Department—retired," he amended. "I was listening to my police scanner last evening when I heard about the commotion here at Artisans Alley." He handed Rose the flowers. "I was impressed with your bravery and your loyalty."

"Why, how very thoughtful of you." Rose beamed, accepting the flowers and inhaling their scent.

"I know it's forward of me, but I wondered if you might want to discuss your part in solving Erikka Wiley's murder."

Rose positively giggled. "Oh, no—I had no part in that. I was just worried about my friend here." However, she didn't introduce Katie to the man.

"Perhaps the two of you should go back to the vendors' lounge. There're a couple of vases under the sink. You ought to put those flowers in water—and maybe sit down and have a cup of coffee," Katie suggested. "I can hold down the fort up here."

"Well...if you're sure," Rose said, her cheeks blushing a becoming shade of pink.

"Go," Katie said and shooed them off.

Rose nodded and the couple started down the showroom's main aisle. Behind Sergeant Tillman's back, Rose gave Katie a jubilant thumbs-up.

It was kind of the sergeant to present Rose with the gorgeous flowers, but it also brought to mind the fact that despite the plethora of cop cars that had littered the tarmac outside Artisans Alley the previous evening, Andy hadn't come to check to see if she was okay. All the local news channels had reported an arrest in Erikka's murder case, with updated stories airing that morning. She knew Andy's viewing habits—he had to have seen at least one or more of them. For a man who'd asked her to spend the rest of her life with him less than twenty-four hours before, he hadn't shown a bit of concern for her welfare.

Katie sighed. *C'est la vie.*

She was still feeling a bit disappointed when Ray emerged from the side vendor entrance and strolled over to the cash desks, carrying a glass jar filled with starlight peppermints.

"Hey," he said.

"Hey, yourself."

He set the jar down and lifted her chin with his index finger to inspect the damage to her face and winced. "I'll bet that hurt."

"I'd be lying if I said it didn't." She indicated the jar. "Is that for me?"

He nodded. "I heard your candy jar was a fatality of yesterday's attack."

"It was." She shook her head. "In fact, I dread cleaning up the mess."

"Already taken care of—Vance was on it first thing this morning."

Frowning, she said, "I'm glad he's on top of something. Have you seen the springy floor in front of Chad's Pad?"

Again, he nodded.

"I should probably have John Healy repair it, but I don't want to hurt Vance's feelings...." Her sentence trailed off.

"Vance and I can handle the floor. In fact, tomorrow morning, we'll assess what it needs to be fixed ." Ray reached into his pocket and took out the butterfly ring he told her he'd tossed into the lake. "Would you like this back?"

Katie glowered at him. "No, thank you. I don't even think it belonged to Erikka, given the fact that Schuler's wife gave them out by the dozens at a gala not long ago and still has a half a box full of them at her agency."

"I don't know about that, but when I turned it over to Captain

Spence, he said there was no way of knowing whether or not the ring had belonged to Erikka and that since Schuler had already confessed to the murder, it was irrelevant anyway."

Katie gave him a lopsided grin. "I knew you wouldn't throw away evidence."

"Not even for you."

So, there were limits to his adoration.

"What will happen to Schuler?"

"Knowing him, he'll say his confession was coerced and plead innocent. If his wife stands by him and pays for the best criminal attorney money can buy, there's a slight chance he may get off."

"Oh, Ray, no!"

"I said slight. But my guess is old Bethany will abandon the jerk in a heartbeat. I'm pretty sure Schuler was only given the promotion to detective because his wife's parents pulled some strings. Just about everybody in the Sheriff's Office knew he was never qualified for the job."

"The Sheriff's Office is better off without him."

Ray nodded and gave her a sad smile. "Despite looking like you went a couple of rounds with a boxing champ, you seem happy."

"Pretty much," she said. "Erikka's killer will be brought to justice, and it looks like Rose found the mystery man Moonbeam promised would come into her life."

Ray's gaze dipped to the desk. "And you've made up with your man."

She barked out a laugh. "Where'd you get that idea?"

"I just happened to be looking out my shop window yesterday morning and saw the two of you with your picnic basket heading off somewhere."

"It was a nice lunch," Katie said. "The conversation, however…."

He gave her a quizzical look.

She sighed. "I didn't get closure with Chad, but I now have it with Andy. That's a good thing. We shared our lives for a while, and even though it didn't work out, I don't hate him. I wish him the very best life has to offer."

"Says the martyred saint," Ray muttered sarcastically, his gaze dipping once more, but she could see he was trying to suppress a smile. "He had the best life has to offer, and he blew it."

Katie shrugged and managed a wry smile. "I doubt he thinks so. But even if he does, he'll get over it."

Key-Lime Cookies

Ingredients

½ cup butter
1 cup granulated sugar
1 egg
1 egg yolk
1 ½ cups all-purpose flour
1 teaspoon baking powder
½ teaspoon salt
¼ cup fresh lime juice
1½ teaspoons grated lime zest
½ cup confectioners' sugar for decoration

Preheat the oven to 350°F (180°C, Gas Mark 4). Grease or place parchment paper or a silica mat on a baking sheet. In a large bowl, cream butter, sugar, egg, and egg yolk until smooth. Stir in lime juice and lime zest. Combine the flour, baking powder, and salt. Blend into the creamed mixture. Form the dough into ½-inch balls and arrange on the prepared cookie sheet. Bake for 8 to

10 minutes or until lightly browned. Cool on wire racks. Sift confectioners' sugar over cookies while still warm.

Yield: 3 dozen cookies

Chocolate Chip Cookie Bars

Ingredients

1½ cups packed brown sugar
½ cup butter, melted
2 large eggs, lightly beaten, room temperature
1 teaspoon vanilla extract
1½ cups all-purpose flour
½ teaspoon baking powder
½ teaspoon salt
1 cup (6 ounces) semisweet chocolate chips

Preheat the oven to 350°F (180°C, Gas Mark 4). In a large bowl, mix the brown sugar, butter, eggs and vanilla until they're just combined. Do not over mix them. In a separate bowl, combine the flour, baking powder, and salt. Then, mix the dry ingredients into the wet until a thick, brownie-like batter forms. Fold in the chocolate chips until they're evenly distributed throughout the batter. Grease a 13×9-inch baking pan with butter or shortening. Spread the batter in the pan then pop it into the preheated oven. Bake the bars for 18 to 20 minutes or until a toothpick inserted in the middle comes out clean. Take the baked bars out of the oven and allow them to cool completely on a wire rack. Once cool, cut the bars and serve. Serve the cookie bars by themselves or with a scoop of vanilla ice cream and a drizzle of hot fudge for an indulgent sundae.

Yield: 3 dozen cookies

Almond shortbread

Ingredients
1 cup all-purpose flour
¾ cup raw almond flour, toasted
8 tablespoons (1 stick) unsalted butter, softened
¼ cup light brown sugar
¼ cup granulated sugar
½ teaspoon kosher salt
1 teaspoon vanilla (or almond) extract

Whisk together both flours in a small bowl. Set aside. In the bowl of a stand mixer fitted with the paddle attachment (or in a large bowl, using a hand-held mixer), cream the butter and both sugars on medium speed until light and fluffy, about 4 minutes. Add the flours ½ cup at a time, mixing thoroughly after each addition. Add the salt and vanilla and mix for 30 seconds. Turn the dough out onto a cool surface and divide it into four pieces. Roll each piece into a log measuring 1-inch thick and 6-inches long. Wrap the logs in plastic wrap or waxed paper and refrigerate until firm, about 1 hour.

Position the racks in the upper and lower thirds of the oven and preheat the oven to 350°F (180°C, Gas Mark 4). Slice the logs into rounds approximately ⅓-inch thick and place them on an ungreased large heavy baking sheet, spacing them about 2 inches apart. Bake for 10 to 12 minutes, until the edges are golden. Let the cookies cool on the baking sheets on cooling racks for 10 minutes. Using an offset spatula, transfer the cookies to a cooling rack to cool completely. The cookies can be stored in an airtight container for up to a week or transferred to freezer bags and freeze for up to 2 months.

Yield: 4 dozen cookies

Cinnamon Coffee Cake

Ingredients

For the Topping:

½ cup brown sugar, packed

¼ cup sifted all-purpose flour

¼ cup salted butter (at room temperature)

1 teaspoon cinnamon

For the Cake:

1½ cups all-purpose flour

2½ teaspoons baking powder

½ teaspoon salt

1 large egg (beaten)

¾ cup granulated sugar

1/3 cup melted butter (salted or unsalted)

½ cup milk

1 teaspoon vanilla extract

Preheat the oven to 325°F (170°C, Gas Mark 3). Butter and flour an 8-inch or 9-inch square or round layer cake pan. In a small mixing bowl, combine 1/2 cup of brown sugar with 1/4 cup of all-purpose flour and the cinnamon. Stir to blend, then work in the 1/4 cup of softened butter with a fork or your fingers until the mixture feels crumbly. Set the streusel aside.

In a medium bowl, combine the 1 1/2 cups of all-purpose flour with the baking powder and salt; blend thoroughly with a whisk or spoon, then set it aside. In a mixing bowl with an electric mixer, beat the egg lightly and then beat in the sugar and the 1/3 cup of melted butter. Add the milk and vanilla and blend well. Stir in the flour and mix the batter on low speed until well-blended.

Spread the batter in the prepared baking pan. Sprinkle the brown sugar streusel topping evenly over the batter. Bake for 25 to 30 minutes or until a toothpick inserted in the center comes out clean. Partially cool it in the pan on a wire rack. Cut the coffee cake into squares while it's still warm.

Yield: 8 to 10 servings

Cinnamon Walnut Scones

Ingredients

1 ¾ cups all-purpose flour
½ cup finely chopped walnuts
4½ teaspoons granulated sugar
2¼ teaspoons baking powder
½ teaspoon salt
½ teaspoon ground cinnamon
¼ cup cold butter
2 eggs
⅓ cup whipping cream
¼ cup buttermilk*

Preheat the oven to 450°F (230°C, Gas Mark 8). In a bowl, combine the flour, walnuts, sugar, baking powder salt and cinnamon; cut in the butter until the mixture resembles coarse crumbs. Combine the eggs and cream; stir into the dry ingredients until just moistened. Turn onto a floured surface. Gently pat the dough into a 7-inch surface, ¾-inch thick. Cut into eight wedges. Separate the wedges; place on a lightly greased baking sheet. Brush the tops with the buttermilk. Let them rest for 15 minutes. Bake for 14 to 16 minutes or until golden brown.

Yield: 8 servings

No buttermilk? Take your ¼ of milk and add 1 tablespoon of white vinegar or lemon juice. Let it sit for about five minutes before you add it to the recipe.

ABOUT LORRAINE BARTLETT

The immensely popular Booktown Mystery series is what put Lorraine Bartlett's pen name Lorna Barrett on the New York Times Bestseller list, but it's her talent--whether writing as Lorna, or L.L. Bartlett, or Lorraine Bartlett—that keeps her in the hearts of her readers. This multi-published, Agatha-nominated author pens the exciting Jeff Resnick Mysteries as well as the acclaimed Victoria Square Mystery series, the Tales of Telenia adventure-fantasy saga, and now the Lotus Bay Mysteries, and has many short stories and novellas to her name(s). Check out the descriptions and links to all her works, and sign up for her emailed newsletter here: http://oi.vresp.com/?fid=aee11a8d64

Not familiar with all of Lorraine's work? Check out **A Cozy Mystery Sampler**, which is FREE. Just click this link.

If you enjoyed ***A MURDEROUS MISCONCEPTION,*** please consider reviewing it on your favorite online review site. Thank you!

Find Lorraine on Social Media

www.LorraineBartlett.com

ALSO BY LORRAINE BARTLETT

The Lotus Bay Mysteries

Panty Raid (A Tori Cannon-Kathy Grant mini mystery)

With Baited Breath

Christmas At Swans Nest

A Reel Catch

The Best From Swans Nest (A Lotus Bay Cookbook)

The Victoria Square Mysteries

A Crafty Killing

The Walled Flower

One Hot Murder

Dead, Bath and Beyond (with Laurie Cass)

Yule Be Dead (with Gayle Leeson)

Murder Ink (with Gayle Leeson)

A Murderous Misconception (with Gayle Lesson)

Recipes To Die For: A Victoria Square Cookbooks

Life On Victoria Square

Carving Out A Path

A Basket Full of Bargains

The Broken Teacup

It's Tutu Much

The Reluctant Bride

Tea'd Off

Life On Victoria Square Vol. 1

A Look Back

Tea For You (free for download)

Tales From Blythe Cove Manor

A Dream Weekend

A Final Gift

An Unexpected Visitor

Grape Expectations

Foul Weather Friends

Mystical Blythe Cove Manor

Blythe Cove Seasons (Free for all ebook formats)

Tales of Telenia

(adventure-fantasy)

STRANDED

JOURNEY

TREACHERY (2020)

Short Women's Fiction

Love & Murder: A Bargain-Priced Collection of Short Stories

Happy Holidays? (A Collection of Christmas Stories)

An Unconditional Love

Love Heals

Blue Christmas

Prisoner of Love

We're So Sorry, Uncle Albert

Sabina Reigns (a novel)

Writing as L.L. Bartlett

The Jeff Resnick Mysteries

Murder On The Mind (Free for all ebook formats)

Dead In Red

Room At The Inn

Cheated By Death

Bound By Suggestion

Dark Waters

Shattered Spirits

JEFF RESNICK'S PERSONAL FILES

Evolution: Jeff Resnick's Backstory

A Jeff Resnick Six Pack

When The Spirit Moves You

Bah! Humbug

Cold Case

Spooked!

Crybaby

Eyewitness

A Part of The Pattern

Abused: A Daughter's Story

Off Script

Writing as Lorna Barrett

THE BOOKTOWN MYSTERIES

Murder Is Binding

Bookmarked For Death

Bookplate Special

Chapter & Hearse

Sentenced To Death

Murder On The Half Shelf

Not The Killing Type

Book Clubbed

A Fatal Chapter

Title Wave

A Just Clause

Poisoned Pages

A Killer Edition

Handbook For Homicide

WITH THE COZY CHICKS

The Cozy Chicks Kitchen

Tea Time With The Cozy Chicks

ABOUT GAYLE LESSON

Gayle Leeson is a pseudonym for Gayle Trent. Gayle has also written as Amanda Lee. She is currently writing the Kinsey Falls chick-lit/women's fiction series, the Down South Cafe cozy mystery series, and the Ghostly Fashionista cozy mystery series, and co-author of several Victoria Square Mysteries (with Lorraine Bartlett). Her book KILLER WEDDING CAKE won the Bronze Medal in the 20th Anniversary IPPY Awards.

Gayle lives in Southwest Virginia with her family and enjoys hearing from readers.

Visit her website to join her email newsletter list!

ALSO BY GAYLE LEESON

WRITING AS GAYLE LEESON

Down South Café Mystery Series

The Calamity Café

Silence of the Jams

Honey-Baked Homicide

Apples and Alibis

Ghostly Fashionista Mystery Series

Designs on Murder

Perils and Lace

Kinsey Falls Chick-Lit Series

Hightail It to Kinsey Falls

Putting Down Roots in Kinsey Falls

Sleighing It in Kinsey Falls

The Victoria Square Mysteries (with Lorraine Bartlett)

Yule Be Dead

Murder Ink

A Murderous Misconception

ALSO BY GAYLE LEESON

WRITING AS AMANDA LEE

Embroidery Mystery Series

The Quick and The Thread
Stitch Me Deadly
Thread Reckoning
The Long Stitch Goodnight
Thread On Arrival
Cross-Stitch Before Dying
Thread End
Wicked Stitch
The Stitching Hour
Better Off Thread

WRITING AS GAYLE TRENT

Daphne Martin Cake Decorating Mysteries

Murder Takes the Cake
Dead Pan
Killer Sweet Tooth
Battered to Death
Killer Wedding Cake

Myrtle Crumb Mysteries

Between A Clutch and A Hard Place
When Good Bras Go Bad
Claus Of Death
Soup...Er...Myrtle!
Perp and Circumstance
The Party Line (A Myrtle Crumb Prequel)

Stand-Alone Books

The Perfect Woman
The Flame
In Her Blood (as G. V. Trent)

CONTENTS